The Sword of Knowledge
Book II

WIZARD SPAWN

C.J. Cherryh
Nancy Asire

BAEN
FANTASY

WIZARD SPAWN

Copyright © 1989 by Tau Ceti, Inc.

A Baen Books Original

Baen Publishing Enterprises
260 Fifth Avenue
New York, N.Y. 10001

ISBN: 0-671-69838-9

Cover art by Larry Elmore

First printing, September 1989

Distributed by
SIMON & SCHUSTER
1230 Avenue of the Americas
New York, N.Y. 10020

Printed in the United States of America

CHAPTER 1

The midday sun managed a brief deception, illumining the Great Hall of the ducal palace, casting illusory warmth on grey stone walls. For a moment tapestries and banners blazed out above the crowded tables. High in the sooty rafters, smoke from the great cooking fires eddied about like a man-made mist.

Members of the ducal court packed the tables set beneath the high seat, their garments a sea of color highlighted in torchlight. Grey-clad priests of Hladyr sat elbow-to-elbow with richly dressed lords of the Duchy; dark blue robes of court wizards contrasted sharply with the House artists' polychrome. Several alchemists sat together, a knot of black in the midst of the tables.

Facing them all, His Grace Duke Hajun vro Telhern sat at the center of the high table, his wife at his left, his eldest son and heir, Brovor, at his right; the other royal children, daughter Alwisa,

1

and son Saladar, his youngest, sat to the wife's left.

Sated and drowsy from rich food and drink—to say nothing of the cups of wine he had downed—Hajun would have nodded had ducal dignity permitted.

But outside, the clouds closed, and once more the hall grew shadowed. A sudden gust of rain slatted against the windows and Hajun winced: *Shining One*, he prayed silently, *keep the winds furled. Guard my ships, Hladyr . . . keep them safe.*

He met the eyes of a grey-haired man sitting at the table closest to the high seat. "Jorrino," he said. "Attend me."

The man rose from his chair, bowed, and walked to the table to face Hajun.

"It's raining again," Hajun said unnecessarily: the sound of it on the window panes behind him was audible over the conversation in the hall. "I'm sick to death of this weather. What are my wizards doing about it?"

Jorrino drew an uneasy breath, met Hajun's gaze squarely. "What we always do, Your Grace. Wish it off on another city."

Hajun scowled. "Dammit, wish a little harder then."

The wizard spread his hands. "My lord, I assure you, we're doing all we can."

An old, old doubt came back. "Could someone— some enemy of mine—be responsible for the storms?"

"Possibly, lord. While we aren't sure one can

ill-wish the weather, we aren't sure one can't: we keep searching."

"For what do I fund you? For *aren't sure?*"

The chief wizard bowed distressedly; and stood in silence.

"Well?"

"There are whispers, lord,—"

"Whispers. Gold to my wizards . . . and they bring me whispers. . . ."

Jorrino gnawed at his mustaches, folded his hands, bowed. "Sabirn, Your Grace—somewhere in this city, a gathering of powerful Sabirn wizards—"

Hajun let go his breath and fell back with a wave of his hand. "Gods, if I've heard that one once—"

"My lord, they say this information *is* from a Sabirn."

Sabirn: little dark people of the alleyways and back streets of Targheiden, people good for little else than the most menial of tasks. Hard to think of any of them as being wizards . . .

"And who was this Sabirn who so freely whispers these dire plots?"

"A fortune teller—"

"Gods . . ."

"In the market. The Guard caught him stealing and put him to the question. *He* admitted to fakery, but he swore—*swore*, lord, that genuine wizards among his people have powers—"

A small, icy snake uncoiled in Hajun's stomach. "Do you believe him?"

Jorrino edged closer, dropped his voice. "Lord, the Sabirn have no love for us."

Hajun started to protest, but frowned and thought

on it, on the weather, the ill winds—inconceivable
that Sabirn might have wizards powerful enough
to bring the kingdom down . . . but they were
secretive, they were ancient: wizards, legend said,
long ago . . . before Targheiden stood—

Before Hajun's duchy existed . . . prosperous,
powerful . . . holding a place of importance in the
Ancar realms that Hajun's cousin, the king, fully
recognized: the king might hold control of the
plains and the trade coming from them, but it was
up to Hajun to keep that trade moving in and out
of the kingdom of Ancas.

And now Hajun's chief wizard echoed rumor of
a Sabirn rebellion, some alliance of powerful
wizards.

Hajun gnawed his lip. "I want you to keep me
advised on this, Jorrino. I want to hear everything
you hear, is that understood?"

The wizard bowed. "I do, Your Grace."

"And, whatever it's worth, keep wishing this
weather onto someone else. For our trade's sake."

"Aye, lord." The wizard bowed again and returned to his place.

"Sabirn?" a deep voice asked.

Hajun glanced sidelong at his eldest, Brovor—
like looking at himself twenty years back: the same
height, blond hair, broad shoulders, blue eyes.
Like himself if only, Hajun thought, Brovor could
find more use for his brain and less for his physical
strength. The days when lords ruled by might of
arms were fading; more often now, prosperity settled on the lord who was smart enough to use
diplomacy to get what he wanted. The nurturing

of trade, not the conduct of war, was the new business of princes. . . .

"Speaking of Sabirn," Brovor said, leaning toward Hajun. "Did you hear about the near riot in the Slough?"

"Damned nasty. Several of the Guard knocked about."

"They got the bastard who started it," Brovor said, "and he was Sabirn. Nailed his butt to the wall, from what I heard."

Hajun lifted an eyebrow. "I thought it was a crowd out of hand, a crowd chasing down a thief."

"Ah, but the thief was Sabirn." Brovor poured himself another glass of wine, took a long drink, and belched. "We ought to burn all of them. Damned demon-worshipers!"

At which Saladar stared meaningfully at the ceiling, lost in thought. "Saladar," Hajun asked sharply of his youngest. "What's your opinion?"

"Regarding the Sabirn or the riot?" Saladar's smile did not touch his eyes. "I certainly don't agree with Brovor."

"And why not?" Brovor leaned forward on one brawny arm. "You never *were* much of a warrior, brother."

"Hush, Brovor," said the duchess. "Saladar's matched you in every feat of arms he's been set to."

"Fah!" Brovor took another gulp of his wine. "Book-reading. Scribbling."

"Saladar?" Hajun said, ignoring his eldest son's grumbling. "Why don't you agree with Brovor?"

"Slaughter the Sabirn? Who would we find to

sweep the streets, then?" Saladar asked, smiling again. "Or collect the slops? I say, keep the Sabirn around. They have their uses."

Brovor made a rude noise. "*I* say kill them all. Let the commons sweep and slop. Then you won't have to worry about rumors. Or the dole." He reached for the pitcher of wine.

"Enough wine," Hajun said quietly, stopping his son's hand. "You don't want to trip over yourself when you leave the table."

Brovor's face went red. He took a deep breath, but subsided back into his chair.

"Tomorrow's your name-day feast." Hajun released his son's shoulder. "Surely you don't want to wake with a headache that will keep you from enjoying your festivities."

"No." Brovor's eyes wavered slightly. "But you won't mind, sire, if I celebrate tonight with my friends. . . ."

Hajun sighed, his eyes flicking down the tables at his eldest scion's company. Stories had filtered back to him of the parties Brovor had attended in the company of these young lords.

"I won't keep you from it," he said, as Brovor relaxed. "But in your cups, do possibly remember the ceremony at the Temple starts not that long after midday. If nothing else, grant your future subjects the sight of a man fully in control of himself."

Brovor nodded, then grinned widely. "I won't disgrace you, Father, and I won't trip over my own feet. I promise."

"Let him have his night," Tajana said, a smile softening her face.

"I'll be back before the midnight bell, Father." Brovor grinned again. "Don't wait up for me."

"Ladirno, what do you think . . . about the Sabirn wizards?"

Ladirno glanced sidelong at the alchemist who had spoken.

"Do you believe it?" the other pressed him.

"I reserve my judgement." Ladirno met his colleague's eyes. The man who sat to his left was elegant as any lord in the Duke's hall, his black robes as rich, if more somber. "And you, Wellhyrn?"

Wellhyrn's lips curled. "Sabirn? Wizards with the power to bring down a kingdom. If malice could serve—"

"I wonder what our Sabirn-lover would say about this?" asked one of the younger alchemists.

Ladirno shrugged. "One has to guess what Duran's thinking. Years since he's been to court."

"Maybe there's reason." Wellhyrn waved a languid hand. "If anyone might know what's going on with the Sabirn—"

"He hires them to go out into the country with him to gather herbs," said the other alchemist.

Another: "Maybe he's sleeping with them."

Wellhyrn snorted: "Herbs. Midwifery, next."

Ladirno said: "With his father banned from court—"

"Consorting with Sabirn. A man of the Profession should have standards—"

"What *does* he do?"

"Midwifery. He runs an apothecary." Ladirno reached for his wine-cup and drank. "He's been making his living that way for over thirty years. Lives in a garret. Looks twice his age. Deals for pennies. By now, it's probably the only thing he knows."

Wellhyrn leaned forward on the table, his arms crossed before him. His eyes glittered in the torchlight. "He'd have money, he'd have a good deal else if he weren't out to spite the Profession. He's got his father's books, the gods know what he's got. *He* deals for pennies, he hands it out free, hands physic to any beggar in the quarter. Free! Hands out his cures, *tells* them to midwives—the gods know who they poison, who knows what he hands out? Or think what would happen if he stumbled across some great alchemistic secret. Gods, he'd hand it out on the streets."

"A fool." The younger alchemist chewed on his lower lip a moment. "And where would the Profession be, colleagues, if we all gave away our secrets?"

"Folk poisoning each other all over town. Burning the town down to melt metals. *We're* highly trained, my friends, the gods only know what this fellow is."

Ladirno said: "He doesn't experiment. As Wellhyrn says, the only thing he's interested in is medicine."

"Oh, aye . . . and look what he did with his great discovery." Wellhyrn toyed with one of the heavy gold rings that graced his right hand. "The fool discovers a cure for the sexual pox, and what does he do, but come to court and tells everyone. Now *any* quack doctor can treat the pox. Think of it! Duran could have made himself richer than all of us combined if he'd kept the cure to himself."

"Thank the gods he's a fool." The older alchemist scratched at his beard. "He could imperil all Targheiden if he *does* discover something big in alchemy. There's no sense of professional ethics in the man."

Ladirno shrugged. "Small danger. Right now he's so damned poor he's barely making ends meet."

The light in the hall brightened as the sun slid out from behind the clouds. Wellhyrn leaned back in his chair and crossed his long legs out under the table.

"I'm off to the harbor," he said. "I'm expecting a shipment. Come with me, Ladirno?"

Ladirno contemplated the long walk from the upper city to the wharfs. "Ah, why not. We've been cooped up long enough as it is with these damned storms."

After a brief hour of sunlight, the clouds had gathered again and, accompanied by thunder, rain fell on Targheiden in sheets. Duran looked out the open door at the water rushing by in the street and gave up on the notion he might have any customers this afternoon.

Despite the open doorway, the thick clouds cast the interior of his shop into deep shadow. Duran walked back to the counter, reached for his flint, and struck a light. Cupping an oil-soaked rag between his hands, he carefully lit the lamp and drew the glass down around it.

Its feeble glow barely reached the walls of the

narrow shop. A large yellow dog rose from its place on the other side of the counter and ambled through the shadows toward Duran, its tail swinging side to side.

"So, Dog," Duran said, glancing out the doorway to the street, "*now* you want to go out. Well, go then, though gods know you won't like it much."

Dog nuzzled Duran's knee in passing, stood for a moment on the rain-spattered threshold, then carefully ventured onto the overflowing walk. The rain was easing somewhat, but Duran did not expect the dog to go far.

He turned away from the door and found a long splinter of wood. Lifting the glass side of the lamp, he kindled the splinter and lit the lamp that hung over the counter. *No more,* he cautioned himself, *unless customers come. Fish-oil's not getting cheaper.*

Wind gusted through the doorway, setting both lamps to flickering. Duran considered closing the door for warmth but that would reduce the light and discourage customers. He sighed quietly, and sat down on the high stool behind the counter to wait, disconsolately, for business. In the street, water overflowed the gutters, poured off roofs.

Ha. The only people who will visit me this afternoon are the drowned.

Behind him, neatly arranged on wooden shelves that ran up the wall, sat his herbs and medicines, each resting in small pottery jars. He was not rich enough to afford glass, so he had labeled each jar in small, neat printing. His more precious medicines sat in a locked cabinet toward the rear of the shop; he kept the key on its chain around his neck at all times. Certain crazies would kill a man for what rested in that locked cabinet.

He laughed to himself. From the Queen of Sciences to herb-pottery. Here he sat in a narrow shop, surrounded by herbs, poultices, and whatnots, visited by the poor folk of Old Town, for whom he was the only thing coming close to a doctor. He healed their fevers, their sores, dispensed drugs that took away pain, and even more dangerous drugs that ended unwanted pregnancies. *Those* he never admitted to having, and the women who sought him out—even the whores— knew that blackmail worked both ways.

There was his cure for the sexual pox; gods knew he saw enough business from the poor who could not afford to go elsewhere, but he occasionally treated richer folk who desperately wished to protect their identities, *and* keep the knowledge of their disease from the High Town doctors—in which cases, Duran never asked any of his clients more than the most general of questions, and they were happy to return the favor, and to pay at least what kept the shop going. Not more. There were ways and ways to guarantee a poor apothecary's silence: one preferred a modest coin—and risked no higher fees.

Oh, Father, Duran thought, settling back against an upright in the shelving. *What would you say of your son now? How far have I fallen?*

Thirty-five years in Old Town sat on a man, made him gray and grim and bent with study in dim light. Duran's blond hair had whitened, his gaunt shoulders stooped more than in his youth, and he had to hold things decidedly farther away these days to see them clearly.

Time, and time—the marks of which were deeper in Old Town than in the High City up the hill, despite that his art had kept him free from sickness and hunger: rain still caused his joints to complain. He grimaced, realized he had not had his midday meal yet, and got down from the stool.

A hunk of cheese and a fresh loaf of bread sat on the shelf under the counter. He cut a slice of that bread and the end off the cheese, wishing he had something besides water to wash the meal down . . . naturally, as if drawn back on a string, Dog appeared at the doorway, dripping rain-water, tail wagging in hopes of his share.

The rain had nearly stopped by the time most folk in Old Town closed their shops. Duran stood in the opened doorway, watching a grey steady drip off the second story overhang onto the street . . . the rush of the gutters grew quieter as the storm rumbled off to the north. Duran snorted: save for old Mother Garan, not one customer had darkened his door all afternoon, and the old woman had only bought willow tea for her headache, one of the simpler and least expensive of Duran's physics.

Dog lay curled up by the doorway, dreaming in the late afternoon, his ears twitching and his tail thumping now and again on the wooden floor— chasing rabbits in his dreams, Duran guessed, though in this part of town it might as likely be mice or the occasional young cat unaware of where Dog's territory began—Dog, just Dog, because Duran had never come up with a name that fit his companion: and Dog had never complained.

Neither had Duran repented the expense of Dog's healthy appetite. Dog's presence served as a deterrent to burglars, and gave Duran a sense of security. Though he never made much of what he kept in his locked cabinet, a large, protective animal on the premises eased his mind somewhat.

Duran sighed, giving up hope of making more than his one afternoon sale, and looked at the inn that sat across the street from his shop. "The Swimming Cat" was the inn's name—a name given it generations back by its owner whose cat had fallen into a half-full rain barrel one night. Old Puss had survived the ordeal, and the innkeeper found her the following morning, clinging claws hooked to the side of the rain barrel, water up to her neck—a stubborn talisman for a tavern always borderline on ruin.

The "Cat" was somewhat seedy now, but still reputable. As the largest inn in this section of Old Town, it catered to travelers who could not afford the better inns farther away from the harbor— excellent food for the price, a gathering place for the neighbors, as well as passers-through from the harbor.

Duran took his cloak down from behind the door, gathered up his keys, blew out the lamps, and stepped outside—Dog, lost in dreams, opened one eye, yawned, stretched, and went back to sleep. Duran locked the door, put the keys in his belt pouch, and started across the street to the inn.

"Bad rain, eh, Duran?"

The woman's voice made Duran wince and turn: it was his neighbor, the seamstress Zeldezia.

"Aye," he said. "Nearly drowned coming back from the docks."

Zeldezia leaned against her door jamb, shoving a long lock of her brown hair back over one shoulder. She was near Duran in age—not ill-favored, but one seldom saw her smile. "We been having more rain than usual, don't you think? Them as says it's witchery—"

"Aye, that we have. Perhaps it will end soon." Duran put on a stubbornly pleasant smile, nodded to her, and turned away. A conversation with Zeldezia was the last thing he wanted on a gloomy afternoon. Damned woman. Enough to curdle a man's appetite.

He stepped over the stream of water flowing down the gutter and made for the "Cat's" doorway. One benefit of the rain, even Old Town smelled better for it, washed and clean, refuse swept away in the gutters—redistributed down the block, generally. But not near the "Cat." Tutadar, the innkeeper, kept his frontage and his alley clean, holding it bad business to have his clients stepping over garbage.

He kept the inside the same—scrubbed. The inn was more crowded than usual for this time of afternoon; doubtless the rain had kept folk indoors who would have otherwise been elsewhere. Duran paused at the doorway steps, letting his eyes adjust to the dimmer light inside.

"Greetings, Sor Duran."

He glanced down, just inside the doorway, at the man who had addressed him. The fellow sat on the floor, a walking stick leaning on the wall of the tavern behind him. He was white haired, clad in clothes patched, but quite clean. The dark eyes that looked up at Duran were full of intelligence and wit.

"Greetings, Old Man," Duran said. "Do we have another story from you tonight?"

The old man shrugged. "Perhaps. If I feel in the mood."

Duran smiled. Old Man was always in the mood. The locals in the tavern had heard all his stories time and again, but no one seemed to grow tired of them. For a few coppers, the old fellow would spin tales that kept his audience enthralled, despite their familiarity with the stories. But Old Man truly shone when the common room was full of travelers who had not heard his tales before. It was then that Duran could swear he was hearing new stories, not those he had listened to for years.

Old Man was Sabirn. But Tutadar had even allowed him inside the inn. Despite a few nervous glances from newcomers, Old Man had become such a fixture of the neighborhood that locals hardly took account of his race.

"So." Duran dug in his belt pouch and came up with a copper . . . one of the three that Mother Garan had paid him for the willow tea. He placed the coin in Old Man's upheld hand. "For a story, then . . . *if* you're in the mood this evening."

Old Man's smile was most engaging. "For you, Sor Duran," he said. "I'll tell it for you."

Duran nodded and walked on into the common room—quiet at this hour, due to grow noisier after evening traffic had had a few cups. He saw a few of the tables occupied: Bontido, the potter, for one, who lived on the other side of the seamstress; Ithar, whose smithy neighbored the inn; a few rain-soaked, better-dressed passers-through from the harbor warming themselves . . .

"Your usual, Duran?" the innkeeper called out from across the room.

"Aye." Duran sat down at his accustomed table, shrugged his cloak back from his shoulders and stretched out his feet. It was then that he got a look at the two well-dressed men who sat at a table a few paces away from his.

Ladirno and Wellhyrn! What, by all the gods, were *those* two doing in "The Swimming Cat"? Duran considered ignoring the two, thought, actually, of changing his table or coming back later, but that was a coward's choice, not to mention it would draw attention from his neighbors. The pair turned their heads to stare at him: he smiled, tight-lipped, nodded a perfunctory courtesy, intended thereafter to pay his attention elsewhere, deliberately.

But: "Ah, Duran." It was Ladirno who spoke, the older of the two. With silk-lined cloaks, softly woven tunics above supple hose and neatly shod feet, the two were totally out of place among the local trade. "We've heard this is where you spend your time."

Duran nodded again, jaw set.

Ladirno's companion lifted an elegant eyebrow— Wellhyrn, the younger, the more handsome of the pair (and he knew it, Duran thought). His clothes were that much richer, gods, velvet and silk in the somber colors of the Profession, and he bore himself with an easy arrogance. "Duran," Wellhyrn said, pitching his voice loud enough to be heard by the other customers. "What a surprise—in a seedy place like this—"

"*I* like it," Duran muttered.

"Really?" Wellhyrn turned to his tablemate. "Shall we be going, Ladir? The wine's sour, the storm's delayed the ship until at least tomorrow. We can certainly do better than this uptown . . ."

Ladirno shrugged, shoved his chair back from the table and stood, gathering up his cloak. "And when can we expect to see you at court again, Duran? Or in the guild meetings?"

"Sometime soon," Duran promised, making an effort to sound friendly.

Wellhyrn had risen to his feet. He swept his cloak up from the back of his chair and settled it around his shoulders. "I'm sure we'll all look forward to that day. And the guild fees. But that can't be in your way, can it? —Coming, Ladir?"

Duran watched the two men cross the room and saw the glint of the coins they tossed to the innkeeper. He could have lived on such extravagance for days.

Damn, damn! He knew he should not let them bother him, but by Hladyr the Shining he could not help it. Fellow alchemists. Ha! Ducal favorites, they spent their days at court, amusing the nobles with petty tricks . . . sleights of hand that kept gullible patrons interested in funding. Tricks of the Profession—all honorable, of course: research materials came dear, and one could hardly explain the *real* secrets. . . .

The hell. Duran took several deep breaths and settled back in his chair. He would not call the present elite of the Profession charlatans, but by his lights they came close. In his father's day—

In his father's laboratory—

Lalada, the cup girl, brought Duran his ale. He took the mug, smiled a silent thanks, and drank. The brew tasted bitter on his tongue, less the fault of the ale, he was sure, than of his mood. There was nothing wrong with what the "Cat" served, damn, there was not.

He took another drink, waiting for his supper— meat pie tonight, an extravagance: every fourth day, Duran allowed himself real meat . . . beef from the herds of cattle that grazed to the north of Targheiden—that much a one-time nobleman allowed himself, every fourth day, no oftener.

Tutadar himself brought Duran's supper to him. "Don't let them gilded donkey-butts get to you, Duran," he said, straightening and crossing his arms on his chest. "Bet them black crows never saved any kid like you did Sora Mitti's son. Think on that 'un, Duran. Them folk ain't got nothin' on *you.*"

"Thanks, Tut," Duran said, cutting open his pie and sniffing the sweet smell of beef. He glanced up, remembering the innkeeper's wife. "Is Anha's hand better tonight?"

"Aye, thanks. She wanted me to tell you that, Sor Duran. She's puttin' that salve on the cut like it'd save her, she is."

"If it flares up again, have her see me." Duran reached for his belt pouch to pay for the pie and ale, but Tutadar nudged his shoulder.

"No, no, this 'un's on Anha and me. For bein' a good neighbor." He glanced over his shoulder at the doorway. "And for not bein' snot-nosed like them two. Enjoy your meal."

Duran stared for a moment, then nodded and smiled. He set to his pie, aware now that he had it before him just how hungry he was.

CHAPTER 2

Well into dark, the warmer for beef pie and ale, Duran finally quit the inn. More of his neighbors had come to the "Cat" for their dinners, and their company had lightened his mood—after-dinner talk had flowed from table to table, warm friendly talk, for it was all Old Town in the tavern this evening: the few uptowners and harbor trade who had come in had returned to their rooms, or gone off uptown and down.

Duran fumbled for his keys and felt for the lock: hard to see, though the "Cat" had torches burning by its front door so long as they lasted. The key habitually stuck in the ancient lock. Duran cursed, jiggled the key, shoved the protesting door open.

Dog stood waiting by the door, uncomplaining as usual. He leaned up against Duran's leg, inviting a quick scratch on his head, then trotted off into the deepening night, about his own necessities. Duran lit his lamp, set it down on the counter,

21

and hung his cloak behind the door. Full of meat pie and ale, he sat down on his stool to await Dog's return, so he could lock up his shop for the night.

Then his eyes fastened on a packet that lay on the floor: someone had slipped something under his door. He stared for a moment, got down from his stool, and picked the packet up. It was made of paper—a fine grade of paper, not the coarse stuff one purchased here in Old Town. He took it back to his lamp, leaned close, and opened it.

Two silver donahri slipped out of the folded paper and dropped ringing onto the counter-top.

For you, our poorest brother. May this small sum keep your body and soul together. The note was signed, with an artistic flourish: Wellhyrn.

Duran cursed and flung the packet down on the floor. *Damn Wellhyrn! Can't he leave me alone? He still goes out of his way to torment me. Why should he bother?*

Dog came back and stood in the doorway, his tail wagging. Duran glanced up from the paper, noting that the butcher must have left bones on his doorstep: Dog held one in his mouth.

"Come on, Dog . . . in, in!" Duran shut the door behind Dog, locked it, and then contemplating the two silver coins glittering in the lamp-light, thought that if he had more pride, he would have sent those donahri back to Wellhyrn with a terse note suggesting how to apply his charity. But pride had long ago found its proper place in Old Town: these two silver coins could keep him and Dog in food and drink for days upon days. Adding the coins to what he had seen Wellhyrn and Ladirno toss about at the inn, he suspected the Duke had given both men another grant to pursue their research.

I could use that. I could do more good with it.

But I don't play the game. I don't cater to the desires of the nobles at court.

Besides, the nobles dislike me. They remember . . . at least those of them old enough to remember my father.

Duran signed heavily, swept the two silver coins up into his fist, and dropped them into his pouch. So be it. If the gods chose to gift him with this silver—though the method of that gift was less than palatable—who was he to turn it down?

Duran gave Dog a goodnight pat on the head, and, lamp in hand, walked to the back of his shop, and to the steps that led upstairs.

It is the nature of all things, Duran read, *that they belong to one class or another. There is the prime matter which is the basis for all substances found in the world. It is the interaction of form with matter that gives rise to the elements: earth, air, fire, and water. They, in turn, through various combinations, produce all the objects that surround us. Therefore, if an object has a preponderance of earth, it is solid in form. The presence of water in an object gives us the ability to produce liquids, or to melt what seems solid. Fire allows us to unlock other forms of matter through combustion. And air, the material of ideas, of the very soul, gives us the intelligence to see all these things.*

Granting the above as undeniably true, then it

is easy to see that changes in the proportion of the elements may result in a change of the form of prime matter. It then follows that, if this is true, any substance may be changed into any other substance if the right conditions can be found. . . .

Duran signed and set his notes aside. All this was basic, first-year study, but it was one of his dreams to turn the language of alchemy into something any learned person could understand. He longed for a return to the old days, when alchemists labored in their laboratories, dabbling less with mysticism and more with metals he could not, in his present estate, afford. . . .

And he would be damned if he was going to go back, hat in hand, apply to the duke and the guild, pay his fees to strut around court, mouthing nonsense that sounded learned, blithering about the mystical union of all things in the great aether beyond the stars. That he left to the other alchemists, the astrologers . . . them with their ducal grants and their rich patrons, that they kept duly astonished or alarmed by sleights of hand and dire predictions.

Not that he discounted astrology: he believed in the macrocosm, the wonderful world of the sun, stars, and planets reflected in the microcosm, the tiny world where man lived. Man grew and changed, so it was natural to believe that other things did the same. It stood to reason that under the proper astrological influences, certain metals might be changed to others. Even lead might turn to gold . . . Theoretically. Not, the gods knew, that he or anyone else had ever seen.

Time and again, when he had been younger, he

had gone to this small furnace and "killed" metals, melted them down over and over, trying to stumble across a purer form. Gold, his teachers had taught him, should lie at the end of numerous "killings." *If* the conditions were right. *If* the moon was in the proper quarter, the planets in the most advantageous houses, and the wind was blowing just right. If, if, if.

Small chance he would ever find the solution. He had received no grants from the Old Duke, though the present Duke honored his late father's invitation for Duran to attend court. What he needed was access to the great furnaces, the fires hotter than he could produce, the help of assistants nearly as knowledgeable as he. And that, he knew, was held from him because he did not— could not—play the game Ladirno and Wellhyrn played.

And years back, he had given up practicing all but the medical side to alchemy. Maybe one day, if the gods smiled on him, he would take the study up again.

Maybe.

He leaned forward in his chair again and shoved his notes aside. Another pile of papers rested on the desk: his writings also, but not devoted to alchemy—pages full of his small, neat handwriting, back and front, with hardly any margin to them. What he had written here concerned the Sabirn, herbs, and Old Man's stories.

He held to the notion that somewhere in their legends and the stories they told, lurked a kernel of truth . . . the learning that had once made the Sabirn a world power. So, when he took Sabirn

helpers with him into the countryside to gather
herbs, he always asked them to tell him stories of
their people—fanciful tales, gods and heroes; some
of the stories he sensed truer than others, but he
did not know enough yet to separate fact from
fiction. Or to know if there were deeper secrets.

One asked the sweepers of streets, the pickers
of garbage, the carriers of slops—one disturbed
one's neighbors with such inquiries; and aware of
that disturbance, Duran tried to keep such jour-
neys to a minimum, talked lately with Old Man,
whom none of the neighbors considered a particular threat: Old Man had lived in the neighborhood
so long, had become so *ordinary* . . .

But Old Man, the consummate storyteller—his
stories were of events that had taken place far in
the past . . . great heroes, quests, the intervention
of gods whose worshipers had died long ago, fables
all, tales for children and the curious. But when
Duran questioned him closely about what the Sabirn
empire had *really* been, the old fellow had gone
silent on him, shaken his head, refused to answer.

Duran flipped through the pages of his notes.
He saw in his mind's eye the way life might have
been in the Sabirn empire. Gods. If he could only
journey back through time—

He rubbed his eyes. Tonight he was plagued by
the "if's." He could only deal with what he had at
hand, instead of what he did *not* have, or could
never possess. And the alchemy he practiced had
more to do with the pot bubbling away over the
small flame, that filled the air with the stench of
sulphur and herbs and lard—hence the window
braced slightly open: more of Anha's salve, an

improvement, if his notion was right, to keep a wound supple and yet healing—

Dog barked downstairs, and barked again. Duran sat up straighter: he recognized that bark, a noise Dog made only when strangers came near.

"Damn!" Duran stood, and took up his lamp, blew out the fire beneath the lard—the front door was locked, he was sure he had locked it. He heard the sudden hammering of a fist, Dog's deep barking. "Who in Dandro's hells could be after physic at *this* hour?"

But children got sick, old folk took spells: an apothecary did have night calls, and they were generally the bad ones.

Duran opened the peephole, discovered two cloaked men on his doorstep, hoods drawn up so he could not see their faces in the lamp-light. "What's the matter?" he called out. "Who is it?"

"Business," one said. The accent was uptown. "Discreet business, dammit, open."

One made the best judgment one could of such visitors. Duran carefully unlocked the door, pulled it open. Dog stood to one side, fur raised along his spine, growling deep in his throat.

"Call off your cur," one of the men said: the voice was young, cultured, and arrogant. The other said: "We won't hurt you."

Duran lifted the lamp higher, but the hoods still shadowed the faces. "Dog, . . . back off, that's a good fellow. Go on now. Go lie down."

Dog growled again, retreated to the center of the shop. Duran stepped back and gestured the two men inside. "How may I help you?" he asked, setting the lamp down on the counter.

"We hear you have the cure for the pox."

So, Duran thought, two high-born, most likely. High-born with high-born liaisons. No wonder they had come to his shop in the dark of night, cloaked to protect their anonymity.

"Aye," he said, closing the door. "I have the cure. Which of you has the pox?"

A pause. Then the taller of the two tapped his chest.

"So," Duran said. "Please bear with me. I must ask you certain questions, and I'm afraid they'll be rather personal. Be assured, Sor . . . I mean no disrespect."

"Ask," he said gruffly.

Duran sighed quietly and lit the hanging lamp above the counter. "How are you certain you have the disease?"

"I . . . I visited a whore," the fellow said, sounding frightened and belligerent at the same time. "Two ten-days ago. Today I noticed a sore."

"Where?"

The tall man gestured briefly at his crotch.

"Is it weeping?"

"Aye. Somewhat."

"Have you visited this whore before?"

"No."

"Do you know anyone else who has?"

"No." The man folded his arms. "Listen, fellow, are you going to cure me or talk to me all night?"

Duran ducked his head, a small bow. "Please don't be upset. The questions are to help you."

The tall man's companion set a hand on the

fellow's arm. "Easy, m'lord. I know this man's reputation. Trust him. He's the one who *discovered* the cure."

Lord, was it? Duran tried again to get a glimpse of the man's face, but failed.

For a long moment, the tall man stood with face downcast, then moved his shoulders slightly in an attempt to relax. "This man looks familiar," he said at last, looking up at his comrade: one could see a young, squarish chin.

Duran tried to place his voice, but could not. "Perhaps you've seen me in the market."

"Hardly." The chin jutted. "*I* don't frequent such places."

"Ah, well." Duran spread his hands and omitted to mention the young man's consorting with whores. "Perhaps somewhere else, then. But that's no matter. You want to be cured of the pox, and with this disease time is of the essence. You said you visited the whore some twenty days ago. Have you noticed any swelling since then?"

The young lord nodded briefly. "Some."

"Around your groin area?"

A pause. "Aye."

"Anywhere else?"

"No. —It's only a slight swelling."

"Does your sore hurt?"

"No." The chin went squarer and squarer.

Duran thought a moment. The disease had obviously not advanced beyond its first stages, much easier then to effect a cure. "I'll treat you," he said, looking up slightly into the man's hidden face, "but you'll have to agree to return for further treatment. This is very important. You *must* return each time for a new application of the paste. Do you understand?"

"Why?" The belligerence entered the young lord's voice again. "Why can't you give me enough of this paste of yours to treat the pox myself?"

"Because it will kill you if it's misused."

"Gods! What kind of medicine is this?"

Duran kept his voice very level. "This is a particularly virulent disease. It calls for a cure equally strong. I can't agree to treat you unless you return to me for the subsequent applications: omitting that, we'd as well not begin."

"He's not lying, lord," the tall man's companion said. "I've heard what he says about this treatment before. Remember Khaldori . . . his doctor told him the same thing. Trust him, m'lord. We can find excuse to get back, your father won't find out."

Khaldori? Duran blinked, but kept all expression from his face. Old lord Khaldori, Duran knew all too well from his early days at court: he had heard sniggering rumor that Lord Khaldori's son had picked up the pox not a year past.

And his visitors spoke so casually of a member of the Khaldori family.

"All right." The tall man sighed quietly. "I've no choice, and I'm told you're the discoverer of this cure. Get on with it then, man. I'll pay you."

Duran dipped his head in a small bow. "I have no doubt. But I do want to impress on you certain things: you realize you're highly contagious now, don't you?"

The young lord glanced sidelong at his companion. "So others have led me to believe." He swallowed heavily, and a note of fear entered his voice.

"And that this is extremely serious. Consequences—"

"I haven't waited too long, have I?"

"No, I don't think so. But don't be tricked by the pox. It can seem very mild at first. Untreated, it can kill you surely as any sword or spear. Not mentioning—"

"I'm ready. Do you want me to remain standing?"

"It would be easier to treat you that way." Duran walked around his counter to the shelves that ran up the wall. He pulled the stool over to one side, and climbed it. The lamp-light cast his shadow against the shelves, but he knew exactly what he was hunting for.

"This won't hurt, will it?" asked the young lord.

Duran picked up his sealed jar of mercury paste and carefully descended the stool. "No," he said, turning to face the tall man. "Not excessively."

The other fellow had stepped back into a darkened corner to give his companion some privacy. Duran set the jar down on the counter and slowly opened the lid, while the young man wrapped a scarf the more closely about his lower face.

"Don't worry," he said quietly, taking a thin paper wand from the shelf behind him. He dipped the end of the wand in the paste: he saw eyes beneath the hood, dark and anxious. "I've cured far worse cases than yours."

The two young lords left as heavily cloaked as they had arrived. Duran watched them go, standing in his doorway, Dog sitting vigilant at his side.

The light from the torches outside "The Swimming Cat" dimly lit the two figures walking away down the street. Duran turned to go inside, then halted. Snatches of what the two men said as they walked away came to him on the breeze.

". . . my father would kill me if . . ."

"Don't worry." This from the shorter man.

The other young noble had said something, only the last of which Duran could understand. ". . . my brother would say."

"How's Sal to know? He's not . . ."

Duran stiffened, and very slowly drew back into his shop. His pulse beat in his ears and he felt his face go hot. Sal? Saladar?

That was the Duke's youngest son.

Which would make the tall young man—

Brovor. Heir to the Duke of Targheiden.

Duran's mouth went dry. He had just treated the second most important man in the Duchy for the pox. For a disease that, if left untreated, could have robbed the Duke of his chosen heir.

"Gods!" Duran shut the door, and stood leaning his forehead on it. No wonder Brovor had all but recognized him. Though it had been years since he had been at court, and the light in his shop had not been the best—Brovor had seen him many times as a child . . . a square-faced, obstinate boy, a bad temper—

A grown man with a dynastic marriage to make, a secret to protect . . .

Hladyr protect! What did he do now? The two men had taken great pains to hide their identities; but the companion had let slip one clue by mentioning the Khaldori family, a second by a refer-

ence to Saladar . . . and Brovor was no fool: some
small, nagging sense of recognition might set him
to asking discreet questions, closer questions that
might turn up a name—an association—that might
make him believe his secret in danger—

Himself vulnerable to blackmail . . .

*O gods! Why did I answer my door? They could
have found other doctors to treat the pox, other
physicians who would keep secrets. Why me?*

They had paid in gold. For silence as well as
treatment. An ordinary apothecary would be over-
awed, have no notion what the scandal was worth,
politically—but a disenfranchised nobleman, an alchemist with guild connections, a son of a disgraced father—with possible motives for political
revenge, or alliance . . .

Not mentioning the chance of the heir dying if
he miscalculated in his dosage—forget all hope of
claiming it was the disease. . . .

He would have to be careful, *very* careful, both
in his treatment and in keeping his identity secret—
and the chances of doing that seemed frighten-
ingly slim. . . .

The one who discovered the cure, the companion had said.

Gods, *hope* the companion never mentioned
names, *hope* the companion never understood his
previous court connections, never connected Duran
the Apothecary with Duran the Alchemist, Duran
vro Ancahar . . .

Nothing to be done. Absolutely nothing to be
done. One walked a narrow line and hoped—and
did not look for much sleep this night.

*   *   *

A day of better trade, a quiet day, thank the gods. But it drizzled. There was a brisk trade in febrifuges, in willow tea. One could forget about ducal heirs, keep one's eyes on Old Town, put palaces and princes out of one's mind and worry about the Wirrin baby, who took colic; and Eemi, from harborside, with a knife-cut from one of her customers: Eemi feared scarring . . . Duran wanted a test for the herbs and lard . . .

It seemed dishonest to charge, the girl being out of work and all . . .

Dog barked downstairs, and barked again. Duran sat bolt upright in his chair where he had all but fallen asleep, his notes on his lap, another experiment bubbling away in its pot. This was Dog's most unfriendly bark, a bark more vicious than that reserved for mere visitors.

Another chorus of barks.

Duran walked across the room to a side window. The clouds had fled and a full moon rode above Targheiden now, and by its light Duran could see movement in the alleyway below. He stared through the darkness, trying to make out what was going on.

And then he saw and stepped back from the window. Someone was being beaten in the alley. Though he had heard no cries for help, the scuffling, the heavy breathing, and the muffled sounds of blows were easy enough to hear in the intervals of Dog's barking.

"Damn!"

Without thinking, Duran grabbed for his lamp and took to the stairs at a run, down the steps, across his shop as he fumbled for his keys. He snatched up his heavy walking stick, the only weapon the law allowed commoners. Hefting the staff in one hand, he unlocked the door and jerked it open wide as Dog joined him, his back bristled, a low growl rumbling up from his chest as he loped out into a street deserted at this late hour, light from the "Cat's" torches shining on damp cobblestones. Duran followed Dog, staff in hand, around the corner of his house and into the blind alleyway.

The combination of moonlight and distant torch-light showed him who his opponents were: mere boys, three of them, probably no more than four-teen years old—and running up behind the young toughs, he was upon them before they heard him coming. He lashed out with his staff—once, twice—hitting two of the boys, then jabbing up at the stomach of the third.

"Damn you!" He spun around to take a blow on his staff from the first tough he had hit and to deliver the butt-end into an unguarded kneecap. "Don't like the odds now, do you?"

One of the boys sprinted off into the darkness: Duran heard a snarl and a yelp of pain—Dog had entered the fight, one remaining thug attempting to tear from Dog's hold, the other, lamed, sidling around Duran, his back to the wall of the building on the opposite side of the alley.

"Hey, Grandpa!" the other taunted, and Duran saw the dim glint of light on metal in that hand. "See if you can get this!"

The young tough stabbed out with his knife, but Duran had expected the move and, jumping back, brought the end of his staff around in a blow that

sent his opponent staggering back against the wall.
A second swipe of the staff knocked the boy's knife
from his hand—at which, with Dog chasing after
the second thug, the boy Duran faced spun and
lurched off into the dark, decidedly the worse for
wear.

Panting, Duran leaned on his long staff, his ears
ringing. Damn. He had not lost his touch.

Dog gave up the chase and trotted tamely back.
Quiet descended on the block. Somewhere shutters banged closed again—none in this lane but his
own, that cast a wan light to reflect on the walls.
The victim of the toughs' attack sat leaning up
against the wall of Duran's house, arms wrapped
around his chest.

"Boy?" Duran said, walking closer. No response.
"Are you all right?"

The boy looked up, nodded briefly, once.

Sabirn. The hair, the features were distinctive
even in the dim light. A Sabirn out walking in this
district. *That* explained the attack.

"Can you stand?" Duran asked. The boy nodded, gathered his feet and made an attempt. After
a brief moment, he subsided. "Here." Duran held
out a hand, grasped the youth under one arm, and
helped him to his feet. "Got you pretty bad, did
they?"

The Sabirn youth nodded again and stood swaying
on his feet. Dog had come back from investigating
the battle-site, and snuffed at the boy's shoes.

Duran looked across at the "Cat," at the end of
the alleyway, but the tavern lay silent: many of its
customers had gone home by now, and the travelers who were staying the night would have likely

gone to bed: too late to rouse Tutadar, no sign of Old Man, who might be some use.

"Lean on me," Duran said, taking some of the boy's weight on his left side. He took the lad toward the street, toward his front door—gods, he had left it open. But Dog trotted ahead and stood waiting on the doorstep, tail slowly wagging back and forth, evidence of property unmolested.

The Sabirn boy balked at the threshold, wobbled: Duran insisted, Duran helped the youth across the doorstep, Dog complicating matters by trying to enter the shop at the same time.

"Go on, Dog. Good boy. Lie down now." Duran nodded, let the boy lean against the counter, picked up his lamp. "Then let's take it slow." He reached out to put the other arm around the boy: the youth flinched. "Easy. *Mehciya.*"

The boy looked at him, set-jawed, scared-looking in the lamplight.

"That's the limit of my Sabir. But I'm a friend. Try to help me if you can."

Slowly, taking as much of the boy's weight as he would give, Duran walked him to the rear of the shop. The steps leading upstairs were steep and narrow; he took them one at a time, pausing now and again to let the youth gather strength for the next. Finally, Duran gained the second story, and led the boy into his room, to his bed.

Another hesitation. "Easy now, take it easy." He insisted, brought the boy to the bedside, let him slide from his arm to sit on the bed. Duran set his lamp down on the table close by, looked down at the Sabirn youth. "Well, now. Let's take a look at you. . . ."

The boy flinched as Duran brushed his long black hair back from his forehead. His gaze flicked back and forth across the room, toward the window—

"Dammit, lad, I won't hurt you. Don't fight me now. *Mehciya,* understand? I'm trying to help."

The boy murmured something inaudible, but sat silent as Duran inspected the cut. That was not as bad as it looked, just bloody. Duran knelt and looked at the youth's ankle: sprained and swelling— if it was not broken. The ribs—the gods knew. The boy had no inclination to let him see.

"All right." He stood and walked across the room toward a small cabinet. "I'm going to get you something that should make you feel better." He glanced over his shoulder. "For Hladyr's sake, boy . . . I'm not your enemy. Relax."

Duran always kept a few essential herbs and poultices upstairs in case he found the need for them. He came back with a splinter of kindling, lit it from the lamp, moved his current project off the stove and set on a clean pot, from the stores on the shelf, wormwood mixed in wine. He waited patiently while the mixture heated, then dipped a clean rag into the steaming solution.

"This may sting some at first," he said, "but it will take away the pain." He met the youth's eyes. *"Amegi?"*

The boy nodded, and Duran set to work on the lad's cut forehead. The boy's hands clenched on the edge of the bed.

"I'm almost done . . . There. Now. You want to let me see the ribs? Mmmn?"

The youth frowned, hesitated—then untied his belt, and set aside a small wooden flute he had kept bound at his waist. Gingerly lifting his tunic, he revealed bruises that had already darkened his thin torso.

"Huhn. Wrap in the sheet. I'll mix something stronger." He went back to his shelves and took out another jar, filled this time with white vinegar and a stronger tincture of wormwood. This, too, he heated a little, poured half into a pan he set to heat, then returned to the boy. "I'll be gentle as I can."

The youth shut his eyes and nodded. Duran generously swabbed the bruised areas of the boy's chest, side and back, then with strips of rag tied the soaked cloth against the lad's bruises.

"That should do it for now," he said as the youth lowered his tunic. "The ankle's what worries me." The water on the stove had begun to steam: Duran brought the pan back, encouraged the lad to slip off his ragged shoe and put his foot into the water.

The boy winced at the heat. Slowly, keeping his eyes closed and his jaw clamped tight, he lowered his foot into the water.

"Ahh!"

"I know," Duran said. "Hurts like Dandro's hells, doesn't it? Patience, lad. The pain will start to go away."

Dark eyes followed Duran as he went back to the stove. "Why're you doing this?" the boy asked.

Duran shrugged. "Why not?"

"I'm Sabirn."

"Aye, that you are." Duran came back to the bedside.

"You're Ancar."

"That I am. I'm also an apothecary. Sometimes a doctor."

"Nobody else'd help me." The boy's eyes were steady. "Why're you different?"

Duran cocked his head. "I'm me," he said. "And I don't like to see folks hurt. How'd you end up in that alley anyway?"

The boy frowned. He remained silent.

"Don't answer if you don't want to. Have you ever seen those three toughs before?"

"No."

"Chase you far?"

The boy nodded. "*Chochi*. My fault." He wiggled his toes in the water. "Damn stupid to get caught like that."

Duran fetched the chair from against the wall, and set it by the bedside. He lowered himself down and crossed his legs. "Have you got any family? Anyone who will worry where you are?"

The boy stared at Duran in sudden, stark suspicion.

"All right. You've scores and scores of relatives. All of them formidable. What's your name?"

After a long pause, the boy replied, "Kekoja."

Duran waited, but that was all. Kekoja. "I'm Duran," he said. "Is that ankle feeling any better?"

The youth frowned, looked at him sidelong. "Doctor, huh?"

"Of sorts. A herbalist and an apothecary. An alchemist, by professional— Mmmn, you don't trust me, do you?"

The boy kept his gaze level. "Why're you doing this?" he asked for the second time.

Why indeed? Duran had asked himself the same

question. He had always been kind to the Sabirn,
but he had never had one of them in his house.
He thought of the neighbors . . .

And felt just the least apprehension.

"Why're you doing this?" the boy insisted to
know.

"Humanity," Duran said. "Was I to leave you
lying in an alley?"

"I'm Sabirn," the boy repeated, as if that explained it all.

Which, Duran thought, maybe it did.

CHAPTER 3

Duran woke, the morning sun just slanting through the shutter-slats. He stretched—gods, he was stiff; and ached in more places than he thought possible. He grimaced, rubbed his eyes, rolled over on the pallet and glanced over to his bed.

The boy was still asleep; curled up in a little ball, he had kicked the rest of Duran's blankets down toward the end of the bed. Duran snorted softly. From the still air, the lack of draft from the window, there would be small need of those coverings tonight. Warm, moist air, no morning wind from the sea—it promised a muggy, nasty day.

Duran sat up, arms on knees and stared at his sleeping charge. The boy had had his suspicions—extreme suspicions—for which Duran did not blame him. Hence the night on the floor—but only one night, damn the young fool. And what in hell could he do with the boy? Turn him out on the streets? Good as Duran knew his medicines to be, that ankle would take several days to heal, maybe need more than wormwood. Maybe need rest— else the boy would limp his way through life: and a Sabirn lad had no prospects but portage and a hand to mouth existence. Lame, he had no hope but beggary.

He wiped the hair back from his face and sighed, feeling all the indiscretions of last night. Maybe he *was* getting too old to be fighting in alleyways. Forty-five. He shook his head, remembering his youth, when he thought anyone who was forty-five had one foot in the grave, and the other one slipping in behind it.

But he did not *feel* old. Inside, he was still in his twenties, still at the prime of his life. He scratched his beard, raked a hand through his hair, and levered himself to his feet, by degrees.

He nudged the table, grabbed after the edge, for balance. Kekoja stirred, stretched his legs out, and groaned softly.

"Hladyr bless," Duran said in morning greeting. "You're better?"

Kekoja rubbed his eyes, sat up in bed, and yawned. He glanced at Duran, then eased his foot out to the side of the bed and looked at it. It was spectacularly puffed, red, and angry.

In addition to which, the boy looked decidedly uncomfortable.

"Chamber pot?" Duran asked, feeling the need for the same.

Kekoja squirmed his way to the edge of the bed and slowly lowered his feet to the floor. He winced, his eyes narrowed in pain.

Duran knelt and drew the pot out from under

the bed. He held out an arm and helped the boy to his feet. "I won't look, if it makes you feel better," he said.

The boy shook off the help, turned his back, balanced gingerly against that foot . . .

No trust of him. No.

Traffic was beginning to stir in the streets below. Duran kept his eyes fixed across the room as Kekoja performed his duty, thinking if they did not both hurry, the slop gatherers would be come and gone—*not* a pleasant prospect for an upstairs bedroom on a hot day . . .

"Shit!"

Duran glanced around just as the boy wobbled and fell sidelong onto the bed, slid halfway to the floor.

He hauled the Sabirn lad up to his knees, trying to be careful of the ribs—helped him lie down then. The boy's eyes were slightly glazed and his face had turned decidedly pale, broken out in sweat. But he shoved the help away.

"Boy?"

Kekoja was breathing hard. He wiped his face, glassy-eyed, said, thickly, "Lost my balance."

"Lie still," Duran commanded, despite the boy's hazed objections lightly running his fingertips over the boy's skull.

"Yeow!"

Duran jerked his hand back. "You've got a lump on the back of your head the size of an egg. Where else did they hit you?"

"Don't remember." The Sabirn lad took a deep breath. "I'm dizzy."

"I'd expect. People who get lumps that size on

their heads don't feel especially wonderful after-
ward. —Does it feel better when you lie down?"

"Not as dizzy . . ."

"Listen, son. You stay put in that bed until you
can stand up and not fall all over yourself. Head
wounds aren't anything to treat lightly."

Kekoja nodded slowly, eased his head back on
the pillow, and looked at Duran, his eyes still
glassy. Duran ignored him, used the chamber pot
himself, took it toward the door.

"Stay put!" he ordered the boy.

The Sabirn lad nodded.

"I mean it. Don't try to get up. You'll do yourself lasting harm. Do you understand?"

"Aye." Faintly.

"Good." Duran started down the stairs. "Remember it. —I'll go get us something to eat."

Dog stood waiting at the doorway, excited and
turning around in circles.

"Poor fellow," Duran said, opening the door
and letting the dog outside. "Don't have your own
convenience, do you?"

He set the chamber pot on his doorstep, stood
up and stretched, with a deep breath of the morning air, paused for a glance up the street. Zeldezia
had opened her shop and was now busily sweep-
ing around her front door. Efdin, the baker, had
already started his day: the sluggish air carried a
scent of fresh bread. There was the rattle of chains
as Ithar opened his smithy. Apprentices began to
gather at the doorways of the other shops on the
street, laughing and calling out to one another.

Duran thought of Kekoja waiting upstairs on the

bed, with not a little worry, having the lad alone with his shelves, his medicines, his personal things—

Damn it all, anyway. Here he, who had always been courteous and kind to the Sabirn, was worried about robbery—on the part of an injured boy. *With an ankle like his, and that knot on his head, he'd be lucky if he could make it down the stairs.*

He closed the door behind him, locked it, and crossed the street to the "Cat." The door stood open, food was cooking. Old Man had stirred out of his night-time place on the floor inside to sit on the wide doorstep, a bowl of food in his hands.

Duran nodded at Old Man in passing, and entered the common room of the inn. This early in the morning, there were no people at the tables. Tutadar stood behind the bar, going over last night's take, arranging the coins in neat rows before him.

"Morning, Duran," Tutadar said, glancing up from his work. "Want your usual today?"

"Aye. A double portion. I'll take it with me if I can."

Tutadar shot Duran a questioning look but said nothing, and walked back toward the kitchen. Duran leaned up against the bar, keeping his eyes to the street outside. Should he tell Tutadar about his unusual guest, or not? Double portions alone of his breakfast would serve as a clue that something odd was going on.

"Got company?" Tutadar asked casually, returning from the kitchen, carrying two covered metal plates. He set the plates on the bar, and filled two mugs with wine.

"Aye." Duran glanced around the common room.

He and Tutadar were still alone. "Last night three toughs beat up a boy in the alleyway. I chased them off, but the boy's in a bad way. Won't be able to move for a couple days."

Tutadar snorted something under his breath. "Damned punk kids are startin' to make life miserable. Himself the Duke better do somethin' about it. Bad for business." He met Duran's eyes. "Got any idea whose kid? Some 'prentice?"

"No." Duran risked it all. "He's Sabirn, Tut. About fourteen. Nice looking boy, smart—"

"You left that kid in your house? Alone?" Tutadar leaned forward on the bar. "I know you don't mind workin' with them Sabirn, Duran, but don't let 'em fool you. Once your back's turned, they'll take you for everythin' you got."

Duran signed for quieter voices. "This one's in no condition to do that right now. Those toughs really knocked him around. Hit him hard enough on the head, he's still dizzy. On top of that, he's got an ankle sprained bad enough to keep him from walking for at least another day or two."

"And what're *you* going to get from this, Duran? 'Sides another mouth you can't afford to feed."

"I couldn't leave him out in that alley, Tut. And I don't think you would have, either. I thought of Old Man—"

"No!" Tut said, waving his hand. "No! Old Man I don't mind, Old Man's got his place here, he's *our* Sab, all right? He's old, he knows his place, he don't make no trouble. But there ain't no kid comin' in here, no. You've got too good a heart in you, Duran. One of these days, it's going to cause you trouble."

"Tut,—keep it quiet, will you? He's just a kid."

Tutadar set the covered plates and two mugs in a well-worn basket. "Just a kid," he muttered. "Listen," he said, then, leaning forward on the bar, his eyes locked with Duran's. "You ain't helpin' yourself by keepin' company with them Sabirn. *I* know you're too damned good-hearted, but—tongues is going to wag, Duran. They already do. It's one thing, hirin' some Sab to dig herbs, port baskets and all, but there's a limit, man. There's a limit t' what folk will understan'. You get my drift? Ain't *me*, you know that . . . but you know you can't keep that kid in there much longer without *everybody* findin' out."

Duran nodded. What Tutadar said was all too true. Because of his uptown ways, because of the . . . odd smells from the apothecary shop, lights at all hours, the occasional midnight customer, his neighbors already considered him peculiar. There were apothecaries who dabbled in . . . elimination of persons unwanted; there were those who sold things . . . unapproved by the clergy and against the law, as murder was . . .

A man who dealt with harbor trade, who treated whores, a large part of whose trade was harborside, in diseases law-abiding folk disdained to name—

"I hear what you're saying." He dug in his belt pouch and set out four coppers on the bar. "I'll bring the plates and basket back after I'm done," he promised.

"Keep your eyes on that kid," Tutadar warned, setting Duran's money aside for the first of his morning sales. His voice grew gruff. "Don't want anythin' to happen to you. You're a good neighbor."

Duran smiled sadly, lifted the basket and went outside. Old Man was finishing his breakfast, his dark eyes roving up and down the street. Duran nodded again in passing, nothing said, and crossed over to his shop, where Dog sat waiting on the doorstep. Duran juggled the basket in one arm, took out his keys, and opened the door—

While the seamstress, Zeldezia, stood leaning on her broom, her sharp eyes watching his every movement. Duran nodded a dour good morning to her as he went inside. Damned nosy woman. Before the hour was out, she would have told all the neighbors that Duran was eating in his house this morning, rather than at the tavern, and *probably* know exactly what he had for breakfast . . .

The slop gatherers had already been down his side of the street: the chamber pot sat empty by the steps. Later, Duran advised himself. Breakfast first. He waited for Dog to come into the shop, shut and locked the door, and went upstairs.

Kekoja sat propped up in bed, pillows stacked between his back and the wall, silently watching Duran lay out the two plates and set out mugs of watered wine on the table beside the bed. Duran noticed a glitter in the black eyes: hunger, most likely. He wondered how long it had been since the boy had eaten a good meal.

"Fish," Duran said, removing the covers from the plates. "Fresh fish. Straight up from harbor. The 'Cat' is fastidious. Are you still dizzy?"

The youth carefully shoved himself upright on the bed, his eyes moving from the dishes to Duran's face. The scowl persisted.

"What do you want?" Kekoja asked, turning to the edge of the bed, carefully putting his swollen ankle off the side.

"What do I want what? What kind of question is that?"

"You got something in mind, or you wouldn't be doing all this."

"Eat your food," Duran said, shoving a short knife across the table to the boy. "It's going to get cold."

Kekoja hesitated, then accepted the knife and began cutting up his fish, spearing small bites of it.

"Why do I have to want something from you to feed you?" Duran asked.

"Never had any Ancar treat me decent before." Kekoja took another bite, chewed hurriedly, and shot him a scowling look. "An' if they did, they'd want something."

"Well, I don't. So take your mind off it." Duran drank and set his mug down. "Now I'm going to ask you again—seriously: do you have any family or friends who will be worrying about you?"

The boy's black eyes measured Duran with a look too mature for his apparent youth. "Hundreds of 'em."

"Hladyr's Light, boy! You'd think I was out after—"

The boy stared at him, jaw clenched.

"I'd *like* to find your kin, boy, let them know where to find you, get you *home*, for Hladyr's sake, I've no other motives. Why would I go to this trouble? There's whores harborside. So what would I be after?"

Kekoja's eyes dropped. He speared another bite of fish. "I don't know," he said, his words muffled by the food in his mouth. "Sell me, maybe."

"Nothing worth the night on the floor. —Lad, I don't bother boys. And I don't sell them, either."

Kekoja looked at Duran again. "I got a grandfather," he said at last.

"A grandfather. Where does he live?"

" 'Cross the street."

"Across the— You don't mean the old, white-haired man who sits in 'The Swimming Cat,' do you?"

A nod.

Duran leaned back in his chair and regarded the boy with renewed interest. Old Man's grandson? He had never thought of Old Man as anything but Old Man. That he had once been married and had a grandson . . .

Not here, Tut had said. . . .

"You want me to tell him you're here?" Duran asked. "He can't take you in, but, hell, wouldn't he like to know you're here?"

A brief flash of emotion passed behind the boy's black eyes. "Aye. If you'd do that . . ."

"After breakfast. And before I go, I'm taking another look at that ankle. Can you wiggle it? Wiggle the toes?"

Kekoja moved his foot carefully. Toes moved. "Hurts."

"Then we'll soak it again." Duran finished off his fish and drained his mug. "I have to run my shop," he said, leaning back in his chair as the boy ate the last of the fish. "I'll open up, heat up some compresses. Will you be all right up here?"

"Afraid I'll steal something?"

"Not really."

"Everyone else thinks so."

"I'm not everyone else," Duran said, putting his plate into the basket and following it with Kekoja's. "The sooner you realize that, the more comfortable you'll be. Besides, you try that window, lad, you'll break your neck. Hear me?"

Old Man sat on the doorstep, his face relaxed as he leaned his head back against the wall, outside, this warm morning. Duran looked all directions, saw no one he knew, hunkered down on his heels. "Greetings, Old Man."

"A good morning to you, Sor Duran." If Old Man was astonished at this behavior, he failed to show it.

"Last night three toughs beat up a boy in the alleyway next to my house. I ran them off and took him upstairs. He's got a sprained ankle, a knot on his head . . ." Duran waited for a response, but Old Man kept silent, his gaze as placid as ever. "This lad *says* he's your grandson. Says his name is Kekoja."

Old Man's expression hardly changed. "Where is he?"

"In my upstairs. In my bed. Eating my breakfast. He's not fit to walk. I don't know where else to send him. Or how."

Old Man's black eyes strayed from Duran's face to the shop across the street. "That's who you took the food to this morning?" he asked.

Old Man missed nothing. "Aye. Where shall I take him?"

"Did he ask for me?"

"He said you were related. He didn't ask for anything."

"He's got his reasons."

"Do you want to see him?"

Old Man's black eyes scanned the street about. Came back to him. Old Man nodded faintly, reached after his stick.

Duran stood, took Old Man's walking stick from the wall, and gave it to him. Old Man rose walked beside him across the street.

Zeldezia's door opened. She shook a dusty rug into the street, stopped, mouth open. Duran cursed inwardly, fished out his keys, opened the door to his shop, and followed Old Man inside. Dog waited by the counter and ambled over to sniff Old Man over.

"Go, Dog. Lie down. You know Old Man. That's-a-boy." Duran shut the door and waved a hand at the stairway. "Upstairs."

Old Man nodded, limped to the stairs, slowly ascended them. Duran came behind, indicated the doorway, which Old Man opened.

"Grandfather!"

Kekoja sat on the edge of the bed, his foot soaking in water and salts. Old Man took another step forward, and spoke rapidly in Sabirn, of which Duran could understand only a few words, none significant to him: the boy responded with words equally swift.

"He says you helped him last night," Old Man said, turning to Duran, "that you don't want anything from him. Is this true?"

"I *don't* want anything from him." Old Man's

look at him seemed too sharp, too careful. "Anybody would have done the same, if they'd heard
the fight. No one in Old Town likes thugs."

Old Man squared his shoulders. "No one likes
thugs, aye. But some of your neighbors, Sor Duran,
like Sabirn even less. He says he ate your breakfast."

Duran shrugged.

"You fed him. Do you know what that means to
us?"

More than he knew, by Old Man's stern look.
Duran shook his head, embarrassed, confused.

"You are willing for him to have this food?"

"Of course I'm willing. He doesn't owe me
anything."

"You are bound by that giving. He is bound.
We Sabirn do not take other people's food will-
ingly."

"I didn't know. And I don't feel that he's bound
to me, if that makes any difference."

"What's done, is done," Old Man said. "Since
you offered him food out of concern for him, and
since you don't know our customs, I don't hold
you to the rules we live by." He gestured briefly.
"But the boy knows. He knows."

"Look, Old Man, debt or no debt—he's clear.
He's free. Where shall I send him? Where's his
father? Where's his mother?"

Old Man shrugged by way of answer.

"Where does he live?" Duran asked. "He comes
from somewhere."

"He lives on the street. So do most of us Sabirn."

"He's not going to be using that ankle for the
next few days. He's not going to be living on the
street."

Old Man shrugged.

Duran stared.

"I'm all right," Kekoja said from his place on the bed. "I can walk."

"Be still," Old Man muttered. "Pay your debts."

The boy set his jaw. "But, I—"

"You know I can't let you stay with me. Don't argue."

The lad's face turned red, and he angrily launched into a rapid stream of Sabirn. Old Man replied in the same language, making a few cutting motions with his hands. Duran watched the exchange, wondering what in the hells he had managed to get himself mixed up in.

"My grandson," Old Man said at last, turning away from Kekoja, "has a mind of his own . . . and a sharp tongue to go with it. I'm sorry, Sor Duran, but he must stay with you. He has no choice."

"Grandfather—"

"No choice, Kekoja!"

The boy frowned, his shoulders still stiffened in anger.

"Since he's staying here," Old Man said, "I insist that you let me pay you something . . . at least for the food he eats."

Duran drew a long breath. *With what?* he wondered. Aloud he said: "Can't either of you understand that I'm trying to help? That I don't expect anything in return?"

Old Man lifted his chin.

"All right," Duran sighed. "Pay for his food, if that's what bothers you."

"You're a very strange one for an Ancar," Old Man said, leaning on his walking stick. "You al-

ways have been, as long as I've known you." He
looked Duran directly in the face—which no Sabirn
did. "You've given more than you understand, Sor
Duran. You don't know our customs, but let me
say that what I'll give you in return means much
to us." He spread a hand over his heart and bowed.
"My name is Dajhi."

Duran reckoned suddenly—he *knew* fewer Sabirn
names than he did Sabirn words. "Dajhi," he repeated, and then, making a blind leap of logic:
"Your name is safe with me. So is your grandson.
Whatever his real name."

Old Man's eyes softened. "You *are* a strange
one," he said. He turned to Kekoja. "You've heard.
Trust this one. Do what he says. Behave yourself,
tehiji."

The boy looked sullenly at his grandfather.
"Aye."

"You have your shop to run, Sor Duran," Old
Man said. "I've taken enough of your time. Take
me downstairs and I'll leave you."

Duran nodded and led the way down the steps,
stood by the doorway as Old Man left, thinking.

He dragged his mind back to his business. Hladyr
send him a few more customers today. The silver
Wellhyrn had given him would only last so long.

The gods—even the Shining One—seemed to
have better things to do than listen to one man's
prayers. All morning long Duran sat behind his
counter, waiting for customers who never materi-
alized. Mother Garan, alone, returned for another
dose of willow tea, saying her head felt better.

Duran charged her the usual three coppers, and sent her off with strict instructions. One worried. Like many others in Old Town, she could not afford a doctor of the kind that practiced uptown. Duran was the next best thing . . . affordable. Knowledgeable enough to worry about the old lady—to ease the pain as he could. To do as much as he could and refrain at least from doing harm.

Duran thought of Kekoja upstairs, and wondered what the Sabirn boy was doing to pass the time. He had not heard the lad leave the bed; his floor had several singing boards, and someone not knowing them it would alert a listener downstairs.

"Duran," Ithar said, entering the shop. "Got me a cut that don't seem to heal."

Duran got down from his stool. "Where?"

Ithar extended one burly arm. "There. Got cut t'other day . . . well, three, four days back, and it ain't healed up like it should. Thought you might have somethin' to help me."

"I might." Duran looked at the sore: it was red and swollen. "Did you wash it good after you got burned?"

"Hells, I didn't have time. Had a man comin' to pick up his goods and I was runnin' late. I just smeared some mud on it."

"Washing's better." Duran turned around and consulted the shelves of neatly labeled jars. He pulled one out and pushed it across the counter toward Ithar. "This ought to help."

The smith eyed the jar. "How much d'you think I need?"

"Not the whole thing." Duran looked at the cut again. "Maybe a quarter jar will do."

"Just rub it on?"

"Aye. And when you're working, —keep the cut covered with a clean cloth. Does it hurt?"

"Sommat. Not as bad as when I did it . . . but it don't seem to hurt any less lately."

"Huh." Duran stooped, reached under his counter, and pulled out a small earthen bowl and its lid. He carefully poured some of the oil from the larger jar into the bowl and set the lid in place—the tangy smell of cinnamon filled the air. "When you get back to your shop, heat some water hot as you can stand it. Soak the arm till the water cools. Then get a clean—clean! stick, drop some of this on."

"Aye. Clean stick." Ithar took the bowl. "What do I owe you, Duran?"

Duran calculated. "Five coppers should do. If you should have some oil left when you're healed, keep it clean and sealed with wax, and it should keep."

Ithar nodded, dug in his belt pouch one-handed, and set the copper coins on Duran's counter. "You ain't gettin' rich doin' this, Duran. I charge *twice* that to fix a broken anchor chain, and that don't take no mixing with foreign stuffs."

"Your customers can afford it," Duran said, pocketing the coppers. "So."

Ithar stared at Duran a moment, then grinned. "Hladyr bless," he said, then turned and left the shop.

Duran sat down on his stool and looked down at Dog. "Eight coppers so far today. We might not do badly."

Dog merely wagged his tail, turned around several times, and stretched out at the end of the counter.

Eight coppers. Duran remembered when he and other noble children spent more than that on sweetmeats at market. He now lived on less than he could have ever conceived, and not all that badly, either—as poor went.

He caught movement out of the corner of one eye: Zeldezia stood in the doorway, holding her apron in one hand.

"Better business today than yesterday," she said, coming inside. "Rain scared off all but the determined, or the desperate."

Duran's contentment vanished. "That's true. You're doing well today?"

"I should be," the seamstress said, lifting one eyebrow. "After all, I *am* the best in this area."

Duran nodded. Obnoxious as Zeldezia could be, she was justified in her pride: she was by far the most talented seamstress in this section of Old Town: people came to her from better sections of the city, knowing they could get a bargain; and went away happy, too.

But Zeldezia never was.

If she didn't spend so damned much time telling everyone how good she is, Duran thought, *someone* might *find a chance to tell her.*

"You still got that boy in there?" Zeldezia asked bluntly.

Duran started. Damned if the woman had not seen him take the Sabirn lad upstairs last night. But he should have known . . . not much went on in the neighborhood that Zeldezia could not ferret out.

"Aye."

"Got beat up bad, did he?"

Duran shrugged. "Bad enough."

Zeldezia cocked her head and looked up at Duran. "Not very talkative today, are you? Who beat him up? You recognize 'em?"

"No. Three boys. Tut calls them 'punk kids.' "

"Well, we don't need them sort here in *this* neighborhood. If they move in, we'll be no better than the Slough."

The Slough . . . the roughest part of Old Town; lair of thieves, whores, and bullies. It lay to the west, by the marshy side of the river, a breeding place for vermin—human and otherwise.

"Hladyr forbid they move in," Duran said, for once in total agreement with his neighbor.

"That boy *is* Sabirn, ain't he?" Zeldezia asked, eyeing Duran closely. "That why you brung Old Man up?"

Duran nodded, knowing he could not deny what she had seen.

"Gods, Duran! Them folk ain't no good. An' you've got one in your house? In your bed? On your *sheets*?" Zeldezia's lips thinned into a frown. "Lady bless, Duran! He'll steal you blind. He'll have all his friends comin' in. You think about your neighbors? *We* don't want no Sabirn hangin' 'round here."

"Old Man doesn't steal," Duran pointed out, trying to keep his temper.

"Old Man's different. He don't bother no one. Besides, he's a cripple and he wouldn't be able to steal nothin' without *someone* noticin'."

"If it makes you feel any better," Duran said, "the boy's Old Man's grandson."

Zeldezia lifted both eyebrows at this news. A tidbit always excited her. He instantly regretted saying that. Especially as her face settled back into its angry expression. "They're devils, them Sabirn. Necro-mancers. Demon worshipers. Ain't no good come of 'em. I tell you, you're a gods-fearin' man, Duran, but you come close to damnin' your soul, havin' anything to do with 'em."

"Now, Zeldezia . . ."

"You got to think! Think what could happen to your business . . . to *my* business if folk found out you're hangin' around with Sabirn, that you got one of 'em in your house, fer Hladyr's sake! Think o' my uptown clients! What'd they think? We hob-nob around with them dirty Sabs? We could lose all our customers!"

"Well, we don't have to worry, do we?" Duran interposed smoothly. "If *you* don't tell anyone, and *I* don't tell anyone, no one will know, will they?"

Zeldezia frowned the darker. "I'm tellin' you, Duran, you're makin' a mistake. You can't trust 'em. Nowhere. Nohow. They'll get you so's you like 'em, an' then they'll run off with everythin' you own. Gods, drinkin' out o' your cups and eatin' off your dishes—"

Duran got down from his stool and walked to the corner of the counter so he faced Zeldezia. "I've dealt with Sabirn for years now," he said, "and not one of them has ever been anything but polite. —Why do you hate them, Zeldezia? What have they ever done to you?"

"They're wizard-spawn!"

"There's nothing they do that the Temple wizards or the Duke's wizards don't do."

"Oh, that's what they want you to think! Them Sabirn wizards practice the dark arts." She lowered her voice. "Priest says anyone who has anything to do with 'em is in peril of his *soul!*"

"Horseshit!" Duran exclaimed, hoping the vulgarity would chase Zeldezia off. As usual, it had no effect. Vadami. Damned snot-nosed district priest. Always spreading *his* version of the Eternal Scheme of Things. . . .

"Well, if *you* end up knifed in your bed one night, I won't be surprised," Zeldezia said. "An' let me tell you, Duran . . . if you know what's good for you, you'll get rid of that boy 'fore folks find out he's up there."

"Not until he's healed," Duran countered, drawing himself up to his full height. "If anyone finds out, I'll know who told them. And it won't have been me!"

Zeldezia threw back her head so she could look Duran in the eyes, set fists on ample hips. "I can see I ain't going to change your mind. Just think on what I said, Duran. Your business an' mine could suffer for your stupidity! Folks ain't going to take medicine you mix with no Sab kid slinking 'round this shop!"

Duran clamped his jaws together, afraid of what he would say if he spoke.

"So." Zeldezia shifted her apron to her other hand, and straightened her dress. "I'm going to the Temple. The Duke's going to be there, him an' his family. It's the Heir's name-day."

Duran's heart went thump. The Duke's heir, resplendent at the ceremony—

Due, soon, for his next treatment for the pox.

Zeldezia turned to go, then looked back over her shoulder. "An' while I'm at the Temple, I'll pray Hladyr that he give you some good sense!"

With that, she swept out of the shop. Duran let loose his pent-up breath and stared after her. Gods! He had told Tut about Kekoja, knowing the innkeeper would keep his mouth shut. How in hell had Zeldezia . . .

Duran glanced upstairs, hoping with any kind of luck, Kekoja had heard nothing. Damned woman. But she could be right.

Dammit all anyway. He had never flaunted his dealing with the Sabirn—the way Tut had said, one hired them—there were few people besides them he could afford to hire. Besides the stories—about which no one knew. He started pacing up and down in front of his counter. He would have to be less obvious in dealing with the Sabirn, possibly cease talking with them at all till this blew over. All of them except Old Man. Old Man was safe . . .

People knew Old Man. They would surely take it better, if they knew the boy was Old Man's grandson.

CHAPTER 4

Storm bore down on Targheiden: Duran heard the rumble of thunder out on the sea; the sunlight faded as clouds moved over the city. He thought of the ceremony taking place in the Temple, and of how this storm would not be viewed as a particularly good omen . . .

As for the main participant in the ceremony, the Duke's son had promised to return for another treatment this very night—punctually: Duran had stressed that. He was sure Brovor had understood. But the dates added up to today, to name-day—not easy, he feared, for Brovor to slip away from the feast held in his honor, but the young man was terrified enough of his disease that Duran hoped escape for the short time it would take to come to Old Town—

Hoped the secrecy would hold up. And that Brovor would ask no questions—nor come to any sudden recognitions.

And the Sabirn boy upstairs—

Duran looked out his open door, gnawing his lip. In one uncalculated act, his life had become more complicated than he could have ever imagined. The Duke's son, then the Sabirn lad. Gods! If his neighbors only knew *half* of what was going on in his shop, if Zeldezia—gods!—if *that* rattle-tongue looked out her shutters tonight—

The thunder grew louder. Duran looked up at what sky he could see. Dark, menacing clouds rolled in over the rooftops; a stiff wind had begun to blow, rattling the apothecary's sign over his door, setting signs to swinging on their chains all up and down the street, a worn-out basket blowing and tumbling down a street rapidly emptying of traffic.

Evil weather . . . aye, the summer had been plagued by it, folk talked in the streets and taverns about it. What was bad for trade was bad for Targheiden, merchants worried, tempers flared over insignificant things; small fortunes vanished each time a ship went down. There was only one bene-fit of the rain: cooler weather this summer kept disease from running rampant through the poorer sections of town.

It also kept customers from his door.

He sniffed the wind. Rain would fall very soon now, rain which—

CRASH!

Duran spun around in the doorway; Dog had risen to his feet and stood growling, glaring at the stairs.

"Oh, Hladyr bless!" Duran ran to the steps, hurried upstairs, and stopped in the doorway.

Kekoja lay on the floor by one of the side windows, his eyes closed, an upturned table and the shattered remains of a porcelain wash bowl scattered around him.

"By all the gods!" he cried, "what in Dandro's hells are you doing?" He rushed to Kekoja's side and knelt to touch his face. "Are you all right?"

The Sabirn looked up at Duran with an unsteady gaze. He tried to sit up, but fell back into Duran's arms.

"Dizzy," he mumbled, closing his eyes again. "Damned dizzy."

Duran sighed, glanced at what remained of his late wife's wash basin, and helped the boy to his feet.

"What were you trying to do? Climb out the window? I *told* you to stay in bed! Why did you disobey?"

The boy kept silent as Duran set him down on the bed; he rubbed his forehead and groaned softly.

"You don't want me here," Kekoja said at last, leaning back so he lay stretched out on the bed. "Thought I'd leave."

"By the window? Gods, boy! That thump on your head addled your brains. You could have *killed* yourself trying to go out the window. And who told you I—"

God. Zeldezia. Shrill voices carried.

"Nobody needs to've told me. *I* know. I'm Sabirn. Nobody wants me." His eyes shimmered with tears; he angrily blinked them away. "Not even my grandfather!"

So there lay the crux of it. Duran propped the boy's head up on the pillows. "Don't talk like that.

I'm sure your grandfather has a good reason for what he's doing." *Does he, or is he not as kind-hearted as I think he is?* "And I never said I didn't want you here." *I'd much rather you'd gone with your grandfather, though. It would have made my life a damn sight easier.* "Take a couple deep breaths. You'll be all right."

Kekoja did as Duran instructed; after a few moments, he seemed calmer.

"Now, listen to me. I don't want you out of this bed except to use the chamber pot, you hear? And until you're steadier on your feet, I want you to call me when you have to go."

"Aye."

"And stay away from windows." Duran straightened the boy's hair gently. "Hear?"

The boy said nothing. Duran went to shut the window, pick up the pieces.

Perhaps if he found them all, he could barter Bontido the potter into fixing the basin.

No. The glaze had splintered. No hope that the basin could be reconstructed. The shards were too small.

He let the pieces fall. Another tie with the past . . . gone . . . shattered like his youth. . . .

"Can you fix it?" Kekoja asked.

Duran rose, looked down at the jagged pieces of the basin. "No. It's beyond repair."

The Sabirn lad bit his lower lip. "I'm really sorry. I didn't mean it."

"I know. It's just that. . . ." Duran waved a hand full of broken porcelain. "It was my wife's, and she's been dead for. . . ." His voice trailed off. He met Kekoja's dark eyes. "You stay in that bed, hear?"

"Aye," Kekoja said faintly.

Raindrops spattered against the roof, sudden gust of storm.

"I'm going back downstairs. You need anything, you call."

"I will." Kekoja stirred on the bed. "Sor Duran? —I won't break anything else. I promise."

Duran forced a smile to his lips. "See that you don't," he said, and turned toward the stairs.

The rain had slacked off to a drizzle. Duran sat on his stool, gazing out the opened door at passers-by hurrying to dryer destinations before the next spate. A ship must recently have made port: he had seen travelers entering "The Swimming Cat." One wondered . . . one dreamed . . . where those folk were from, what their business in Torgheiden was, and where they were going.

One might have had a dream of voyages—of travel to far places—in one's golden youth, when such things were possible . . .

But the farthest he ever went was to the country.

And, god, that was not far enough for his troubles, not far enough for safety from a duke's son, his father's past, his own damnable stupidity—

He had made another ten coppers since his midday meal, which brought his total day's take to eighteen. It was not the most he had ever made in a day, but—considering the rain and the fact summertime brought fewer illnesses than winter—not bad. He had broken even and seen a modest profit.

But medicines did not happen by magic. Nor come out of moonfluff. Fees bought supplies. Customers did. And he was running low on both.

Ah, well.

Duran walked to the back of his shop, drew a large earthenware jug out from under a table, and lugged it back to the counter, poured white vinegar from the large jug into a smaller one, dropped wormwood leaves into the vinegar.

Now, for the next two months, those small jugs would sit high on his shelves, the wormwood steeping in the vinegar. Duran plugged the large jug, carried it back to the rear of the shop—

The bang of a door down the way said, considering the direction and a familiar sound, that Zeldezia had returned from the Temple ceremony and was reopening her shop. Hladyr keep him from the woman's thoughts . . . a prayer, he knew, that would likely go unanswered. By now, she had probably told everyone she had met that her neighbor was harboring a Sabirn in his home, a wizard, no less, a practitioner of dark sorceries. . . .

He had known the risk he ran in taking Kekoja in: or at least he had *thought* he had known. His neighbors were good folk, all of them, working as did he simply to make a living in Old Town. But Tutadar's words came back to him: no! Absolutely not! Not here! Not in my tavern—

Damn. Why were people so fearful of what they did not understand or what was different? In all his years of dealing with Sabirn, Duran had not seen one genuine wizard. The Sabirn played a good game, some of them, and had people convinced they had far more powers than was true— any alchemist uptown knew *those* tricks; and any temple wizard could do sleight of hand, conjure doves—

Or fire.

"So, Duran. How's your afternoon been?"

He winced, turned from his search after alum he *knew* he had, and faced Zeldezia in his doorway. She wore a bright blue gown, graced with some of her finest embroidery, and her hair was neatly done up in braids and coif—a handsome, an impressive woman, in her temple finery: except the sour expression on her face had not changed from several hours back.

"Not bad," he said, keeping his voice light. "I've turned a profit, and the day's not over—not *everyone* went to temple."

She looked at him, then lifted her eyes toward the room upstairs. "Still got that Sabirn kid up there?"

Duran pursed his lips and wished he could say otherwise.

"S'pose I couldn't expect you to come to your senses," Zeldezia said, shaking her head. "You're a stubborn man, Duran . . . you don't listen to good sense. You been upstairs to see what he's thieved yet?"

"I doubt he's stolen anything," Duran replied, sitting down on his stool. "He's in no condition to do much but sit and soak his ankle. Leave it alone, Zeldezia. Leave it be. The boy'll go. He's just a kid with a sprained ankle. Let him be."

"I prayed for you," she said. "I did. Them Sabirn can corrupt you, taint your soul—they got charms can confuse a man, so's he's got to do what they want—and he don't even think any more . . ."

Duran snorted. "Now you're sounding like Priest Vadami," he muttered.

"I told him to pray for you, too."

Duran's heart constricted. "What . . . did you tell him?"

"That you was needing prayers. That this boy's moved hisself in—"

"Zeldezia!" Duran snapped, stepping down from his stool. "Can't you stay out of my business? Who gave you the right to prattle on to Vadami about what I do?"

Zeldezia stepped back a pace. "It's *my* business, too. Damned kid'll drive customers away from *all* of us!"

"And who was to know if you hadn't told? He's not going to be here much longer. He's got a sprained ankle! He's not in anybody's sight!"

"Listen to me, Duran," she said, squaring her shoulders. "You can't even see what's goin' on under your own nose. The boy's bespelled you, that's what he's done. Them Sabirn can do it, turn your mind to helpin' him, then mixin' god knows what, gettin' 'im moonwort and them whore's babies—"

"Oh, good *gods*, Zeldezia!"

"Vadami was shocked. He was real shocked."

"Did you tell him the boy was injured? Did you tell him that, or only what you wanted him to hear?"

Zeldezia's chin lifted. "I told him. Vadami says that don't make no difference. You're still comin' close to corruptin' your soul. You don't even know that kid's hurt. He can make you *think* he's hurt. An' this a 'pothecary's shop, with all these drugs and such—who knows what he can do with his hands on stuff like this? He could put it in the public well—"

Duran drew a short and furious breath. "He's not putting anything anywhere, Zeldezia. He can't walk! He can't stand up! Now I have business to attend to, as do you, I should think. And from now on, I wish you'd keep your nose out of my business, and your damn mouth *shut!*"

"Go on and treat me like this, Duran, but I'll *still* pray for you. Blessed Hladyr will bring you to your senses." She spun on her heel and stalked to the door. "You lissen to yourself, Duran, swearin' at your neighbors, bad-talkin' a priest, bad-talkin' me for prayin' for you—what's that sound like, hey?"

She left.

"Oh, damn, damn, damn!" Duran slammed a fist down on the countertop. "What's she *done* to me?"

A priest. A simple district priest, Vadami might be—but he had the ears of higher placed brethren, some of whom frequented the court.

Duran leaned his head on his hand and rubbed his eyes.

Vadami sat at a small table toward the front of "The Golden Shoe," a High City tavern frequented by well-to-do merchants, an occasional petty lord or two, and lower placed dignitaries of the Duke's court. He sipped his ale, and met the eyes of his companion, another priest—his immediate superior.

Priest Sorgun returned the stare, his eyes calm as the expression on his face. Vadami had chosen the inn as a place to talk because he felt comfortable here, and it was neutral territory, where neighbors paid little attention to him and his companion:

priests from the Temple often came here in the afternoon or evening.

"You wanted advice, Vadami."

"Aye." It was the ale—Vadami knew, in some distant part of his mind, that he had imbibed more than he should. It *was* the Duke's heir's name-day.

"What is it you want to talk about?"

"My feelings, Superior."

"What feelings?"

"Rebellious thoughts, Superior. Discontent. Envy. I—know that's unworthy of me."

Sorgun lifted an eyebrow. "What—kind of thoughts?"

Vadami glanced over his shoulder. Several fellow priests sat at a table toward the back of the room: ducal favorites, those priests, whose parishes incorporated the better sections of town.

"Do you see those men, Superior?" he asked, indicating the priests with a motion of his head. "I've served Hladyr from an early age. I gave up what could have been a promising career as a merchant. *I'm* no less a priest than those court favorites, and yet what do I have to show for it? *My* parish is Old Town, where donations—while sincere—are next to nothing."

"Each according to their means—"

Vadami set his mug to one side, and leaned forward, his hands gripping the edge of the table. "But why have I been allotted such a position in life, Superior? I'm smarter than many priests I know, and I love the Shining One with equal fervor. Why have I been doomed to minister to Old Town?"

"Ah, Vadami . . . not everyone gets what he

wants from life. Hladyr must test some of us more than others."

"But, why me?" Vadami straightened in his chair. "Why not someone else?"

"Patience," Sorgun said quietly. "We all have to start out somewhere. You're young, Vadami, only twenty-five, you have years of ministering before you. Many chances."

"I know, Superior." Vadami lowered his head. "But there are times. . . ." His voice trailed off, and he looked up at his companion. "Patience is difficult."

"Be strong. This is but a test put before you." A faint smile touched Sorgun's face. "And, whether you believe it or not, it's a test other priests have faced."

Loud laughter rode over Sorgun's words. Vadami heard a group of men at the table next to his discussing the near riot that had taken place in the Slough the day before. Vadami made a sign of aversion, turning that fate far from his life. Gods bless! Worse than ministering to Old Town was the saving of souls in the Slough.

"A wizard," the men were saying. "A Sabirn wizard, bold as brass."

Vadami took another gulp of ale. Sabirn. Warlocks! Traffickers in the dark arts! He hated the Sabirn nearly as much as he feared them. And now, from what the seamstress Zeldezia had told him, it was not only the Slough that harbored them. . . .

It was not only the Slough where sedition and riot threatened good folk.

A dismal future. If the temple blamed him—

"You do a good work, Vadami."

Vadami's face went hot. "One tries, Superior. One desperately tries. But there are deaf ears."

"Specifically?"

"Have I ever told you about Duran?"

"The nobleman."

"Ex-noble. He's poor as his Old Town neighbors now. But—"

"Is he a problem?" Sorgun asked.

"His shop is a focus for—midnight visitors. Whores. Persons with—" Vadami felt his face go hot. "Disease."

"He's an apothecary, isn't he?"

Vadami squared his shoulders. "He deals with Sabirn. Trades with them. *Harbors* them."

Sorgun's face went very still. "Have you advised him?"

"Aye. More than once. Duran listens; then—"

"He still sees them?"

"Aye. There's this old man who begs at the tavern across the street, a hanger-on, sweeps up—"

"Sabirn, you mean?" Sorgun's gaze had grown uncomfortably direct.

Vadami chose his next words with care. "A true daughter, a woman named Zeldezia: she's very pious, very reliable, always at temple. I saw her today. She asked for intercession, for—prayers for the neighborhood. She told me Duran actually has a Sabirn boy living in his house."

"Go on."

"Zeldezia said there was some kind of attack. Duran beat the attackers, drove them off, took the boy into his shop—" Vadami stammered, looked at the table. "Into—" He coughed. "Into his bed, by what this good woman says."

Sorgun said, "Tell me about this—resident at the tavern."

Vadami blinked, felt his face still over-warm. Sorgun's question was hardly the shocked response he expected. "Everyone calls him 'Old Man,' and he lives inside the door of the tavern. 'The Swimming Cat.' He's a storyteller. A menial. Aside from that, I don't know much about him."

"How long has he lived there?"

"Years." Vadami shrugged. "No one pays much attention to him. He's obviously harmless—but this boy—"

Sorgun nodded slowly. "Vadami . . . I want you to feel you can talk to me like this at any time, for any reason. That's what I'm here for. Isn't it?"

"Yes, Superior."

"Keep an eye on this Duran." Sorgun lifted his mug of ale. "I do want you to keep careful watch on this Old Man."

"The old man's no problem. He's been there for—"

"Just watch him. I want you to tell me if you see him talking to anyone who doesn't live in Old Town."

"Aye." Vadami drained his mug to cover his confusion. If Sorgun was concerned about Old Man, then—then, all things considered, it certainly would do him well to be equally concerned.

Ladirno flung open the windows to catch what breeze blew in from the harbor, but there was little of it: the air even in this large room was stifling in its closeness. He sat down in his chair, loosened the collar of his tunic, and stretched his

feet out before him. Temple bells had just rung
out, announcing the tenth hour, well into afternoon, but Wellhyrn had not appeared yet.

*Making me wait, just like he does everyone.
Damn! He can get to anyone with his airs . . .
even me, who first championed him at court.*

At times Ladirno questioned his friendship with
the younger man. They both shared the same
attitudes and philosophies of life, but there was a
malicious streak in Wellhyrn that Ladirno did not
share.

And a self-centeredness and carelessness of others' annoyance.

He yawned, drowsy in the summer afternoon
heat, and shook his head. As long as he had his
place in life established and felt moderately un-
threatened, he was fairly content. Wellhyrn, on
the other hand, was always busy trying to keep
anyone else from the same step of the ladder.

Steps sounded in the hallway outside, and
Ladirno looked up.

Wellhyrn at last . . . he would recognize those
footsteps anywhere. "Come in," he called out,
before the knock.

The door opened. "I've got it!" Wellhyrn said
with uncharacteristic fervor, stepping into the room.
He opened his belt purse and took out a lump of
something that looked vaguely, from Ladirno's viewpoint, like a rock.

Ladirno took the object Wellhyrn gave him.
Weighing it in his hands, he smiled. "It looks
good, very good. It should fool the Duke, or anyone uninitiated."

Wellhyrn's green eyes sparkled in the sunlight.

"Damn right it should. It took me long enough to bury that lump of gold in mud and coat it. But it took the firings. Now, when we set up our furnace and insert this 'rock' of ours, a little tap of the tongs and we'll have gold to reward the Duke's patience."

"After which the Duke, of course, will reward *us*." Ladirno handed the object back to Wellhyrn. "Well, sit down. Sit down. Wine? I have a new bottle."

Wellhyrn put the "rock" back in his belt pouch, nodded and took a chair, expecting to be waited on as usual. Ladirno smothered angry feelings: if the relationship he shared with Wellhyrn was not so profitable, he would gladly put the younger man in his place.

He got up, poured two glasses of wine, and walked to Wellhyrn's side. "It's a masterful job you did," he said, as Wellhyrn took the glass.

"Of course. After all, I *am* a master at what I do." Wellhyrn took a sip of the wine, then leaned back in the chair, a thin smile touching his too-handsome face. "I wonder what old Duran did when he found my two silver pieces?"

Ladirno shrugged, sitting down again, and drinking his wine. "Kept them, I'll bet."

A momentary expression of anger twisted Wellhyrn's face. "That's not what I meant, Ladirno," he said, swirling the wine in his glass. "I *meant* . . . I wonder what he thought."

"Hard telling." Ladirno looked carefully at his companion: Wellhyrn had something on his mind, something bothering him. "Why are you so angry at Duran all the time?" he asked casually. "He's certainly no threat to folk like you or me."

"Ah, but you don't know that, do you?" Wellhyrn sat up straighter, leaned forward, one elbow on the chair-arm. "I think he very well *could* become dangerous. You know how he talks to those damned Sabirn all the time."

Ladirno lifted one eyebrow. "That's a threat?"

"Have you forgotten what we heard at court? The Sabirn plot? The wizards trying to bring down the kingdom?"

"Gods. Sabirn with wizardry. Pigs will fly."

"Use your head, man," Wellhyrn snapped. "You and I both know that once the Sabirn ruled an empire, that they enjoyed a level of life that we haven't rivaled."

"Aye . . . but that was a thousand years ago. Their empire fell, man! What good were their wizards?"

"Did *they* fall?" Wellhyrn cocked his head. "Or did they somehow preserve their secrets, their knowledge? *Do* they have wizards who remember techniques from their past? What if—" He lifted a hand to keep Ladirno silent. "—they actually *are* able to do things that we can't? What if their wizards *are* stronger than ours?" Wellhyrn leaned forward, jabbed Ladirno's arm with his finger. "More to the point, dear colleague, —what if they have alchemists among them? What if *that's* what Duran's after?"

Ladirno made a rude noise and took another drink. "Rumor. Rumor on both counts. Nothing's ever been proved that alchemy ever predated—"

"Not if the secrets went with them! I'm saying 'what if.' I'm saying what if they *do* have such secrets—or they hold out secrets, what if that's where Duran's father got his information? Duran might make himself quite, quite something, thumb his nose at the Guild—"

"Huhn."

"Listen to me. Duran's got every reason to be angry at the ducal family after what happened to his parents. He could be involved in this plot . . . an Ancar protecting Sabirn in an Ancar city. It makes sense, doesn't it?"

Ladirno contemplated his glass. Wellhyrn might be right; the rumor of Sabirn wizards seemed genuine enough—at least that the Sabirn harbored secrets. At least that few people—save Duran—ever gave them more than an angry glance.

And an alchemist outside the Guild—came up with a cure for the pox—

Plot against the kingdom aside, if Wellhyrn was right, and if the Sabirn *did* possess superior alchemistic knowledge, and if Duran discovered it . . . in the face of the Guild—in spite of the Guild . . .

Ladirno scowled. His position at court, Wellhyrn's, and the other alchemists', would be worthless.

To say nothing of the subterranean power Duran might wield having allied himself with subversives, plots against his own race, his own kind—

"Ah-h-h." Wellhyrn smiled coldly. "So you *do* see it."

"I see a possibility." Ladirno gestured sharply. "But I think you're overreacting, Wellhyrn. Duran's a fool, a virtual hermit, nothing left in life besides ministering to the poor of Old Town. He's dealt with Sabirn for years now. If they had such secrets, don't you think he would have found something more important than a pox-cure?"

"Maybe he has."

"Mmmn."

"I'm simply telling you why I think we should—contain this problem. I don't mean by doing anything—criminal: gods know we don't want a confrontation: but just by doing little things, like leaving the silver in his shop. Keep him unsure of himself and his place in life. Keep him questioning why we're living so well, and he isn't. Let him make a mistake."

"You've got a mean streak in you," Ladirno said. "Do what you want to. I won't stop you. But I still think you're expending a lot of energy on a problem that isn't a problem."

"Yet."

"Yet," Ladirno admitted. "Yet."

Duran counted his take for the day, came up with twenty-four coppers, and congratulated himself. Tonight, he would be able to eat well, to have, yes! a second mug of ale.

Dog stood up, shook himself, and ambled outside. The late afternoon shadows had darkened the street, and Dog knew his master's routine. Duran watched the animal turn down the street, nose to the ground, reading what only other dogs could read. Dog would be back before he shut his shop down for the night and crossed the street to "The Swimming Cat" for his nightly meal.

He glanced upstairs, wondering what Kekoja was doing to pass the time. He had slipped up several times to look in on the boy, found the Sabirn lad asleep, or quietly staring off into nothing. He had shared his bread and cheese with the lad at midday, made up a new pan of hot salts, and instructed Kekoja to soak the ankle again. Kekoja had complied, saying little more than necessary.

Duran rubbed his eyes, and leaned back against his shelves. What in Hladyr's name had Zeldezia told people about the boy? Her talking with Vadami—gods! The priest would certainly be paying more attention to this street after today. . . .

Duran cocked an ear—heard flute music, coming from upstairs; he remembered the small, wooden flute Kekoja kept in his belt. For a moment he let himself be carried along with the music, until the strangeness of the melody made him sit straighter on his stool.

That was no Ancar melody the boy played, or Torhyn either. There was a haunting loneliness to the song, an alienness to it. Sabirn music. Music that spoke to Duran of twilight evenings, places with no names, and gods that had died with their worshipers.

Duran felt the hair at the nape of his neck stir. He glanced out the door, afraid of who might be listening to that playing, and drew a deep breath. He could hear Zeldezia now, complaining to all the neighbors about Duran's Sabirn boy, who played music that trapped souls in darkness.

But it was only twilight the boy played . . . twilight, and a loneliness that could not be comforted.

CHAPTER 5

Two days passed. Duran glanced over his shoulder as he crossed the street, but Zeldezia's door was shut. He had exchanged nothing more than brief greetings with her since their argument that day, and he frankly found her silence a blessing. Hladyr only knew what she was saying behind his back, but at least she had quit trying to get him to throw Kekoja out on the street.

Old Man sat in his usual place by the doorway and, as Duran passed, smiled broadly. Duran smiled back, then carefully erased the expression from his face as he entered the common room. He did not know how far rumor might have spread the story of his guest, but it would not do to rub his neighbors' noses in the fact.

Tutadar looked up from what he was doing at the bar, and lifted an eyebrow as Duran stopped. "Eating here, tonight?" he asked, setting a freshly drawn mug of ale on the counter. "That's a change." A lower voice. "Kid gone yet?"

"No." Duran glanced around the common room, found it not all that busy, filled mostly with his neighbors, and kept his own voice down as he paid attention to the mug Tut offered. "A few more days should do it. His head's a lot better, and he doesn't lose his balance that often. That was a damned nasty sprain he suffered. Came close to breaking his ankle, I'd say."

"You want your usual?" Tutadar asked.

"Aye. —How's Anha's hand, by the by? Any better?"

Tutadar's face broke into a smile. "Oh, aye. Think your medicines got her back to her old self. She been yellin' at me lately just like she used to."

"Good." Duran turned and walked back to his table and sat down.

And noticed a change.

Slight, that change, but a change nonetheless in the atmosphere of the common room; though his neighbors had nodded to him as he passed by their tables, there had been none of the usual good-natured bantering back and forth with him that he was used to.

He leaned back in his chair, cursing himself for seeing shadows where there probably were none. On the other hand, if Zeldezia had been as busy telling people about Kekoja as he feared she had, then there could be a damned good reason.

The tavern girl, Lalada, came to his side carrying his plate. Duran smiled up at her as she set his dinner on his table, and felt his expression freeze: she had not returned the smile, and moved with an uncertainty he was not used to seeing in her— some days ago.

Damn Zeldezia! She *must* have been in the "Cat" the last couple of days, spreading all kinds of rumors about the Sabirn boy. Duran took up his ale, sipped at it, and pretended he noticed nothing amiss.

The smith Ithar got up, came over to his table. That was encouraging. "Mind if I join you?"

"No. Please, sit down. How's your arm doing?"

Ithar pulled out a chair and sat. He extended his arm and, even in the lamp-light, Duran could see that the cut was healing normally, new pink skin.

"Feels lots better," Ithar said, letting his sleeve fall. He took a long drink from his mug. "Wanted to thank you for what you done."

"No thanks needed. You just be careful in the future to wash any cut you get, never mind the mud, and you shouldn't have any more trouble."

The smith nodded, wiped his mustache with the back of his hand, leaned forward on the table. "Want to ask you a couple questions, Duran. Man to man."

"Certainly." Duran's heart lurched. "What?"

"You got yourself a Sabirn kid in your house?"

Duran briefly shut his eyes. "Has Zeldezia been telling *everyone* in the neighborhood, or just a select few?"

"Then you ain't denyin' it?"

"No. Did she also tell you the boy had been hurt . . . badly?"

Ithar's eyes wavered a bit. "No. She didn't."

That figures, Duran thought. "It is true. He was beaten by three young toughs in the alleyway outside my house. I chased them off and I'm keeping him until he can walk again."

"Chased them punks off?" Ithar asked. "With that stick of yours? Them as been hangin' round—"

"Aye."

"You could've been hurt bad, Duran. Any of 'em could have had a knife."

"One did."

Ithar drew a long breath and took another drink of his ale. "Why didn't you call for help? We would've come a-runnin'."

"I was too busy. —Now, let me ask you a question. Did Zeldezia tell you the boy's Old Man's grandson?"

The smith shook his head.

"It seems to me that someone who's so free with other people's business could at least get the story right."

"But, Duran. . . ." Ithar shook his head. "The boy *is* Sabirn."

"So's Old Man! I can't imagine you leaving an injured boy on the street just because he's Sabirn, Ithar. I truly can't."

Ithar scratched his head. "Maybe not. But I wouldn't have let him into my *house*, f' the gods' blessed sake—"

"Ithar, none of the Sabirn I've ever dealt with have stolen from me. That's the truth. None's ever done me an ill turn."

Ithar stared at Duran for a long time. "Tut always said you got too kind a heart for your own good. I agree with him."

"For Hladyr's sake, Ithar! The boy's no demon. He's just like you or me."

"Look, Duran: Old Man . . . he don't worry me. He's old and he's crippled. But a young kid, now, fast on his feet—"

"Ithar." Duran reached out and set a hand on the smith's forearm. "A skinny, fourteen-year-old boy's no threat to you or anyone in the neighborhood. He's been here three days and nothing's happened. Has it? Tell me if it has."

"You're an honest man, Duran, but you got a soft spot's going to do you hurt. You took in that dog when he was starvin' and you was little better. Now, you're takin' in this Sabirn kid when you *know* better, and he ain't got no uses." Ithar's brown eyes were level. "You tell me: you going to stand surety for 'im? Pay us for anything he steals? 'S only fair. . . ."

Duran leaned back in his chair. "He's not going to steal anything from you," he said, "and if he does, *I'll* be the first one to turn him in to the Guard."

"You mean that?"

"I swear to it."

"Well . . . if *you* stand for 'im. . . ." Ithar drank again. "But I'll tell you for damned sure, Duran . . . makes me nervous just thinkin' 'bout one of them little, dark folk livin' this close to me. Gives me the creeps."

Duran chewed and swallowed and reached for his ale. "If you met the boy, Ithar, you'd change your mind. He's intelligent—a good lad . . . polite *and* smart. He's a kid, Ithar. Like any kid. What in hell's everybody spooked for?"

"If you say so." Ithar looked at Duran for a moment, then self-consciously grinned, reached across the table and rested a hand on Duran's shoulder shook it in comradely fashion. "You're all right, Duran . . . you really are. Twenty years I knowed you, an' you been honest. I just hope to hell what you're doin' here won't do you hurt."

"That I can't help. Zeldezia's doing the hurt."

"Feh!" Ithar waved a hand. "She talks too much. We don't believe *everything* she says. . . ."

"You believed this, didn't you? Didn't ask me?"

The smith nodded slowly. "Aye, that's so—but, dammit, ain't nobody took in a gods-cussed Sabirn. Sneaky bunch. None of us likes 'em . . ."

Duran finished his fish and wiped his mouth on his sleeve. "Sneak is as sneak does. Some don't care who they hurt. Some don't care what the truth is."

"Zeldezia? Believe me, Duran . . . I'm going to let everyone know about it, too." His face grew serious. "But that boy give you any trouble, you tell me. Givin' you any trouble?"

"No. For one thing, Old Man's talked to him, and told him mind his manners."

"Dandro's hells . . . you do be careful. You been lucky in the past dealin' with Sabirn. Hope your luck's still with you."

"Come over and meet the boy yourself, if it'd make you feel better. He's a kid. See for yourself. He won't bite."

The smith's eyes wavered. "Not me, Duran. You can keep that kid in your house long's you want to, by me, but don't be tryin' to get *me* to be friendly to 'im."

"All right. But don't worry, Ithar. Your tools will be where you leave them—same as always. If anything *is* missing in this neighborhood, I'd look to the gang that beat this lad. Sure won't be him taking anything. I promise."

"That's all I can ask." The smith finished off his ale, spat into the rushes on the floor, and stood. "Got to be goin'." Ithar lingered, said, on an apparent second thought: "You take care."

Duran watched Ithar return to his table and wondered if Ithar knew something.

Heads got together. By the hour Duran left "The Swimming Cat," a number of heads had gotten together, and the atmosphere in the common room of the inn had returned to near normal. A number of his neighbors still looked at him from the corners of their eyes—still, he felt sure, distrusted him, thanks to Zeldezia's spreading rumors. But Ithar, both honest and forceful, would set the neighbors right, and Duran thanked Hladyr he had known the smith as long as he had. Next to Tutadar, the smith was probably the most respected man in the neighborhood.

As (Duran smiled wryly, balancing the basket containing Kekoja's dinner in one hand, fumbling for his keys) he himself certainly was not.

He opened the door to his shop, set the food down on his counter. He was lighting the lamp when he heard Dog growl a warning.

The two young lords stood in the open doorway, cloaked as before.

"Come in," Duran said. He held onto Dog until both men had entered his shop, then ushered Dog out the door. The animal growled again, and refused to go any farther than the doorstep. "It's all right, Dog." Duran scratched Dog's ear, shut the door, faced the two men. "I have to take something upstairs. I'll be right back down."

The Duke's heir and his companion glanced around the shop. "See that you are," Brovor growled. "We don't have all night."

Arrogant young cock, Duran thought, and lit the lamp over the counter for his customers' benefit, keeping his chin down—god, they had known each other as children, he and Brovor. And he was that much changed. . . .

He picked up the basket of food and the other lamp, and climbed the stairs, opened the door.

"Duran?"

Duran set the lamp down, giving light as the boy sat up and rubbed his eyes.

"I've got a customer," he said, opening the basket and setting Kekoja's food on the bedside table. "I'll be back. It shouldn't take me long."

Kekoja's nose wrinkled. "Fish again?"

"Beef pie tomorrow. I promise you. Eat your food, lad. I'll be right back."

"How many more times do I have to come here?" Brovor asked, from behind a fold of his cloak.

Duran paid attention to his work. "The sore's started to disappear. The swelling's gone down."

"How many times? I asked you a question."

"This will be your fourth treatment," he said. "With luck, ten more."

"*Ten?*" The prince's whole body jerked. "You damn quack, that's intolerable!"

"Lord." The heir's companion spoke from the corner. "It does take time."

"And if I don't come back?" Brovor asked, his voice edged with menace.

"You die," Duran said with a shrug, tossed the swab, got up and wiped his hands. "Sooner or later, you die."

"Damn you!" Brovor took a long breath. "You—" Someone knocked on the door.

"Who's that?" Brovor asked in a hoarse whisper, clutching his cloak about him, his hand reaching for the hilt of the short sword he wore.

"I have no idea." Duran had not heard Dog bark, so he assumed his visitor was someone Dog knew. He put the top on the jar and set the wand beside it. "It's probably a neighbor—"

"No one must know I'm here!"

"I suggest you and your friend go to the back of the shop where the shadows are deepest. I'll try to keep this brief as possible."

"Gods! I'll—"

The heir's companion took Brovor by the arm. "Come, lord. He's right. Patience. Please."

Brovor glared at the door a moment longer, then followed his friend to the rear of the shop.

Another knock.

"Just a moment," Duran called. He glanced once over his shoulder to be sure the two young lords were hidden, then opened the door halfway and stepped outside.

Vadami stood waiting in the street.

Hladyr bless! The priest! Not now! Duran resisted the urge to glance behind him as he held on to the door.

"Good evening, Duran," Vadami said. "Hladyr's blessing on you."

Dog sat a few paces away, tail dropped. He was not fond of Vadami, but he was too well mannered to growl at someone he recognized.

"Good evening, Priest," Duran said, stepped out past the priest, pulled the door shut. "Been boiling up medicines. It's a warm night. Pleasanter air out here, I assure you, Father. —What may I do for you?"

"Just a social call. How are things going here in your neighborhood? Are you and your neighbors in good health?"

Like hell, Duran thought, a social call. Where was Vadami going with these questions, at this hour—

With the prince in the shop. And Zeldezia's going to him about the boy—

"Everyone's doing fine, thank you. Aside from normal complaints, headaches and such, no one's been sick."

"That's good to hear. Summer can bring on bad fevers."

"True, but I haven't seen the fever so far this year. My business isn't doing all that well, but I don't mind if it means folk are healthy."

Vadami rubbed his clean-shaven jaw. "I haven't seen you at Temple in some time . . ."

"Difficult to close my shop—folk do need medicines. I've no help."

"I saw Zeldezia there," the priest said, his voice holding mild reproof. "She manages."

"That may be true, but Zeldezia makes better money than I do. And *her* clients can wait. A sick youngster—"

"Of course, of course." Vadami dismissed the subject with a brief gesture. "But I thought you *had* help. A Sabirn."

Duran bit his lip. "A boy. A boy beaten and left

in the alley. He's not help, Father, far from it. His family's poor, the boy might have died. A work of charity."

"Charity to someone who deals with the dark powers. Do you understand that? You're putting your soul in peril."

"I doubt the boy has anything to do with powers—dark or light. He's a frightened kid—"

"Duran. This boy—this boy sleeping in your house—is an agent of deception. Of temptations—"

Duran snorted. "Why? Because they're dark, short, and speak a different language? This is a fourteen-year-old—"

"They're wizards. Demon-worshipers. Dealers with the Dark. They reject the worship of Hladyr."

"Were they ever invited to worship him?" Duran asked.

Vadami's face tightened. "They could come to the Temple if they wanted to . . . if they evidenced a sincere desire to change their ways. But none of them has ever done that. They've no souls. They *can't* repent."

"That's for priests to say," Duran said, making a desperate effort to avoid controversy. "They're servants in all the noble houses. I see no difference in principle. . . ."

"What's wrong with you, Duran? Of course there's a difference. They're servants. But *you* deal with them, you trade with them. . . ."

Duran spread his hands. "They're the only help I can afford—when I can afford it at all."

For a moment, Duran thought that he might have broken through the priest's narrow view of things, but Vadami's face hardened. "So you take this boy into your employ—"

"Not my employ!"

"They're already starting to bespell you, just like Zeldezia said. Duran, I'm warning you. Don't have anything to do with the Sabirn! If you do, you'll be denying Hladyr and all his works. You know the Book of the Shining One, where it says:

"A fool is he who turns from Hladyr's face,
For darkness shall rise to engulf him,
Birds and dogs shall strip his bones,
And his name shall be taken away."

Duran rubbed his eyes wearily. "I received an excellent education in my father's house. I know the words of the Book, too, like:

"Turn not away the man from your door
Though he be ragged like a thief,
It might be one of the god's come to test
The love of the Shining One's children."

Vadami frowned deeply; from the expression in his eyes, he had hardly expected to be met verse with verse.

"You twist things. You twist them into what you want to believe. Beware arrogance. Most of all beware arrogance. The holy words don't apply here."

Duran worked sweating hands, searched for persuasive argument. "I'd not quarrel, Father. I assure you—I'll be in Temple."

"I fear for your soul, Duran. I truly do. You're better educated than folk hereabout: and because of that you can use the holy words—but don't misuse them. I urge you, *urge* you most strongly, don't let the Sabirn fool you. They're minions of darkness. I'm afraid for your soul, Duran, I'm afraid for all those around you."

"I'll be careful, Father."

"Surely, with all your learning, you've heard stories of their wizards? There was one named Siyuh—feared in all the northlands. They say that Siyuh and his followers could make fire leap from their hands—a pact with the Dark—"

"A thousand years ago."

"Will you wager your soul on it?" The priest shook his robes free, stepped off to the walk and looked back at Duran. "Please, Duran . . . as you hope for Hladyr's heaven . . . have nothing more to do with the Sabirn. Don't think I'm persecuting you. I'll be offering up daily prayers for you."

"Thank you, Father."

"Hladyr save. Good evening."

The priest turned and walked away down the darkened street.

Duran stood, numb a moment. Dog came ambling out of the shadows, sat down and nuzzled at his hand.

O Lord Hladyr, Duran thought, *Shining One, maker of all things. If you are Lord of everything . . . are you also Lord of hate?*

Behind him—muffled by the shut door, he heard a footstep.

Gods! Brovor!

Duran opened the door without letting Dog in, slipped hastily inside—

"Took your own damn time, didn't you?" Brovor walked out of the shadows. "What was that?"

"I'm sorry. It was the local priest. He's the *last* one I'd think you'd want to know you're here."

"Damn!"

"He's gone. It was a chance visit. It's all right."

"He's gone," Brovor's companion said. "Lord, let's be out of here."

"I needn't remind you," Brovor said, "of discretion."

"I am," Duran said, "discreet."

Brovor dug in his purse. Laid down a gold piece. A second.

"One," Duran said. "One is enough, lord. Discretion is part of the charge."

A moment the blue eyes stared at him above the muffling cloak—straight at him. Sweat ran on Duran's ribs.

"Who's upstairs?"

"A sick old man, lord. Quite deaf."

Brovor stared, fingering his sword-hilt. At last, he nodded briefly, motioned to his comrade, left.

Duran stared at the closed door, long after the two young lords had gone. Gods! Vadami on his doorstep, the Duke's heir hiding in his shop, the Sabirn boy upstairs! His knees were shaking, now that he was alone. Dog settled down by the counter, another one of the butcher's bones between his paws, his tail wagging slowly back and forth. Duran smiled bleakly.

"Dog, you have the answer to an easy life, don't you? When things start getting bad, go off into some corner, curl up with a good bone, and watch the world go by."

Dog wagged his tail again and gnawed at his

dinner. Duran shook his head. One moment's thought, one moment's recollection on Brovor's part, and Brovor might remember him—Brovor might think he had motives—

Brovor seeking a state marriage, on which peace or war might depend—

And a Sabirn boy in the question—he wondered if Zeldezia had any idea what she might have done by telling Vadami about the Sabirn boy. He doubted it. Zeldezia more than likely never thought beyond the moment she spoke.

But who might Vadami tell—and where might it go? Duran rubbed his bearded chin. Again, he did not think he was dealing with a malicious soul; Vadami was merely . . . pious.

And if Vadami told one of his superiors, he might find himself in the Temple answering questions. On the other hand, if Vadami told some of his secular friends, *they* might—

Duran squared his shoulders. No use trying to foretell the future. For his entire adult life he had walked a fine line between respectability and notoriety: an alchemist without guild connections could hope for little else.

Best, he thought, best try to put the best face on things—do things in the open, where it regarded the boy—

Daylight on a sore—worked some cure. So might public exposure of a situation—the boy in some ordinary, harmless context—stop the speculations.

He stooped, patted Dog on the head, took the lamp and walked back to the stairs, up the steps—

To the door where Kekoja sat up in the bed and set aside a—Duran stared. A book? Gods!

The boy—reading?

He set his lamp down on his desk and faced Kekoja. The Sabirn lad stared back, his eyes dark pools in the lamp-light.

"Sorry," Duran said. "That took me longer than I thought. What were you reading?"

Kekoja's eyes wavered. "Just looking at the pictures."

Duran walked over to the bedside and picked up the book. It was one of his philosophy books, a rather dry treatise by a fellow named Artoni who had written several centuries in the past. Duran lifted an eyebrow and ruffled the pages.

"There aren't any pictures in this book, Kekoja."

"Now you tell me."

Duran smiled. "Don't lie to me," he said mildly. "I don't like that. You can read, can't you?"

Kekoja flinched, then grimaced. "Aye. Some."

"That surprises me."

"S'pose so."

"Who taught you?" He thought of a lasting puzzle: the storyteller, the foreigner whose Ancari was sometimes—astonishingly good. "Your grandfather?"

"Aye." The Sabirn boy shifted uneasily in bed, then looked up at Duran. "But I don't read too good, and I can't read fast. I can speak Ancari better'n I can read it."

"I think you're not telling me the whole truth, Kekoja." He took the book back to the desk and laid it down. "I think you're a damned lot smarter than you want to show."

Kekoja lifted his chin. "An' what difference'd *that* make, that I can read, or that I'm smart? Who'd care one way or the other?"

"Your grandfather obviously cares, or he wouldn't have taught you. Knowledge is never anything to be ashamed of."

"You ain't Sabirn."

Duran drew a long breath. "No, I'm not. But I think I understand what you're saying."

Kekoja's wary expression persisted. "Grandfather says you're a fair man. Even when it gets your neighbors mad."

"I guess that sums it up."

"Why?"

Why? The question Duran had asked himself over and over. Why are you doing this? Why are you courting disaster? Why, why, why?

"I'm not sure," he said, falling back on utter honesty before this boy, this street urchin he had rescued from a beating at the hands of other ragtags who looked and lived much the same. "I suppose I don't like to see injustice. I don't like to see things misunderstood." He waved a hand at the books, the shelves. "That's why I'm an alchemist, that's why I operate my shop. Because I want to know what things *really* are . . . I want to understand them. And I can't believe something's bad simply because I don't understand it."

"That could get you in trouble," Kekoja said seriously. "Understanding things."

Duran laughed quietly, folded his arms, lighterhearted, he had no notion why. "You're damned right it could, lad. It has. But I haven't given up trying to understand things."

"You aren't afraid of us Sabirn?"

"Oh, yes, as much afraid of you as I am of my own kind. There's good and bad in all of us, whether we be Sabirn, Torhyn, or Ancar. It's simply easier to overlook our own bad traits and assign them to people who aren't like us. Have you ever been afraid of things like that?"

Kekoja nodded slowly.

"Of something new? Of something strange?"

Kekoja nodded again.

"Because it was truly frightening, or because you'd never seen anything like it before?"

"Both."

"Smart boy. Aye, we can be afraid of something we know all too well . . . or too little. Ah, lad! Now there's the thing—I suppose I'm not afraid of Sabirn because I think I know you better than most folk. I've heard all the tales spread about your people, but so far I haven't seen any of them coming true."

"They say we steal."

"And I imagine some of you do. So do some Ancar. So do some Torhyn. Some have titles." Duran shook his head. "Nothing special in that."

"They say we're wizards."

"Now *that* I would like to see," Duran said. "Most cheat. I haven't met a real one yet, though I suppose that doesn't mean there aren't any."

Kekoja cocked his head. "Grandfather was right. You *are* a strange one."

Duran laughed and drew the chair out from behind the desk so he could sit facing Kekoja. "I suppose I am."

"Why do you talk with Sabirn?"

"I'm interested in your legends, your stories. That's why your grandfather fascinates me."

"Why?"

"I save stories. I collect them like some men collect books. Somewhere in those stories is a key to the past, to what really happened."

"When?"

"Hundreds of years ago—when your people ruled their empire."

The Sabirn boy's face went very hard in the lamp-light. "That was a long time ago."

"Aye. So long ago most of the facts are probably forgotten by now. But legends can hide facts, lad, beneath their fanciful surfaces. That's what I'm after. I'm like a man who sifts sand through a sieve hunting for gold."

The room grew silent. The windows stood wide open to the summer night. Duran could hear crickets, the cry of nighthawks, the barking of a far away dog. He looked at Kekoja, but the boy seemed lost in thought.

"Grandfather knows," Kekoja said finally. "He knows the most stories of any of us."

"Maybe sometime he'll tell me the ones he hasn't told."

"Maybe. You write these stories down? All of them?"

Duran nodded. "What I can remember of them after they're told."

"In these books?"

"In some. I write what your grandfather says. What the other Sabirn say, the ones I've hired to help me when I go to the country." Duran suddenly remembered what Vadami had told him about a legendary Sabirn wizard. "Have you ever heard of someone named Siyuh?"

Kekoja's eyes widened; he sat bolt upright in bed. "Ziya!" he whispered.

"A story you know?"

"No." The boy looked down, leaned back up against the wall, and folded his arms across his chest. "I don't."

"Are you sure?"

The lad would not meet his eyes. "Nothing," Kekoja repeated.

Duran knew he had missed something there. The moment was gone; he could not recapture it.

"I'm tired," Kekoja said, turning his back on Duran and stretching out on the bed. "Let's go to sleep."

"If you want." Duran frowned at the boy, wishing he knew what had happened. One moment, Kekoja had been open and friendly; the next, he exuded all the charm of a stone.

And gave him the floor again.

CHAPTER 6

A huge clap of thunder shook the house the following morning and jarred Duran out of a deep sleep. He sat up in his bedding, rubbed his shoulder, and looked around. It was dark enough outside to be night, and rain had started to fall heavily.

"Damn." He rose to his feet, lit the lamp on the bedside table, and stretched the stiffness from his neck and back. Yawning, he walked across to an open window.

The wind had picked up and blew in off the harbor. Duran could hardly see across the narrow alleyway that divided his block from the building next door. He cursed again, drew the window shut, and hurried over to the other window. Rain blew in there, too, and Duran's sleeves were soaked by the time he got the window closed.

He walked to the window at the front of the room, shut it partially and returned to the bed. Kekoja was sitting up now, rubbing his eyes. Duran

105

nodded a good morning to the Sabirn boy, drew the chamber pot out from under the bed and used it.

"You next, lad," he said, standing and pulling on his hose. He stuffed his feet into his shoes and walked away from the bed to give Kekoja some privacy.

"Slops men'll be drenched to the bone this morning," Kekoja said.

"If they come now," Duran said, looking out the window at the downpour, "they'll be drowned. Is your head better?"

"Aye. Doesn't hurt near as much."

Duran turned around. "How's your ankle?"

Kekoja set the pot down, sat down on the bed and rubbed his foot. "Feels fine. But it felt fine yesterday, too."

Duran crossed his arms on his chest. "Walk for me. Just across the room and back."

Lightning flared, followed instantly by another crash of thunder. Kekoja flinched, stood and made the limping trip back and forth. He waited by the bed, his dark eyes watching Duran's face.

"Looks good," Duran said. "Better than yesterday."

"Then I can go?" Kekoja asked, his face lighting up.

"Where?" Duran waved a hand to the storm outside. "You want to go outside in this?"

"Well, maybe not now. But you think I can walk good enough to let me go?"

Duran sighed softly. "Aye. But I wouldn't go anywhere until the storm lets up." He came and picked up the chamber pot. "I've got to get us breakfast and let Dog out. Are you hungry?"

"Not very." Kekoja sat back down on the edge of the bed. "You go on an' eat at the inn, if you want. Bring me back some of what you have."

"All right." Duran picked up the lamp, too, and started toward the steps. "If you're interested, you can look at any of the books I have up here." He glanced over his shoulder at the Sabirn boy. "Some even have pictures in them."

"Duran," Kekoja said, "I'm sorry I lied to you. You been good to me, and I shouldn't have done it."

"Well, don't lie again. You don't need to be afraid of me."

"I learned that." Kekoja smiled slightly. "You can tell when I'm lying anyway. You got a good eye on you. And, Duran?"

Duran paused on the first step.

"Ask Grandfather if he wants to look at me walk. Even if you decide I can leave, he's the one who'll have the final word."

Duran nodded and descended the stairway to his shop. Thunder boomed again and Dog whined as Duran walked toward the front door.

"Sorry, Dog," Duran said, unlocking the door one-handed. "You stay close to the building, or you'll float away."

Dog stood on the doorstep, sniffing the rain-soaked wind, unsure whether to go out or stay inside. Duran leaned out the door, set the chamber pot on the doorstep, and ducked back. The gutters were deep underwater already, and a steady stream of rain poured down from the second story overhang.

"In or out, Dog," Duran said, reaching behind the door to get his cloak. "I can't wait forever."

Dog wagged his tail, and stepped out into the street, shook his head at the rain and trotted off around the corner. Duran pulled his cloak on, and cursed the weather, for it told him he would suffer another day with few customers. He leaned up against the door jamb, and watched the rain fall. Quicker than he would have guessed, Dog was back, dripping with rain and anxious to be inside.

"Bad day for all of us," Duran said, stepping aside to let Dog in. Dog wagged his tail, distributing rain outside of the puddle he was dripping on the boards, sat down and began to lick the water from his coat. "Stay here like a good boy. I'll be back."

Lifting the hood of his cloak up, Duran stepped outside, pulled the door shut and locked it. Drawing a deep breath, he turned and ran across the street where the door to "The Swimming Cat" stood cracked. Duran entered, stood for a moment dripping in the doorway, and flipped the hood back from his face. Thunder rumbled overhead.

"Morning, Sor Duran," said Old Man from his place inside. "Bad storm again today."

"Aye. I'm drenched from crossing the street. Your grandson wanted you to watch him walk today. He says *you're* the one who'll tell him if he's well enough to leave."

"You think he is?"

"He's a lot better, aye. He's not dizzy any more, and I think that ankle of his has healed."

Old Man's eyes sparkled in the lamp-light. "I'll come," he promised, "when the rain lets up."

Duran nodded and looked up as Tutadar walked in behind the bar, taking his usual morning position. "You're brave," Tut said, looking up from his money-counting.

"No. Hungry." Duran came to lean on the bar and glanced around. "No one else in here yet?"

"Not likely till the storm lets up. You eatin' here this mornin' or takin' out?"

"Here." Thunder rattled the windows. "Hladyr grant it'll slack. I'm not anxious to go back out in that."

"Who would be?" Tutadar walked to the kitchen and bellowed something at his cook. "Can't remember havin' such bad weather at this time of summer," he said, returning to the bar and pouring Duran a glass of wine. He shoved the mug across the bar and leaned forward, his arms crossed. "Trade's gone to hell—'nother ship gone."

Duran took a drink, wiped his mustache. "Another?"

"Word is, I hear it from Efdin, the Duke's got one well overdue. The *Gull's Pride* comin' out of Padis loaded down with spice—likely straight to the bottom in that big storm last week."

Duran frowned. Efdin the baker would know news having anything to do with spices. Last week. That must have been the storm that roared into Targheiden the same day the thugs had chased Kekoja into the alleyway.

"Hladyr bless the crew. I'll bet the Duke's not pleased. The price of clove will go up now for sure."

"*Gull's Pride* ain't the only ship out of Targheiden might be in trouble. From what some of the folk stayin' here in the upstairs say, weather's been foul at sea for the last fifteen days." The door to the kitchen cracked open and the cook stuck his head out, hailed Tut. "Sit," Tut said, "I'll bring you your breakfast. Might join you myself."

Duran picked up his mug and sought his table. Lalada the serving-girl came out from the kitchen, nodded dourly his way, too early for cheer, and began setting up the mugs behind the bar for the morning crowd. Thunder rumbled again, and Duran wondered if there would be much traffic in and out of the "Cat" as long as the rain kept up.

Two men came down the stairs from their rooms and entered the common room; they paused for a moment, as if checking to see who was present, then took a table close to the bar. Travelers, Duran noted, most likely traders from Fresa by the cut of their tunics. They talked quietly to each other and gave brief orders to Lalada, who disappeared back into the kitchen.

Tutadar came back into the common room carrying two plates, and set them down on Duran's table. He returned to the bar, poured three mugs of wine, and set two of them out before the travelers.

"Your food'll be out shortly, Sori," he said with a small bow. "Get you anythin' else?"

"Not unless you have good weather in your kitchen," one of the men said.

" 'Fraid not. You come far?"

"From Fresa," the other man said. "Business with Porandi."

"Luck to you, then," Tutadar replied. He turned away and joined Duran at his table.

Duran started cutting up his fish. Porandi was one of the more successful traders who had few ties to the noble houses. He wondered if any of Porandi's ships had suffered losses.

"Damned weather's bad for everyone," Tutadar said around a mouthful of fish. "Gets me by havin' few travelers in and out. Gets you by havin' fewer folk show up at your shop. —Heard you had a visit from Vadami last night."

"Aye." Duran lifted an eyebrow. "Was he here?"

"No. Efdin saw 'im when he was at bakin' last night."

"He would." Efdin again. The baker, like himself, kept night hours.

"So what'd Vadami want of you?" Tutadar asked. Then his expression changed; he glanced over his shoulder and back, lowered his voice. "Wasn't anything t' do with Zeldezia tellin' 'im about the Sabirn kid?"

Duran frowned. "He warned me." He finished his fish and lifted his mug. "I don't think I've ever done anything that's caused more of a stir than this, Tut. And all because I helped a boy in trouble."

"Ithar told me he'd talked with you, an' you'd told 'im what really happened. Don't like Zeldezia much, myself. Always got her nose stuck somewhere it don't belong." Tut leaned back in his chair, turned his head at another rumble of thunder, then looked back. "She used to be soft on you, Duran, back when she first took over that shop. Thought you was really somethin'."

Duran nearly choked on his wine. "She *what?* Me? You've got to be joking, Tut."

"Ain't." Tutadar leaned forward and lowered his voice. "I knowed you near as long's Ithar knowed you. 'Member when she bought that shop, near seventeen years back? She found out you were pure Ancar, an' thought you'd make a fine catch, her bein' a widow an' everythin'. You never paid much attention to her, an' I think that took 'er down a notch or two."

"Gods," Duran murmured. "I'd sooner lie down with a spider!"

Tut laughed, his eyes twinkling in the lamp-light. "Thought so. Me, too. Woman's got a tongue that'd cut stone. You should'a seen the looks she used to give you. —Ha! Maybe that's why she been so nasty to you. What she cain't have, she don't want nobody else havin' neither."

Duran shook his head and finished his drink. "Save us. —Could you get me another plate of fish and a mug of wine, Tut? The boy's probably starving by now."

"Sure." Tut waited as Duran set out four coppers for his meal and Kekoja's and swept them up in a practiced hand. "That kid healed by now?"

"Near back to normal as far as I can see."

"Good. Now, when he leaves, maybe things'll quiet down 'round here."

"Maybe." Duran watched Tut walk off toward the kitchen, and wondered.

The thunder still rolled. Ladirno sat in one of the chairs by the windows, and stared disconsolately at the downpour sheeting down the mullioned glass. Wellhyrn and he would have to wait at least another day to show the Duke their newest attempt at changing lesser metals into gold. Bad weather had always put the Duke in a foul mood; and now that Hajun had entered the shipping business, storms tended to worry him into depression.

So. Another day, then. Ladirno suspected Wellhyrn was equally disappointed at the turn of weather and the postponement of their demonstration. If there was anything Wellhyrn loved, it was being the center of attention. He probably lay buried beneath his covers in bed, cursing the bad luck—or the wizardry—that had brought another storm to Targheiden.

And since Wellhyrn would be foul company this morning, Ladirno either faced a lonely day in his rooms, or seeking company elsewhere—which meant going out in the downpour.

"Damned rain," Ladirno muttered. He left the depressing view and dressed, choosing dark colors for his hose and tunic that would not show the dampness—or the mud. He took down his cloak from a peg on the wall, blew out his lamp on the way out, and felt his way down the darkened hall.

Cheap landlord.

Ladirno's apartments were on the second floor of a building that housed a well-to-do merchant and several court functionaries. He wished he might have been able to buy the apartment on the first floor, but that place had been occupied for generations by the Farchendi, and—short of the entire family dying at once—they would never give up their rooms. All in all, Ladirno lived at a more than respectable address, only a few blocks from the palace and the Temple—and the damn skinflint Farchendi would not afford a nightlamp in the hall . . .

The rain was falling in sheets when Ladirno

opened the door out onto the street. He considered where he might find company: two taverns sat within equal distance of his building, and his friends frequented both—both served good food. It was simply the direction of the wind that made up his mind; better to walk with the wind at one's back, and to hope the storm might lessen, than to face the driving rain.

Ladirno pulled the hood of his cloak up and dashed outside, ran down the street, hugging the building, protected somewhat by the wide overhangs of the upper stories. Water swept down in torrents: the cobblestones were treacherously slick, the gutters spilling well onto the walks. But Ladirno reached the doorway that led into "The Golden Shoe" with no incident, and shoved his way inside.

For a moment he stood at the entrance to the common room, dripping rain water in puddles at his feet. His heart sank: not one acquaintance in the place: he should have guessed that the bad weather would have kept them indoors: the court functionaries would stay home later than normal given the Duke's mood in stormy weather—not for the first time, Ladirno wished he had a wife, a house of his own, and a gods-blessed cook to make his meals.

But he was well known in the "Shoe" and its ambiance was homey and warm. Sooner or later some crony would show up. Ladirno pulled the hood back from his cloak, unclasped it and held it out to one of the serving-lads who stood close by.

"Breakfast, Sor Ladirno?" the fellow asked, holding the dripping garment at arm's length.

"No. I'm looking for company, not food. I *will* have a glass of wine . . ."

Ladirno walked across the room: his shoes squished water between his toes as he walked.

Taking a chair at a table directly beneath a lamp, Ladirno leaned back and simply took to watching till the wine came—then he took a small book no larger than his hand from his belt pouch, opened it, and began to read.

All this, of course, was calculated to place him in the public eye. He had a reputation for being one of the Ducal favorites, one of the alchemists who frequented court. Sitting as he did now beneath the lamp would show off his rich clothes, the gold chain he wore, and the fact he was always studying. Small matter that the book had nothing to do with alchemy . . . it *looked* impressive.

"Ladirno."

He glanced up: a prestigious senior colleague stood beside the table. "I didn't see you," Ladirno said, slipping his book back into his pouch. He hastily moved a chair. "Do sit down."

"I was in the back." Garvis gestured over his shoulder to the rear of the room. "I've already had my breakfast. I need to return to my laboratory."

"A few minutes won't hurt."

Garvis sat down. The waiter brought more wine; Ladirno paid twice the amount asked, letting the coins fall on the table with a flourish.

"So, Garvis," he said, turning to his companion. "What have you heard regarding the Sabirn plot?"

Garvis shrugged. "Not much more than you already know." He lowered his voice. "I'd say it's a genuine rumor though; the Duke's been set thoroughly on edge—"

"Have they found any other Sabirn who know about the plot?"

"No. They've been staying out of sight. What with the bad weather, they know when it's best to stay hidden."

Ladirno nodded sagely, recollecting his discussion with Wellhyrn the day before—decided if *Garvis* saw some seriousness in the matter—

Mnnn. "You remember Duran, don't you?"

"That one!" Garvis drew in a breath. "Like his father. Stubborn. What's he to do with it?"

"Sabirn. He's searching for something. Sabirn alchemy."

"Sabirn alchemy! No such thing! They were sorcerers! Black sorcerers!"

Ladirno shrugged, not willing to seem—incorrect with this man.

"What have you heard?" Garvis asked.

"That he—has resentments against the court."

"The stiff-necked fool *chooses* Old Town. His father's banishment—was ameliorated and his father left him sufficient, I hear, but Duran thumbed his nose at respectability, set up this shop—to 'pursue his father's studies.' So-named studies. The fabled notes."

"Do you honestly believe his father ever kept such notes?"

"I've heard he did a lot of experimentation . . . of what sorts no one knows." Garvis leaned forward, jabbed the table with a gaunt finger. "A few of those experiments went wrong. *That's* why the Old Duke banished him."

Ladirno's eyes widened. "Dark sorcery?"

"I'll lay odds—mark me, those notes had Duran's 'discovery' of the cure for the pox. He's nothing!" Garvis exhaled a heavy, wine-laden breath. "Sabirn, is it?"

"So the rumor goes. Digging in the hills. Going off with Sabirn hired help. For days."

"Looking for herbs."

"So they say."

"Being a fool, he'd immediately give all the knowledge away."

"A *dangerous* fool," Ladirno murmured.

"Dangerous indeed," Garvis said, looking to the front of the tavern. "The rain's slacked. I've a meeting. *See* me about this."

"Absolutely."

Garvis pushed back his chair, stood, and left the common room. Ladirno sipped at his wine. He was beginning to sound like Wellhyrn, talking about shadowy plots and Duran's possible connection with them. But connections with Garvis, Garvis whose favor with the duke was—very sure . . .

Ladirno had never considered the Sabirn more than a nuisance; he discounted tales of their powers, their abilities to foretell the future and cast curses. Certainly they must have wizards: everyone had wizards, but—

Still. There was the unseasonable, the most unreasonable weather—

The rain slacked: other patrons began to filter in, rain-soaked. Ladirno took a long drink of his wine, thinking of ducal favor . . . of funds that had nothing to with Wellhyrn's inventions—of an apartment with well-tended lamps in the hallway—

He looked up from his glass. The priest Vadami passed his table, his grey robes dark with rain.

"Vadami," he said.

This priest he knew from his connections. *This* priest dealt with Old Town—

If anyone would know the gossip—

"Join me, Father?"

The priest looked mildly puzzled, drew out a chair and sat down.

"May I buy you a glass of wine then?" Ladirno offered. At Vadami's nod, he lifted his glass, caught the waiter's eye, and held up his other hand with one finger extended.

"Thank you, Sor Ladirno." The priest kept silent until the waiter had brought the wine to the table, taken Ladirno's coins, and left. "You're very kind."

"It's nothing."

Vadami drank deeply, wiped his mouth with the back of his hand, and sighed. "Warms the insides, doesn't it? Excellent."

"It is that." Ladirno leaned back in his chair and studied Vadami. "Your district is Old Town, isn't it? You know 'The Swimming Cat'?"

"Aye."

"Do you know a man named Duran?"

Vadami's cup hesitated on the way to his mouth. "Aye."

Ladirno swirled the wine around in his glass. "One wonders—we've fallen—out of touch. I worry about him, being poor as he is. I'd like to help him."

"*You* may worry about his being poor, Sor Ladirno, but *I* worry more about his soul."

"In what regard?"

The priest frowned, a very troubled look passing over his face.

"Ah." Ladirno's heart lurched, but he kept his face only concerned. "Is he—in some difficulty?"

"His associations. With the Sabirn."

"He's always been friendly to the Sabirn. We twit him about it—his friends do."

"Are his friends aware—he has one living in his house."

Ladirno's eyes narrowed. "Really? How odd. A man or a woman?"

"A boy." Vadami's face colored. "I've warned him. I told him I was afraid for his soul. He quoted me scripture."

"Scripture?" Gods above and below! If Duran had a Sabirn living with him—

Was Wellhyrn onto something? Could this boy be involved with the plot? What if Duran—was dealing with—some ancient knowledge?

"Overmuch learning," the priest was saying, his voice pitched to quiet complaining, "can lead a man to pride, master alchemist."

Ladirno smoothed down his mustaches, hardly hearing a word the priest said on dogma. Damn! Interesting in the extreme—

The storm had decreased from a downpour to a steady rain. Gusts of wind still blew in off the harbor, several tiles from a roof near the "Cat" lay scattered and broken on the cobblestones.

"Hladyr bless," Duran murmured, glancing up at the dark sky. He tucked the basket containing Kekoja's breakfast under one arm and quickly crossed the street, hopping across its flooded edges. He made his front door, took out his keys, and let himself into the shop.

Dog got up, stood in the doorway and inspected the lessened storm with canine disdain. Duran set the basket down on his counter. "Make up your mind, fellow," Duran said. "Inside or out. I want to go upstairs."

Dog wagged his tail, evidently decided another foray into the puddles was not worth it, and curled up in front of the counter.

Duran closed and locked the front door, and took breakfast upstairs.

Kekoja was sitting on the edge of the bed. He had lit the lamp, opened the shutters, and sat with a book open on the table.

"Breakfast," Duran said, leaving the stairs and crossing the room to Kekoja's side. "You're probably starving by now, aren't you?"

"No." Kekoja set the book aside and dug into the fish and bread. "You see my grandfather?"

"He says he'll come over and watch you walk soon as the rain stops."

"Way it's still raining, that'll be five days from now." He sipped the watered wine. "Thought the windows'd blow in."

"I know. If it happens again when I'm gone, close the shutters on the outside. Reach out and pull them." Duran walked over to his desk, sat down, and opened his belt pouch. He took from under the desk lid a small purse where he kept the shop money and spread the coins out on his desk. Twenty-one coppers. He opened a battered notebook, unstopped his inkwell, dipped his pen.

"Doin' your accounts?" Kekoja asked from across the room.

"Aye. And I didn't do too bad yesterday. Made a profit."

Kekoja took a drink of wine. "You as kind to all your customers as you been to me?"

Duran smiled. "I try to be. My job's different than most people's. I see folk at their worst . . . when they're sick. It never hurts to be kind to people who don't feel well."

"Grandfather says you're the only thing close to a doctor this part of Old Town ever sees. You could get more 'n coppers."

"Maybe so." Duran wrote down the total of yesterday's take, returned the coins in their purse to his belt pouch, and capped the ink. "But Hladyr knows how much each item I sell costs me. I have to live with myself, lad, and overcharging people makes me angry. I take just enough to make a profit some days."

"Today'll hurt you, won't it?"

"Aye."

Kekoja stood up and walked to Duran's side, wine-cup in hand. "I could help you," he said, "if you'd trust me with your numbers. I've got a good head for doing sums."

Duran leaned back in his chair and looked up at the Sabirn boy's face. "Who taught you numbers, Kekoja? Old Man?"

"Aye."

"Five plus six, plus twelve, minus eight, plus two equals what?"

"Seventeen."

Duran lifted an eyebrow. "You *are* fast. —But you know what I could use more than someone helping me with my books? A runner."

"A runner?" Kekoja cocked his head. "For what?"

"I'm tied down to my shop all the time it's opened. If I had someone to take medicines to people too sick to come see me, or someone who would brave weather like today to go around to people's houses and take orders—this summer, that could mean something."

He watched the Sabirn boy think that through.

"Mother Garan, for example," Duran said. "She's old and she has a lot of headaches. I give her willow tea for them and that makes her feel better. But she can't get in if it's raining like it's been today. Do you see?"

"Aye," Kekoja answered, nodding his head. His eyes met Duran's. "But you couldn't pay much, could you?"

"No." Duran smiled. "That's why I'll probably never have a runner. No one would work that cheap."

"What'd people say if you had a Sabirn runner?"

Duran looked at him steadily. "People might get used to it. People might get used to the idea you're here. People might use their heads, instead of their mouths—maybe decide this *isn't* some great secret. It's secrets people are really afraid of—"

"I'll do it," Kekoja said. "I'll be your runner."

Duran frowned, shook his head. Help the sort the boy offered—that was always out of reach for him. And even for a good reason, with the best of thought behind it—he could not, he told himself, expect a fourteen-year-old Sabirn to take on the burden of community distrust. "There's some actual physical danger, the toughs that gave you trouble, for one. And people are bound to—say things, especially at first. Besides which, I can't pay much."

"I'm a damn sight cheaper than anyone else you could find."

"I thought you wanted to be out of here."

"That don't mean I never want to see you again. I *like* you."

Duran looked at the boy, found an unexpected longing in his heart. The house had not been so quiet these last few days; there had been a bright, quick wit to deal with—there had been someone . . . waiting for him at home . . .

Besides which—the boy out in the open was no threat to the neighborhood, the boy would quickly be like his grandfather, just a Sabirn who worked for someone . . . a Sabirn who had a place and a reason to be on the streets . . . for the boy's own sake, as much as his . . .

"Let's deal," he said to Kekoja. "What I can pay you is this: if I make a profit for a day from your running my medicines, I'll give you a third of it. Does that sound fair?"

Kekoja thought for a moment. "Aye. And if you don't make a profit, we both suffer. I'll work hard."

Duran drew a deep breath. *Gods! Could this actually be happening to me?* "You know Old Town at all?"

"Aye."

"Well enough to make deliveries and pick up orders at places you've never been before?"

"You tell me how to get there, an' I'll do it."

"What about those thugs? What if you run into them?"

Kekoja stiffened; Duran could see the visible effort it took the boy to relax. "I'm not afraid. Was damn stupid of me to get caught like that in the first place."

"Remember, you'll be carrying money. Not a lot

of it, but money that will pay me *and* you. Do you think you can skin out of a fight?"

"If I have to, I have to." Kekoja's shoulders squared. "When I'm on the job, I work for you, Duran. When I'm off the job, you don't hold anythin' over me."

Duran nodded slowly. "That sounds like a fair exchange. But if you aren't staying here—where will you be staying?"

He hoped Kekoja would say—*I'd rather stay here*. But Kekoja glanced away. "I got places," Kekoja said. "Don't worry 'bout me, Duran. I lived on the street 'fore you found me in that alleyway."

The house would be empty again. So. One settled for half, if there was no hope of the whole. "I can't help but worry, but I won't ask you where those places are. But if I need you—if I do have to find you, what should I do?"

"Ask my grandfather. He'll know where I am."

"I'll also want to tell your grandfather what we've agreed to," Duran said. "I think he should know, don't you? I think he should agree."

"Aye."

Duran stood and faced the Sabirn boy. "Then let's strike our bargain, you and I."

Kekoja held out a hand and Duran placed both his around it.

"Hladyr witness: I promise to abide by my word, to give you a third of the profits you make for me in return for your services as my runner."

"Gods of my people witness: I promise to work hard for you."

Duran grinned widely and pressed Kekoja's hand. "Done, boy! We're in business together now."

"When you want me to start?"

"Tomorrow. This afternoon, I'll tell you where my customers live. I've got medicines to mix. You'll help me."

"Will you teach me herbs?"

"Aye, if you've a mind to learn it." Duran walked over to the bed and put Kekoja's plate and empty mug into the basket. "I've got to open my shop. Someone might need something. Will you be all right up here?"

Kekoja sat down on the bed and lifted a book. "I can always look at the pictures," he said with a lop-sided grin.

Duran smiled, picked up the basket and went downstairs, where Dog was waiting to be let out. The rain was still falling heavily when Duran opened the door.

Duran leaned up against the opened door and stared at the rain-hazed street.

Now that he had done it—now that he had actually *hired* Kekoja—a chill of misgiving knotted in his gut. He *hoped* he understood his neighbors. He most sincerely hoped that.

CHAPTER 7

"Duran!"

Duran looked up from the alembic he was heating: Kekoja stood before the counter, soaked to the skin, a growing puddle spreading beneath him on the floor.

"I've got orders, Duran! People actually give me orders!"

Duran set aside his book and smiled widely—so a little talk up and down the neighborhood had worked, his customers did have faith in him—

"Anyone seriously ill?"

"No."

"Good." Duran remembered the alembic, picked the head up in thick rags, poured out his decoction from the cucurbit, wrinkling his nose. "Who ordered what? You remember them all, I hope?"

"Aye." Kekoja closed his eyes and cocked his head. "Young Filland's teeth are bothering him again. Says he needs what you usually give him."

"That would be watercress," Duran said, taking down a jar from the shelves behind him. "Who else?"

"Sora Mitti's son's got a toothache. She says it hurts him real bad."

"All right. What she needs is clove seeds." Duran got out another jar. "And she'd better have him to Heimid, get that seen to. Are you paying attention to what I'm giving them? You said you wanted to learn herbs."

"Aye, I'm listening. Cardilla says you know what you give her."

Another jar came off the shelves. "Hemp tea for Cardilla."

"And Mother Garan's headache's back."

"Poor woman." Duran shook his head. "Willow tea for headache. Any more?"

"No. That's all." Kekoja's dark eyes looked suddenly worried. "But it's a start, isn't it?"

"It certainly is. You did marvelously. You have an honest face. Now pay attention to how much I'm giving to each of these people." Duran started making heavy paper packets into which he inserted the various remedies. As he worked, he briefly named off the dosages and how to figure, while Kekoja watched every move. "You *are* a help," Duran said. "None of these folk would have come in today. They'd have suffered. Especially Mother Garan."

"Why don't you sell the old lady a big lot? She says she's got it all the time."

"Because—she only affords a bit. And I'll tell you a secret: I'd *give* it to her at cost—except she'd take too much, she'd take it all the time—

and willow tea hurts the stomach if you take too much, too long: and she'd be worse off."

"She says she really hurts."

"If it doesn't clear up—if it gets worse—there are stronger things. You give them—if you have to. If there's nothing else can be done. And they'll ease the pain—but that's all they'll do."

"You mean she'll die . . ."

"People do." He finished wrapping the last of the packets, and carefully placed them in the small waxed basket he used when gathering herbs. "Try to stay as dry as you can," he said, handing Kekoja the basket. "And take your time. Don't slip on the cobblestones."

Kekoja grinned. "If I do, I know a good 'pothecary to treat me." He drew his cloak over the basket held tight under one arm. "Don't worry, Duran. I won't get into trouble."

Duran watched the boy step back out into the rain and disappear down the street. Dog lay by the opened door, his tail thumping against the wall.

"Dog," Duran said, "if this works, I *might* see a comfortable living."

Dog whuffed once, and settled down for a nap, unconcerned whether Duran made a profit or not.

Two more days of storm and rain. The first day, Kekoja returned with twenty-five coppers off his orders; the second day, it was twenty-two. Duran immediately paid the boy his share: eight coppers— a couple of good meals at an inn like the "Cat."

Now, sitting on his stool and watching the afternoon sunlight break through the clouds, Duran congratulated himself. The deep dark secret was out on the streets—no wizard, a bright-eyed, cheerful boy: folk relaxed, he had given the boy a chance to do more than . . . gods only knew *what* Kekoja had done before Duran had rescued him from the thugs.

And, gods, if his business continued to hold—if having Kekoja's healthy legs to run for him could bring orders in from streets up and down Old Town—he had always lived so frugally and saved every copper he could; he kept his small hoard hidden beneath one of the boards in the floor upstairs. *If* he continued to make the profits he had seen in the past two days, he might—

A scratching at his door brought Duran out of his daydreaming. He looked up at the skirted shadow in his doorway.

"Afternoon, Duran," Zeldezia said, stepping into the shop. Dog lifted his head, sniffed twice, and the beat of his tail stopped. "Never seen the like of this weather."

Duran put on a polite expression and nodded. He had not seen much of Zeldezia lately, a state of affairs he considered most fortunate. He had *not* talked with her since the boy had taken to the streets, he was sure she had that on her mind, and he vowed he would not let her make him lose his temper, that he would be polite to her no matter what she said.

"Sure been strange," she said. "All them storms comin' in. More like spring."

"Aye. It certainly has," Duran replied. "I hope you're doing well."

"Pfft." Zeldezia waved a hand. "It'd take more'n

rain to keep business from *my* door. Folks got to have clothes to wear." She walked over to the counter and leaned up against it. "Seen that Sabirn kid up and down the street. He stayin' here?"

Duran drew a deep breath. "He isn't staying here any more, Zeldezia. I promise you."

"Then where's he livin'? He stole anything?"

"No."

"He's taking medicines to people." Zeldezia's dark eyes narrowed. "Who knows what he's pilferin'. Duran, where's your good sense? How, by all the gods, can you trust 'im?"

"I trust him. He's a good runner, *and* an honest one."

"Ha! Honesty an' Sabirn ain't even in the same *world* with each other. I bet some o' your stuff ain't ever *gettin'* to your customers. You ever checked?"

"He hasn't done anything of the kind." Duran shifted on his stool, determined not to be angry. "I know how much I charge, and he's returned with every copper of it. I know my doses, I sell exactly what's required, and it gets there."

"But how you know he's been tellin' you the truth? How you know he ain't got more orders than he tells you? That he ain't takin' money for 'em and not givin' it to you?"

"I'd find out."

Zeldezia snorted something under her breath. "You're a damned trustin' man, Duran, if you think that kid ain't stealin' from you. An' what do you think he's doin' for your reputation? It's a little uppity of a Sab, runnin' medicines! Ain't never heard the like."

"Uptown shops use Sabirn all the time," Duran said. "As for my reputation—my good customers take care of that."

"Huh. Next you'll have 'im mixin' and boilin'. —You *don't* let him, do you?"

It hit too close. Morally he hated the lie. "Of course not." He arched an eyebrow in her direction. "And he saves people time . . . which *most* of us who work don't have in abundance." As usual, Zeldezia did not rise to his pointed remark. Duran doubted she understood him. "You know how it is. Old folk needing medicines and can't get out in the bad weather; and I can mix or I can be running up and down the streets getting soaked."

"Huhn." She straightened her skirts. "I still say you're out of your mind, Duran. An' I don't like havin' that kid runnin' in and out of your shop. Some of my uptown customers might see 'im."

"So? Your uptown customers wouldn't blink. They're used to Sabirn. And you certainly haven't been shy about telling everyone you know *I'm* responsible for the boy's presence. What's to keep you from telling your customers the same thing?"

An odd look passed across Zeldezia's face. "Do you honestly think I'm nothin' but a gossipy busy-body? That I don't care what happens to you?"

"I don't know what to think," he said sternly. Gods, could Zeldezia be softening?

"Believe me. I *am* concerned."

"You certainly have a strange way of showing it. I'd far rather be left alone."

"—I'm concerned for your *soul*, Duran . . ."

"Listen, what I do is between the Shining One and myself . . . not all the neighbors!"

"But Vadami. . . ."

"He's already talked with me," Duran said, keeping his voice even. "At your instigation, no doubt. Zeldezia, I wish you'd let it lie! Trust me to know whether my soul's mine or not!"

Zeldezia's face darkened. "I talked to him about you, aye, I did, an' I *told* you so. An' I told you what Vadami said to me." She drew a sharp breath. "I been outright and plain, everythin' I done. I care about you! But nothin' I've said, an' nothin' he's said, seems to've made any difference."

"Gods! Is that how you care? Who made you that way?"

"An' what do you mean by *that?*" she asked, drawing herself up and crossing her arms on her chest.

"Just what I said. Someone must have been damned nasty to you for you to be so bitter. And it wasn't Sabirn. I doubt you ever knew any Sabirn. Why can't you leave people alone, Zeldezia? Why can't you keep your nose out of other folk's business?" He lifted a hand. "Before you say the Sabirn lad I hired is your business, too, let me remind you he doesn't come into *your* shop. He doesn't even pause by your door. And as for you . . . you don't have to come over here and talk with me. You don't have to associate with someone who's obviously a damned soul!"

"That's not fair!" she cried. "Not fair at all. I done fair with you—"

"Even the Sabirn?"

Zeldezia's dark eyes glittered. "Them folk ain't got no souls! They sold 'em to demons and other crawlin' things of darkness in exchange for their nefarious powers!"

Hardly Zeldezia's own words. He saw Vadami in that. "And do you know that for a fact, Zeldezia?"

"Don't have to *know* it: Vadami told me so."

"If Vadami told you a country pig would be our next duke, would you believe him?"

"You be careful, Duran." Zeldezia's voice dropped to a harsh whisper. "You're comin' close to heresy. Vadami's a priest! You should have respect!"

"I won't dispute that. I talked with him that night . . . we quoted scripture. He quotes at me, I can cite him holy words that say the exact opposite of what he says."

"You a priest, too, you an' your uptown ways?" Zeldezia looked ready to be impressed. A lie tempted him; a dangerous lie, but:

"No." Duran allowed a small smile to touch his face; and he remembered that Old Town *had* no sense of humor about the Temple. "But I had a fine education in my father's house. Surely you know that."

For some reason Zeldezia's face went red. "Oh, aye, Duran . . . lord it over the rest of us, you bein' Ancar and noble. Well, you're poor as us, now, ain't you? An' as for bein' Ancar . . . if I remember what the priests told me, it was Ancar destroyed the Sabirn empire and put them demons down! That's why there's the Duke, Hladyr bless 'im! Don't you snigger at prayin' an' tell *me* you know more'n Hladyr's own priest!"

Duran nodded toward Dog, who lay asleep by the doorway. "Once all dogs were wolves. They preyed on man's livestock, and man himself when they were pushed to it. Now some of them live with us, guard us, and are our friends. Just because two of Hladyr's creatures were enemies once doesn't mean dogs were demons. Or that old enemies can't change. Hladyr can change them. Maybe Hladyr has. Would you hate his creation? Because he put the Sabirn here. Would you say demons are powerful as Hladyr? I don't. So what happens is *his* doing, isn't it?"

Zeldezia snorted. "Very pretty, Duran. You're even tryin' to *sound* like a priest." She turned toward the doorway. "Mark my words, you're huntin' for trouble keepin' that boy workin for you. One of these days it's all goin' to come home to you, your jokin' an' your lookin' down your nose at folk an' you're sendin' this slinkin' Sab kid around so's poor sick folk got no choice but deal with 'im, that's the respect you got for your neighbors. I tell you, some woman alone, she's got cause t' be scared of that kid, *sure* she's goin' t' pay 'im, *sure* she ain't goin' t' tell if he ask't more money than you said—she's scared!"

"Tell me when this happened! Name me names!"

Zeldezia would not meet his eyes. She flounced toward the door. "Any decent woman! Any poor old woman or ailin' old man, for that matter! You deal with your neighbors with that Sab kid, you go right on, and when it does come home, you remember what you done, 'cause not a one of your neighbors'll come to help you!"

She walked out of the shop, nearly stepping on Dog as she did so.

Dog scrambled out of the way, looked reproachfully at Duran, then shook himself and ambled

outside. Kekoja was due back any time now, and
Duran felt relieved the boy had not returned to
find Zeldezia in the shop.

Duran shook his head. With people like Zeldezia
in the world, it was no wonder one of mankind's
favorite pastimes was war.

Thunder over Targheiden as Duran locked his
door and ran across the street to the inn. The rain
had started falling heavily just as he left his shop
and, by the time he ducked inside the "Cat's"
opened doorway, his cloak was wet.

"Good evening, Sor Duran," Old Man said from
his place on the floor. "Do you think this rain will
ever stop?"

Duran shook his head and gave Old Man a
copper. "For your story tonight, if you're in the
mood to tell one."

Old Man smiled and slipped the coin into his
belt pouch. "I may tell one you've never heard
before," he said.

Duran paused, looking at him. But Old Man
looked elsewhere.

Duran walked to his table. The mood of the
customers in the "Cat" was subdued tonight, the
gloom of yet another day of rain, Duran thought.
Tut came, took his order, and vanished back toward the kitchen without more than a few polite
words.

During which Duran found himself the object of
several furtive stares. Hladyr bless!

Then he thought sourly: Zeldezia.

Damn her.

He sighed, rubbed his eyes, and glanced up as a red-nosed Lalada brought him his ale.

"You don't look like you're feeling well," he said.

"Not," she sniffed. "Got a bad humor in my head."

"Come over to the shop, and I'll give you something to make you feel better."

Lalada stared for a moment. "Only if *you* give it to me. Don't want no Sabirn handlin' it."

Duran matched the ale-girl's stare. "You'll get it from me," he promised, "and no one else."

"Then I'll stop by tomorrow. 'Fore I come to work. You up that early?"

"I can be."

"I'll be there."

Duran watched her go back toward the bar and shook his head. Damn Zeldezia! Gain a bit and that woman's mouth undid it all again . . . He had gotten around her before. He dropped his chin on his hand and thought. . . .

Tut came up with the beef pie—beef pie more often these days, thank the boy for that: nothing wrong with fish . . . in fact, he *liked* fish . . . but, gods, a body could get tired of second-choice . . .

The door to the inn opened, a momentary rush of rain-sound, a rumble of thunder overhead.

Ladirno and Wellhyrn entered the common room.

Gods . . . not tonight.

What in hell brings them down on the harbor-route?

The two Ducal favorites made quite a show of shaking the rain from their costly cloaks and slowly walking to take a table near Duran's. In a perverse way, it warmed Duran's heart that none of the "Cat's" customers paid any attention to the newcomers' fastidious settling-in.

"Duran." Ladirno nodded slightly as he took a chair close by. "I hope you're doing well."

"I am. And you?"

Ladirno smiled. "Excellently. We did an experiment for the Duke a few days back—in between the storms—and produced him gold from a stone."

"And received quite a handsome gift from His Grace for doing so, I might add," said Wellhyrn, inspecting his fingernails. He looked at Duran and lifted an eyebrow. "We've just come back from the harbor. My shipment's been delayed again by the weather. —How are you doing in this dreadful summer? How are the finances?"

Duran tried to keep his face expressionless. "I'm doing all right. Thanks for your concern."

Tut came out from the kitchen; Ladirno and Wellhyrn placed their orders in loud voices, the "Cat's" most expensive, individually-prepared selections. Duran busied himself with his pie, though neither alchemist seemed interested in talking with him again.

Pompous asses! He chewed a bit of pie, swallowed and took a long drink of ale. He was doing far better than they thought. . . .

But he had no inclination to compare finances and he certainly had no desire for their attention. Ladirno he never minded much; the fellow was competent but all too willing to practice the tried and true without ever seeking the new. It was Wellhyrn who puzzled Duran: there was some-

thing hard and dark and twisted about the man
. . . something Duran did not like or trust.

He kept his head down, eating his pie and drinking his ale, and trying not to pay attention to his
colleagues' conversation. Most of it, he thought,
was aimed directly at him, since Wellhyrn was
recounting events that Ladirno must already know
. . . successes at court, admiration from fellow
alchemists, and gifts of money from the Duke and
other nobles.

Dammit, man! he chided himself. *If you wanted
a life like theirs, you could play the game, too.*

And have them for permanent company . . .

". . . hear about the necromancer they hanged
over on the west side?" Wellhyrn was asking
Ladirno, as the two of them started their dinners.
"The Guard caught her practicing and took her
before the priests. They say she never would admit to anything—but one knows."

"They put her to the question, of course . . ."

"Hot irons," Wellhyrn said. "She cursed the
priests when they were hanging her. Quite a show.
Big crowd."

"In all this rain? Gods."

Wellhyrn laughed, a cold laugh, unnerving to
hear coming from one so young. "Folk know there's
something odd in this weather. You should have
seen it. All these hundreds of people standing in
the storm and the lightning—"

"You saw it?"

"Oh, I did."

"Huh." Ladirno gave a shiver or a shrug.
"Demon-worshipers. I want no part of it."

Enough to curdle a man's appetite, Duran

thought, listening to it. He finished his pie, he had no inclination to be chased out of the warm tavern in the height of the rain, and he hoped they would leave soon—turned slightly away and leaned back in his chair, trying to give the impression he was dozing after a rich meal. He heard Wellhyrn and Ladirno rise, finally, scatter coins on the table in payment for their food, and leave.

But he heard the gossip they left in their wake. He heard people mutter—*sorcery* . . .

"Duran."

He looked up: Ithar stood at his side, a mug of ale in one burly hand.

"Mind if I join you?"

Duran shook his head and gestured to a chair.

"Saw them snot-nosed rich boys tryin' to bother you," Ithar said, sitting down. "Don't you let 'em get to you, Duran. Them kind ain't worth more than fish food." His dark eyes sparkled. "An' maybe the fish'd spit 'em back."

"Sometimes it's hard to ignore them," Duran admitted. "Them and their money."

Ithar cocked his head. "Why?"

"Hladyr only knows. I can't think of anything I'd want from them."

"Fah! You just remember that them kind don't never do nothin' for anyone but themselves. They may have all the money an' importance, but they can't take it with 'em."

Duran drew a deep breath. "I think you're right, Ithar, but there are times when I'd like to punch their smirking faces in, and me, a gentleman."

"Don't waste your time. You got better things to

do." Ithar crossed his arms on the table top. "That Sabirn boy of yours workin' out?"

He looked hopefully at Ithar. So maybe the damage was *not* that widespread. "Aye. I wish I'd thought to hire someone long ago. I never thought I had the money for it."

"An' Sabirn come cheap."

Duran nodded. "I've been doing all right lately than I've seen in years. I might be able to buy some better equipment for the shop if things keep going so well. I might want some smithing . . ."

"Be glad of the work. But you just be careful, Duran. An' tell that boy of yours to keep his head down an' never look like he's doin' anythin' but run for you. You understand?"

"Zeldezia's been talking again."

"It's not only that," Ithar said. "It's that hanging—"

"The boy's nothing but an orphaned kid! He's damn sure no wizard, let alone any—"

"No, no. I didn't mean it that way." Ithar lowered his voice. "We ain't seen no necromancers in years, Duran. Not in years. Now they go an' find themselves one that's probably been spellin' the weather . . . bringin' on the storms an' such . . . An' maybe that's it an' now it'll stop—"

"I don't believe anyone can control the weather," Duran said. "Not even the Duke's wizards, else he wouldn't have lost so many ships at sea."

"Ah, but what if his enemies got themselves a bunch of wizards to counteract *his* wizards? Eh? What then?"

Duran closed his eyes. What had caused his father to fall from power and the friendship of the Duke? Was it wizards again?

"You just keep yourself out of trouble, Duran . . . an' keep an eye on that kid. Whatever that necromancer did, she got caught at it."

"Or, she was an easy one to blame for the bad weather," Duran suggested. "Some poor old soul—"

"Duran. Duran, lissen to me. That necromancer they hung?—She was Sabirn."

Duran left "The Swimming Cat" earlier than was normal for him, while the rain was still falling and lightning played in the heavy clouds. He ran across the street, stood in the windy space beneath his second story overhang, and cursed the key that stuck in the lock. The warm feeling of late afternoon had disappeared from his heart, leaving coldness behind . . . a coldness next to fear.

Gods above and below! If Targheiden's folk decided that Sabirn were at fault for the weather—

He shook the rain from his cloak, hung it behind the door, absent-mindedly patted Dog, who stepped outside to his nightly duties all oblivious to hazards—

He resolved to say something to Kekoja in the morning, warn the boy—gods, how did one explain such lunacy to a boy?—warn the boy to keep the lowest profile he could.

And himself? Damn. He was Ancar. His personal danger was negligible. He was no courtier, had no enemies with political reasons—he refused to be a coward, could not turn back from what he had done, from hiring Kekoja . . . honor forbade that. Pride did. He could not desert the boy—or fling him off, out of some stupid, weaseling fear—

By the time Duran had lit his lamp, Dog came

back into the shop, stopping in the doorway and shaking the rain water from his coat. He sat down, scratched at one ear, then jumped to his feet and whirled about.

"Sor Duran."

Old Man stood in the doorway beneath the overhang . . . Old Man, and Kekoja.

"Come in," Duran said, wiping his hands on his tunic. Gods hope there was no problem. He tried to tell himself it was otherwise, a personal business. Gods, who might be seeing him here, from the "Cat's" door? "Come in, you'll drown out there."

He lit the lamp hanging above the counter and turned up the wick in the other. Old Man and Kekoja came into the shop, shook the worst of the rain from their cloaks, and sat down on the floor.

"What can I do for you?" Duran asked, coming around the counter to face his guests.

Old Man's dark eyes were steady in the lamplight. "You left early tonight, Sor Duran. I've come to tell you that story I promised you."

A sense of guilt washed over Duran—for all his fears. For a woman hanged . . . For thinking—instantly—why? What will the neighbors think?

"Please." He shut the door against the rain—wondering again who might see, as if that door being shut—made it clear it was no case of Old Man as a customer. But he hated cowardice. "Can I get you tea?"

"Tea, yes, thank you," Old Man said; and Duran got the pan he used for tea, lit a spill and fired up the little apothecary's stove at the end of the counter—while Old Man settled into the only chair, while Kekoja settled crosslegged at his feet—

Like some personage with his escort.

"Thank you," Old Man said, when Duran brought the tea, and sipped it while Duran found himself a seat on the stool, his own cup in hand . . .

"This is a story I doubt your neighbors would appreciate," Old Man said after several sips. "You've asked me several times what things were like before our empire fell. Well, I thought I'd tell you a story about those last days, if you want to listen."

Duran's heart beat in fear. "Of course I'll listen." He realized in his panic what Old Man was offering—he knew what he ought to do, and set the tea-cup down on the counter at his elbow. "Did your grandson tell you I keep such stories written down? To prevent their being lost? Do you mind?"

"No. Write anything you like."

Duran hurried behind his counter and pulled out a sheet of coarse paper and a stick of charcoal. Seating himself on his stool, the paper on the counter, he took up the tea-cup again, poised himself anxiously to take notes.

Old Man smiled and began his story. At the first, it seemed a mere recounting of old myths, old accounts reassuringly familiar—agreeing with what the Temple held the world was like a thousand years ago: the barbaric Armu had pushed eastward across the Irdanu River into Pesedur, thrust out of their homelands themselves by the tall, fair Ancar. Kingdom after kingdom fell to Armu hordes and Ancari armies, all advancing toward the west and the heart of the Empire.

Then Jarrya fell, the breadbasket of the inner world, and the Ancar came southward into the

Sabirin peninsula—toward the capital, where authority tottered—as at sea, Sakar harbored pirates and worse, sitting poised to do any kind of damage they could to failing shipping . . . taking advantage of the Empire's weakness, adding to that weakness by raiding ships, ruining the mercantile houses . . . increasing poverty and dissent—

Duran dutifully made brief notes, interested that once Targheiden had been called Cerinde and that fabled Sakar was now known as the Sacarres. But of greater matters, secret matters, he heard nothing he had not been told before, albeit in pieces and disconnected as a whole.

Then Old Man spoke of the Empire itself.

Sabis was the capital of that empire, and the center of the once thriving trade that had made the Sabirn wealthy, drawing substances and goods from all around the Inner Sea. Sabirn ships, far more advanced than those of other nations, carried Sabirn trade into all the surrounding world, bringing back wonders from other countries—arts, slaves, furs and silk and spices. The Sabirn had boasted banks, a class of traders with power in the imperial court, and a beginning guild of artisans. In short, the level of their civilization had rivaled what existed today—in everything but the commonest of conveniences, in everything but the blessings the Temple provided, the knowledge of Scriptures, the work of Hladyr's priests—

There had been other gods.

"And wizardry?" Duran asked, as Old Man paused for a moment. "You had your wizards, didn't you?"

"Ah, wizards. Aye, we had our wizards, as you

have yours. Their methods didn't vary much from yours."

"No more powerful?"

"No more powerful."

Duran found himself vaguely disappointed.

"But there was other knowledge," Old Man said.

"Alchemy?" A chill went down Duran's back. His hand paused, waiting.

"Alchemists . . . who were wizards. Wizards who were alchemists. *That* gave them the power. . . ."

Duran swallowed. "Did you ever hear of any of them who could turn base metals into gold?"

Kekoja ducked his head to hide his expression, but Old Man disdained such subterfuge. He laughed quietly.

"No." His dark eyes glittered in the lamp-light as he looked up at Duran. "Can you?"

"No," Duran admitted, shaking his head. "Not I. And no one I know can—" Thinking of Ladirno and Wellhyrn this evening—and their claim of gold. "—despite what they say." He could hang for what he admitted. The Guild would see to it. "They're simple tricks."

"What we *did* have in the twilight of our empire was a man named Sulun, who called himself a 'natural philosopher,'—and who came close to developing a weapon to drive the invaders out of Sabir."

"A weapon—of wizardry?"

"Of natural force. Sulun and other like-minded folk survived the downfall of the Empire, and went off into the wilderness, taking all their knowledge with them." Old Man smiled slightly. "They were known as wizards, Duran . . . and some of them were. But wizardry only gave them luck. Their wits gave them what they made."

"Then they could have *saved* the Empire—"

"Aye. But when an empire is falling, even philosophers find themselves dealing with time and fools. There was no time. And there was an abundance of fools. So Sulun and his followers took with them a knowledge of medicine, of shipbuilding, of manufacturing . . . of all kinds of things. We remember. We do remember."

"But remembering—" For a moment Duran was conscious of himself as Ancar, tall, fair, blue-eyed—themselves as Sabirn, the dark, ancient folk—who might want their Empire *back*—

Or want revenge for it. . . .

"Your barbaric ancestors crushed Sabis like an overripe fruit," Old Man said, and clenched an uplifted hand. Let it fall. "Say nothing, Sor Duran. You are not your ancestors. We are not ours. Sabis was ready to fall . . . hollow from the inside out. Kingdoms and empires age. They have their lifespans. They breed descendants. Your ancestors happened to be the instrument."

Duran felt the flush on his cheeks. "Nevertheless, the waste of it all—"

"Nothing is wasted—nothing lost."

He stirred on his stool. "You know the priest, Vadami? He told me there was once a great Sabirn wizard named Siyuh—Ziya?—who made fire leap from his hands. Is that a true story?"

Old Man's smile never wavered; only his eyes became hooded, shut off, remote from Duran's questions. "Perhaps that's a story I can tell you one day. But not tonight. I've talked longer than I should."

"What would *you* do," Kekoja asked suddenly, leaning against Old Man's knee, "if you knew what we knew in the days of our empire?"

"Me?" Duran blinked in the lamp-light. "I've never really thought about it. I'd try to make better medicines first, I suppose. When I see people die and I can't help them. . . ."

"And being an alchemist," Old Man said, "you're interested in changing base metals to gold. What would you do if you could?"

Duran studied Old Man for a long moment, trying to guess why he and Kekoja were asking such seemingly unrelated questions. "I'm not denying I'd like to have more money. Money can buy many things, Old Man, and it can help people if it's used right. But consider this: if I was interested only in making money, I'd be up in the Duke's palace with the rest of the alchemists."

Old Man frowned and ducked his head. "I must be going," Old Man said, then, reaching for his walking stick. "At my age, sleep is something I value."

Kekoja stood, drew Old Man's cloak up, and helped him to his feet. The suddenness of this departure puzzled Duran, but he left Old Man's secrets alone. He stepped down from his stool, set his paper and charcoal stick on the counter, and faced the two Sabirn. Should he tell them about the necromancer who had been hanged, and warn Kekoja to keep very quiet? No. Tomorrow. It was quite obvious Old Man and his grandson wished to leave.

"When you come to work tomorrow, remind me to tell you something," Duran said to Kekoja. "It's important, but it will keep."

"Aye."

Duran watched from his doorstep as Old Man and Kekoja walked across the street. Then, just as he started to turn away, he noticed two men standing in the shelter of the building across the alleyway. Dog joined him at the doorway, growled softly, and sniffed in the newcomers' direction.

"Old Man," one of the men called out softly. "It's us."

Brovor, returned with his companion for another treatment.

Aside from the one time Brovor had let Duran know he recognized him, no one had mentioned names again. Duran's estimation of the heir had gone up; the young lord had not missed one night of coming for his medicine, though it meant going out in the rain and visiting a section of town he otherwise might never have frequented. It must have been difficult for Brovor to get away from the palace every night. But fear was a great motivator, and if getting the pox kept Brovor away from the whores, the lad might have learned a lesson.

CHAPTER 8

"Gods-cursed storms!" Wellhyrn snarled, flinging his sodden cloak to the floor of Ladirno's apartment. His light brown hair was plastered to his
forehead where the hood of his cloak had not kept
the rain out. Damp spots marked his expensive
jerkin, and his hose were dark to the knee above
soaked glove-leather boots. "I don't think I've ever
seen the like! Has anyone told you about the river?
It's flooding the lower areas of the Slough."

"Bah!" Ladirno waved a hand. "It could flood
the Slough right into the sea, and the world would
be a better place for it. What in the gods' names
brings *you* out on a day like this?"

Wellhyrn's green eyes caught the light from the
gray, rain-spattered window. "News, Ladir. News
we can possibly turn to our benefit. Do you have
something to drink?"

"Aye." Ladirno walked over to the sideboard,
poured himself and Wellhyrn a glass of wine, then

151

extended one of the glasses to his guest. "What is it now? Gods, you pick up more gossip than anyone I know."

"Duran," Wellhyrn said, dropping down into a chair and sipping at his wine. "I was out early this morning, before the downpour. I stopped for breakfast at the 'Shoe,' and who should drop by but your new friend, Vadami."

"Vadami? *My* friend?" Ladirno snorted. "That fellow's nobody's friend but his own. Well, what about him?"

A thin smile touched Wellhyrn's face. "Vadami, oh, so humbly asked if I'd seen you. He seems to think you're a friend of Duran's."

"Gods."

Wellhyrn chuckled. "Anyway, I didn't shatter his delusion and asked him to join me. I said I might be seeing you later on in the day and if he had a message, I'd be happy to pass it along."

"So?"

Wellhyrn lifted an eyebrow. "Vadami had been ministering to some poor creature in Old Town last night and was on his way back to the Temple. He happened to be walking up Smithy Street by 'The Swimming Cat,' when he noticed—of all things—that old Sabirn from the tavern—*and* that Sabirn kid—"

"—his grandson, by my sources."

Wellhyrn's handsome face was alight with malice. "Both of them at Duran's door. Him *and* this young boy. Now I ask you why. I ask you why Duran let them in and shut the door fast."

Ladirno frowned. "Puzzling."

"Isn't it?" Wellhyrn's mood changed: all humor had fled from it. "It makes me damned nervous, Ladir. What in Dandro's hells is going on in that shop, that's what I'd like to know? Why's Duran buying good ale of a sudden—eating beef like a gentleman? Did you catch that?"

"Did Vadami hear anything?"

"In a storm like the one last night? Hardly. He was afraid of being seen, and only got close enough to make sure he saw what he thought. Then he retreated to shelter at the front of 'The Swimming Cat' to watch what happened next."

Ladirno swirled the wine in his glass, watching the lamp-light in it. "I'd give a lot to know what was going on in there."

"So, dear colleague, would I." Wellhyrn stretched in the chair, his movements graceful and refined. "I'm very much afraid that Duran might be involved in something."

"Such as?" Ladirno asked.

"Sabirn secrets. Such as—hidden knowledge. One wonders what he's doing—and what the Sabirn's price is."

"He's been talking to that old man for years."

Wellhyrn took a sip of wine. "Doing gods know what for years."

"Fah! *I* think there's no secret to be had. If that old man knows secrets like that, if any Sabirn does—why are they so damned poor?"

"I can know many things," Wellhyrn said softly, his voice smooth, "but if I don't have the tools to make use of what I know, I might as well not know it."

"Gods. You don't think—"

"What better cover for a wizard than to appear as an old beggar?"

"Now you *are* grasping at straws. I'd believe Duran capable of searching for Sabirn secrets—but credit him with wanting to bring down the kingdom . . . For gods' sakes, Wellhyrn . . . he's an Ancar noble!"

Wellhyrn sneered. "*Was* an Ancar noble. His father was banished—for treason."

"Treason being the old duke's whim, by what I hear, not Hajun's. And Duran's still Ancar. I can't believe any Ancar—"

"Would do what? Consort with Sabirn? Think about it. Obviously he's after something from the Sabirn. We *think* it's alchemical secrets. It could be worse. But even if it's only the one, they provide him with alchemistic secrets we can only dream of—if only to keep him on the string. And where would that leave us, and the other members of our profession?"

Ladirno stared at Wellhyrn, and rubbed his forehead, fighting down a headache.

"Now you're beginning to see it," Wellhyrn said.

Ladirno stared at the rain-washed window. "I suppose," he murmured, "we'd better brave the storm. It's time both you and I had another conversation with our little priest. I want to get to hear his story for myself."

Vadami stood in the doorway of "The Golden Shoe," abhorring the thought of going out into the rain and wind of Old Town, but if word of his loitering got back to his superiors, they would take his hours here for softness. He sighed deeply in resignation, took a long breath, opened the door and nearly ran head-on into a dripping Ladirno, accompanied by an equally sodden Wellhyrn.

"Ah, Father Vadami," Ladirno said, thrusting the hood of his cloak back and smiling. "The very person I wanted to see. What luck to find you here."

Vadami pushed his own hood back, bowed slightly, and kept a smile on his face, unsure whether he was being mocked.

"A table for three," Wellhyrn said to a serving-boy. "And your best half bottle of wine."

Feeling caught up in something he did not understand, Vadami followed the two alchemists to a table at the rear of the common room, far from the crowd near the windows. Seating himself across from the two hosts, he unclasped his cloak and let it hang over the back of the chair.

"How may I help you, Sori?" he asked, trying to read the expression on their faces, but their smiles never wavered. Hladyr bless! If only *he* could be as important as these men. If only the Shining One would bless him with the luck . . . would bring his love of the gods and his work to the attention of his superiors.

And get him out of Old Town.

"I got your message," Ladirno said conversationally, leaning back in his chair. The waiter brought a carafe of wine and three glasses to the table, left them unpoured at the wave of Ladirno's hand.

"My . . . message, yes." Vadami watched the

lamp-light glitter on Ladirno's gold neck chain.
"About Duran—"

Ladirno tilted his head, implied invitation.

"I'm getting increasingly worried, Sori. He doesn't
want to listen to me—and—considering you have
some concern for him—rather than go to Temple
authorities, you understand—"

"We appreciate this," Ladirno said.

"I thought maybe *you'd* be able to talk some
sense into him. After all, you're his—" Cough.
"—friend in the guild—"

"You mean about his visitors last night."

Vadami nodded. "He's endangering his soul,
consorting with the Sabirn. It's become extremely
serious—this business on the west end—"

"We understand that," Wellhyrn said smoothly.
"Necromancy is a very serious charge."

"I'm trying to rescue him. I can't make any
headway with him, though gods know I've tried.
He doesn't believe they're dangerous."

"What was the old man talking about?" Ladirno
asked, pouring Vadami a glass of wine, then filling
his and Wellhyrn's glasses. "Did you hear anything at all? Can you guess anything?"

"No." Vadami took a sip of the wine, marveling
at its smoothness. "I couldn't get that close. But
whatever it was—it undoubtedly had to do with
the dark arts."

"You think so?"

"What *else* would a Sabirn be talking about?
They're devils! What can they want but to snare
the innocent? I've tried to warn him, Sor Ladirno.
Duran's soul is in my care, it's my duty as a priest
of Hladyr to keep him from falling into darkness."

"Could the old man have been telling Duran secrets?" Wellhyrn prompted, running a languid fingertip around the rim of his glass. "Things the Sabirn might—remember?"

"No one could know. The old man usually tells tales at the inn. But people have seen Duran— writing while he talks."

The two court alchemists exchanged a brief look, one full of obvious concern. Vadami's heart warmed: these were good people. It was good to know that men so powerful still had concern for a friend in danger. Maybe, with their help, he could talk Duran into leaving the Sabirn alone.

Maybe—with their help—and a good outcome for this affair—he could find friends at court—

It was very wise of him—to have gone to them and not his superiors.

"I *am* concerned." Wellhyrn shook his handsome head. "Have you noticed this old Sabirn talking to anyone strange?"

Hladyr bless! Sorgun orders me to tell him if this old man ever talks to anyone who lives outside of Old Town. Now I get the same question from these eminent alchemists. . . .

"No. Not that I can remember. But I'm not in Old Town every hour of every day. I certainly could keep an eye on things—"

"That *would* be appreciated. But don't worry too much. We'll see if we can talk some sense into him. Meanwhile, keep up your watch. We'd like to know how he's doing." He smiled and spread his hands. "Unfortunately, we don't see much of him at court. It's probably very embarrassing for him to attend, poor as he is."

"Perhaps we ought to help him again," Ladirno suggested.

"Aye. Perhaps."

"I—" Vadami hesitated, cleared his throat. "I did—observe the shop last night—out of concern, you understand. Attempting to be sure I understood before I—approached anyone with this information—"

"Did you see him leave the premises?"

"No. But I did see—other traffic that night."

"Be more clear."

"I can't be. Two heavily cloaked men—I'm sure they were men—went into Duran's shop. They—went uptown. I followed them—as far as the palace gate."

"And?"

This was frightening. Vadami wished he had more understanding *what* he had seen. Wellhyrn's eyes frightened him. "They went inside. The guards evidently knew them. They passed without question."

"Anything distinctive about them?"

"One very tall. Broad-shouldered. Both in black cloaks, wrapped up to here—" A measure at his nose. He swallowed heavily, wondering if he was in some danger. He searched his recollection frantically for detail. "One—the small one—had blue boots. Blue with silver piping down the side. . . ."

That got a reaction: both alchemists went very attentive and stared at him.

"Sori?" Vadami asked.

"And?"

"That's all. That's all I saw."

"Interesting." Wellhyrn reached into his belt pouch and pulled out two gold midonahri. "Take this as your donation for the day. And don't worry about Duran. We'll talk with him."

"And you'd best be off for Old Town," Ladirno said. "Just—be as discreet as you have been. This is important."

Vadami reached out and took the coins, trembling. Hladyr bless, it was more than he usually saw in a month from all of Old Town.

He pursed the coins, stood, took up his cloak. Ladirno and Wellhyrn nodded him a courtesy. "Father," Ladirno said by way of parting, as if he *were* somebody.

"The blessings of Hladyr," he murmured, signing them both. "I'll remember you in my prayers."

As the priest walked off to the door, Ladirno met Wellhyrn's eyes, said in a hushed voice, "You *know* who that was."

Wellhyrn's voice was unsteady. "What in Dandro's hells, was *he* wanting with Duran?"

Ladirno's face shone pale in the lamp-light. "Let's get out of here."

And out on the street, in the downpour: "The Duke's heir!" Ladirno hissed. "Gods, man, what's going on?"

"Knowing Brovor, Duran could have been selling him a love potion."

"Don't joke!"

"But we'd better hope it *wasn't* anything more than a love potion."

"What do you mean by that?"

Wellhyrn looked him in the eye, water streaming down a face paler than its wont. "There's another possibility. What's Duran best known for?"

"He's a herbalist—a part-time alchemist."

"Think, man! The famous cure for the pox! What if—"

"O gods above and below!" Ladirno felt his heart lurch in his chest. "You don't think he—the heir—good gods, Brovor's negotiating for Mavid's daughter—the alliance with—"

"Why else would he be visiting someone like Duran? If you were the Duke's son and had the pox, would you call in the court doctor to treat you?"

"Of course not. I'd. . . ." Ladirno rubbed his eyes. "Gods! If Duran *is* treating Brovor, and he cures him—"

Wellhyrn smiled nastily. "He's either rich or dead—when Brovor's the duke."

"Hells!" Ladirno shook his head. "But this Sabirn connection!"

"Worrisome. Damned worrisome." Wellhyrn gnawed at a hangnail and Ladirno stared helplessly at his younger companion, wishing his mind worked with the same speed as Wellhyrn's. He felt certain Wellhyrn had other things in mind, *dangerous* things—

"I think," Ladirno said, cautiously feeling his way forward, "if we mentioned that Duran's tied in with the Sabirn to the prince himself—just happen to mention it—"

Wellhyrn shot him a furious scowl. "*Why* would we just happen to mention Duran? Don't be a fool! That's a way to get both our throats cut!"

"But—"

Wellhyrn's smile dazzled. "But the Duke! His Grace has the rains to contend with, he has the *suspicion* of Sabirn necromancers—if he finds out an Ancar, the son of a pardoned traitor—is dealing with Sabirn—"

"Talk about dangerous! Good gods, Wellhyrn!"

"No, no, if we phrase this exactly right, stressing Duran's Ancar heritage, the Duke might take it personally—personally enough to take action— and uncover this conspiracy . . ."

A cold chill ran up Ladirno's spine. "What kind of *action*, Wellhyrn. We're talking about Duran's *head!*"

"Exile. Exile's what his father got, exile's the most likely thing."

"But what about Brovor?"

"There is the other possibility, you know."

"What?"

"That the heir's in on it—the wizardry—the Sabirn—"

"God, no! Not Brovor."

"Wouldn't be the first son wanted his inheritance early. Say the Sabirn knew that impatience. Say the Sabirn found a way to Duran—who has a way to the heir . . . you know what we're talking about here?"

"Hladyr save—"

"We just talk with His Grace, we just quietly— quietly handle all this. Tell him a non-guild alchemist is . . . friendly with the Sabirn. With all this anxiousness about that situation—the Duke *will* be concerned, the Duke *will* move . . ."

"Gods, this is dangerous."

"Steady. Steady. It's also profitable. For us, you understand. When you play at these levels—you take risks. Brovor's one. But one thing we know—he's not working with the Sabirn. If he's being double-crossed—he'll come to *us* to sound us out—and we can position ourselves—"

"I don't like this!"

"Easy, easy, let's go back in, have something to eat, calm ourselves. Gods only know how long we'll wait at the palace, and I'll be damned if I'm both hungry *and* wet."

The wind rattled the expensive glass windows of the Great Hall, and the Duke—in tedious and sparsely-attended audience—winced at the noise. Another day of storms had swept down on Targheiden . . . another day of weather that could sink a ship and lose all its cargo: more complaints. A minstrel played something soothing in one corner, and the courtiers stood or sat together in small groups, their conversations low enough so that nothing could be heard.

"Damn soggy bore," Hajun muttered to his wife, who sat a few paces away with her daughter and their ladies, all of whom were busy with needle-point. He had not been in the best of moods all day, and it was a wonder she was even speaking to him after he had snarled at her over breakfast.

His two sons sat with a group of friends their own age, other lords' sons, brought to Targheiden to learn manners of the court. They laughed, told jokes, and diced together, the weather preventing their usual summertime entertainments of hawking, arms practice, and hunting. Brovor had been much out on the town lately, going off every night with his friends. Granted he had not stayed out late, and had not returned drunken as he had so many times in the past—such partying worried Hajun: that was the fight at breakfast. His wife dismissed it as the last fling of a young man on the verge of state marriage and true adulthood, counseled him to ignore the late-night outings.

But there were hopeful signs. Today, for instance, Brovor and Saladar were not feuding—an unusual but a pleasant sight.

"Your Grace . . ."

The door to the hall had opened: his steward entered, paused, and ushered two black-clad men into the room: Ladirno and Wellhyrn. Hajun smiled in greeting, though his heart was not in it. He wanted nothing to do with their speeches or demonstrations today; but—in a slow day—they promised, perhaps, diversion . . .

"Wellhyrn. Ladirno," he called out, stirring in his chair. "You attend me in vile weather, gentlemen. I do commend your faithfulness."

The two alchemists bowed and approached the dais, past the idle courtiers, conversations briefly paused, the eternal estimating glances following whoever walked that route. Wolves, Hajun thought, estimating the town dogs.

"Dreadful day, isn't it?" Hajun gestured Ladirno and Wellhyrn to be at ease, hardly interrupted his signing of permissions and warrants, thick on the desk. "What news?"

"The river's beginning to flood the Slough,"

Wellhyrn said. "As I'm sure Your Grace has heard. . . ."

"Good riddance." Hajun signed another document and blotted it, guarding his sleeve. "Surely there's something *else* going on in Torgheiden besides the floods."

Ladirno glanced at Wellhyrn and bowed slightly, lowered his voice. "If it please Your Grace, we've come here today for a reason."

"Aside from keeping me company while the storms rage? Laudable. I need diversion."

Neither man reacted to his sarcasm, and Hajun felt briefly cheated. Town dogs indeed.

"A matter somewhat touching the Guild," Ladirno continued, leaning a bit forward in his chair. "Something—of great delicacy—"

"So tell me, man. Don't let me die of old age before you get around to it."

This time a faint flush stole across Ladirno's face. Hajun chided himself for being snappish: Ladirno and Wellhyrn were hardly responsible for the vile weather. He smiled quickly, to pass off his words as levity.

"It involves the Sabirn, lord," Ladirno said, "and one of your court."

"Oh?" Hajun's quill stopped on its way to the inkwell. "One of my—*court?*"

Wellhyrn cleared his throat, attempted to whisper: "One of our colleagues—"

Hajun beckoned him up a step on the dais. Both advanced anxiously.

"One of our colleagues," Wellhyrn said, "a member of this court—at least—in entitlement, if not in fact—"

Hajun felt his wife's eyes on him, and lowered his voice. "Who's involved?"

"Duran vro Ancahar."

Hajun let out his breath. "So. Duran's hardly one of the luminaries of this court," Hajun said. "In fact, it's been a long time since he's even darkened my door."

Ladirno nodded and gestured quickly. "That may be true, lord, but he has access here. As well as to the Guild."

"He's been known for years—to have contacts among the Sabirn," Wellhyrn said, keeping his voice as low as his companion's. "Being his colleagues, as Ladirno said, we have a professional responsibility to report—" The young man glanced around, and lowered his voice further. "—possible involvement in the dark arts."

Hajun blinked. "Duran?"

"There's perhaps reason he keeps to Old Town, that he's—ignored your late father's generous restoration of his rights. He goes off into the hills with the Sabirn. He's taken a Sabirn into his house. There are rumors—" Wellhyrn coughed. "—of moral nature. He ignores his priest—his closest associates are Sabirn."

"Why?"

"Why indeed, Your Grace," Wellhyrn said. "In this most unusual summer—in this year of disasters—why these nightly visitors, why these strange associations, why this sudden distance from his priest?"

"Which is strange," Ladirno said. "Duran's always seemed to be religious in his own way."

"Huhn." Hajun studied the two alchemists. There was something going on here, something that lurked beneath the surface of their ready concern. He had not seen that concern evidenced so obviously before. Maybe there was a great deal going on he had not paid close attention to.

"It's a matter of concern," Wellhyrn said. "Understand: we know this man. We mark changes in him. And considering his discovery, his trade in—medicines certain individuals might have reason to want in extreme secret—there's such a chance for blackmail. Understand, Your Grace, we've no proof. But we've abundant witnesses of his Sabirn contacts. This boy—a storyteller at a certain tavern—whom he entertains late, behind closed doors—an Ancar nobleman, Your Grace. In these anxious times . . ."

"Your Grace," said Ladirno, spreading his hands, "it's well known that *all* Sabirn practice the dark arts in one way or another. Their very gods . . ."

Hajun nodded. He looked up at the windows—at the perpetual, unnatural spatter of rain.

Wellhyrn said softly: "I know you've been concerned, lord, by the weather. As have we all. Uncommon. Malicious. Flooding in the Slough."

"The necromancer they hanged," Ladirno said, softer still, "Your Grace, she *was* Sabirn. But not the only Sabirn."

"All Targheiden knows you've lost ships," Wellhyrn said. "If it *were* a plot—how better to undermine the duchy? Even the kingdom itself . . ."

Hajun stared at the two men, forcing his face expressionless.

"Why would Sabirn," Wellhyrn said, "woo some-one like Duran? And *why* doesn't he return to court?"

"Jorrino, Chadalen," Hajun said, beckoning the two of his court wizards in the hall. "Master Jorrino. Master Chadalen. These two gentlemen have suggested *Sabirn* agency turning the weather against me. Is there any chance of this being true?"

Chadalen was a tall fellow, his dark blond hair and blue eyes speaking of mixed Ancar heritage. He bowed slightly. "Anything is possible, Your Grace."

Jorrino, the elder of the two wizards shook his head. "We're aware of the hanging. But whether it's so—I can't answer. We simply don't know enough about them to say for sure. It's *very* difficult to locate a wizard by his effects—unless you know his motives, Your Grace."

Hajun leaned on the armrest of his chair and propped his chin in his hand. Everyone knew the Sabirn for demon worshipers, down to the last child of them. He remembered their dark, silent faces, seen from his remote viewpoint of royal carriage or shipboard. He remembered their soft, unintelligible language, the way they seemed to drift from shadow to shadow—servants, even in the highest houses, clinging to dark, ancient gods, even those who professed to convert—one always had to doubt—

"Lord?"

He looked up: the two wizards and the alchemists were watching him, waiting for some reaction.

"*Could* the Sabirn be responsible for the bad turn in the weather?" he asked.

"It's certainly possible." Jorrino shrugged. "They operate outside the jurisdiction of the Temple. We've thought mostly of foreign enemies. But—if there *are* secrets we've not yet met, I suppose—I suppose if one truly dealt in the dark arts, which we do not, Your Grace! being gods-fearing men— one *might* indeed gather enough power to control the weather."

Hajun frowned. Gods above! If the rumor about the Sabirn wizards was true, could they be behind the bad luck that had been plaguing his trade fleet? Was it possible they were powerful enough to ill-wish him in such a fashion *despite* his wizards—who confessed to their own impotence against forbidden, ungodly magics—

The plot . . . always the plot.

When one of those little, dark people looked at him, he had always shuddered.

"Chadalen . . . *if* the Sabirn are ill-wishing this weather on Targheiden, can you and your colleagues deflect their power?"

Chadalen looked worried. "We can only try, Your Grace. Perhaps—abandoning our concentration on *foreign* enemies, directing our attention much closer to home—may make us of more effect."

Hajun rubbed his eyes, looked again at the four men facing him: the two alchemists' faces betraying nothing of what passed in their thoughts; the two wizards, impressive in their dark blue robes, equally expressionless.

Damn! He felt forced into a corner, beset with maybe and might-be.

Duran was hardly a threat to Ladirno's position, or Wellhyrn's, for that matter. They had no reason

for professional jealousy. Duran had bothered no
one, never tried to ease his way back into favor.

But consorting with Sabirn, leaning toward use
of the dark arts, *and* of possibly plotting the end of
Ancar rule over Torgheiden—*could* a son's bitter-
ness over his father's exile go that far?

Hajun took a deep breath. "So be it," he said
and sat up straight in his chair. "I'll bring Duran
in for questioning."

CHAPTER 9

The common room of "The Swimming Cat" stood nearly empty; most of the customers were travelers marooned at the inn by the storm. The neighborhood folk had left a while ago, rain or no rain, to return to their shops and finish out their business day.

Duran sat at his table, taking longer than normal for his lunch. Lunch. He smiled to himself. Hiring Kekoja as his runner had given him enough of a profit that he had decided he could afford lunch. It was fish, to be sure, but it was warm, and the ale that had accompanied it tasted ever so much better than water.

Tut walked up, a mug of ale in his hands. He had finally finished setting out clean mugs behind the bar, and supervising the clean-up of the tables after his noon-time customers had left. Now it was Tut's turn to sit for a while, to relax before preparing his staff for the dinner crowd.

171

"So," he said, sitting down at Duran's table. "That kid of yours doin' real fine for you, ain't he? I can't remember a time when you been in here for a meal other than breakfast or dinner."

Duran nodded. "Aye, Tut. I can afford a mug of ale every noon now, a hot lunch now and again. And perhaps a meat pie for dinner, who knows?"

Tut took another swallow of ale and lowered his voice. "Keep your eyes on that Zeldezia. She been goin' around talkin' 'bout you again."

"Hladyr bless! Now what?"

"She been sayin' you're comin' close to demon-worship yourself. She says even the good priest ain't been able to change your mind."

"Gods, why doesn't she stay out of my business. That boy doesn't bother her at all—he's never been around when she's come to my shop. Why can't she leave me alone?"

Tutadar dipped one fingertip in a puddle of spilled ale, and drew an idle pattern on the table top. " 'Cause you don't pay her no mind, Duran. She don't like people who pay her no mind. Now if you were to tell her you'd *think* 'bout what she been tellin' you, maybe she'd leave you alone."

"For a while."

"For a while," the innkeeper agreed. "But you *don't* tell her what she wants to hear, you see? You ignore her, an' go on 'bout livin' your life, fine as you please. That must be eatin' at her."

"Why can't she bother someone else?" Duran asked. "You'd think she'd grow bored with me."

A wide grin crossed Tut's face. "You're a challenge. I don't think she's ever met anyone who don't pay her no mind." He gestured briefly. "The rest of us . . . we just tell her what she wants to hear an' then go on 'bout our business. You tell her what she *don't* want to hear."

Life was an eternal compromise in Old Town. One compromised with what one bought, not having the money to afford better. Where one lived was a compromise, for the same reason. And, as Tut had said, dealing with people one met or had to deal with on a daily basis, was an eternal compromise.

Duran had learned many lessons living in Old Town, but compromising what he believed in was something he found the hardest. It galled him even more to give in on something when it made, or should have made, no difference to anyone else one way or the other.

"Maybe so," he admitted, "but, gods, Tut!"

"Hey," Tut said, "you want to shut her up, there's one way."

"What's that?"

"Sleep with 'er."

"Good *gods*, Tut!"

Tut shrugged. " 'At's what she wants."

"And then I'd have her for good and all. Thank you, no!"

"Long as you don't—she's got nothin' to do but stew an' be religious. Mostly it's that Sabirn kid. I been tellin' you that, an' I thought you understood."

"I *do* understand, but, gods, she should be able to see the lad isn't driving her business away, that no one in the neighborhood has had anything stolen. None of the *other* neighbors are put out by his working for me—"

Tutadar looked down into his ale, swirled it a

few times, and slowly lifted his eyes. "It ain't exactly that way, Duran."

A cold chill ran Duran's spine. "Are you trying to tell me something?"

"Guess I am," Tutadar said softly.

"By the gods! What is it that they're upset about *now?* I thought between me, you, and Ithar, they'd calmed down."

"They had," Tut said, shaking his head, "but Zeldezia been talkin' necromancy and demon worship. An' nobody's real comfortable with that—"

"Me either, Tut, and you know it."

Tutadar met Duran's eyes. "I know it. I knowed you for years, and you never been into the dark arts that *I* could see, but them Sabirn dabble in demon worship all the time."

"I'm sure they have their own forms of wizardry. So do we. You use what works in this world, and wizardry works. Up to a point." He leaned his elbows on the table. "Beyond that point, it's only conjecture. Period. I've yet to see anyone use wizardry the way it's portrayed in the sagas and poems. That's storytellers' fables. If such things really *could* work, don't you think we'd see evidence of it all around us?"

"Well, you got a point. But most folk don't have your mind, Duran. We never been educated like you. We can only believe what we hear."

"Have you *seen* any wizardry lately . . . *real* wizardry, not street-seller wizardry?"

"No. Can't say I have. But Zeldezia, she been talkin' 'bout the *dark* arts, not somethin' you'd see everyday."

"Dandro's hells! Just because some people are different from others, does that mean they're evil?"

"I s'pose not. But, I still don't like them little people 'round my inn." The innkeeper lifted a hand. "An' before you start in on remindin' me I still let Old Man stay here, you know what I think 'bout that. He's old an' crippled, an' he don't bother no one. *I'm* talkin' the young ones, the ones who don't like us any more'n we like them. Who's to say *they* ain't using the dark arts?"

"You think the boy who works for me is a demon worshiper?"

Tutadar's gaze wavered. "Maybe not him . . . he always been polite and nice to me when I seen him. But that don't mean other Sabirn ain't makin' pacts with demons. You ain't forgotten that necromancer they hung outside town, are you?"

Duran sighed. "No. I haven't forgotten. And I've warned the boy what happened, told him to be very quiet and very polite—"

"He *better* be quiet, if he knows what's good for 'im. If the neighbors suspect he been involved in anythin' smackin' of sorcery, they'll take it out on you."

"I haven't heard any complaints from my customers," Duran pointed out, flinching at another loud boom of thunder overhead. "If *they* thought the boy was a devil worshiper, they wouldn't be letting him deliver their medicines."

"Any of 'em stopped by your shop to talk since he been takin' your physics to people?"

"No. But the weather's been too bad for most people to be out. I haven't seen more than six or seven people a day in my shop lately. Why should they walk in? It's *convenient* for them to have the stuff delivered, that's why I hired the kid, Tut, *convenience!*"

"What do the folk who *have* stopped by your shop think 'bout your boy?"

"They don't seem to mind."

"Huhn. Where's the boy now?"

"I told him I was going to sit a while after my meal. I don't know where he went. But he'll be there when I get back." He sat up straighter in his chair. "In fact, I'd probably better go. Not that I expect to have all kinds of people waiting at my door, but there's—"

The door to the inn opened. Duran lifted his head and Tutadar turned in his chair.

Two men stood at the edge of the common room. Lamplight glittered on their helms and mail; their bearded faces were expressionless, their eyes shadowed.

Tutadar rose quickly and went to greet them. Duran stared. The Duke's own Guard. Two of them. In Old Town. His chest tightened. Why, in Hladyr's name, had they come to Old Town and, more specifically, "The Swimming Cat"?

He shoved his mug to one side and watched the two men brush by Tutadar and come toward his table.

"Duran Ancahar?" one of the guards asked.

"I'm Duran," Duran said, amazed his voice was steady. "May I help you gentlemen?"

"The Duke requests your presence at court," the other guard said. "Sor."

Duran's mouth went dry. He glanced at Tutadar, but Tut seemed speechless. The other customers were watching with unveiled curiosity.

"I'll come," Duran said, standing and pulling his cloak over his shoulders.

The two guards turned, walked across the common room and waited by the doorway. Duran took a deep breath, fastened his cloak and followed.

"Please tell the boy I've gone to the palace," he said to Tutadar. "I shouldn't be long."

Tutadar nodded, his eyes gone very wide. "Hladyr bless, Duran," he said. "I'll watch your shop."

Duran nodded, squared his shoulders, and walked toward the door where the Duke's Guard waited.

No sooner had Hajun sent two of his Guard to Old Town to bring Duran back he had regretted the decision. He glanced around the hall now, saw the two alchemists over by the edge of the room, deep in conversation with two of his courtiers. His wizards had retired to their side of the hall, and stood silent, watching everything that went on around them with hooded eyes.

Damn! he thought. *It's like a battle. One side draws up their troops over here, and the other army deploys its lines over there.* He disliked the image that had come to mind. During his reign, he had put more than a moderate effort into keeping factionalism at a minimum. The last thing he needed now was for there to be "war" between his alchemists, his wizards, and his priests.

With the chance of wizard-war mixed in with it.

He remembered Duran, the Duran he had known as a very young child, the boy with whom his eldest son had studied, played, and learned rudimentary arms. Duran had never seemed anything but forthrightly honest, honest as his father—so much so that one had feared even then that honesty would not stand him well in the future. Politics was the air Hajun had breathed—even in those days; not that he liked it . . . Hajun had much rather return to the fabled past when a man's word was a man's word, and fine shading of meaning did not overlay everything a man said.

But Duran's father, Hajun's friend, had been banished from court and had his title stripped from him, Hajun frankly had never understood why. The old duke had counseled his son, saying: this is what a duke must do sometimes, even when he doesn't like what he's doing . . .

By which Hajun had taken it that his friend had powerful enemies at court, and knew that placating those enemies had been more beneficial to the duchy at the time than protecting a long-time ally.

Politics stank.

And now Hajun was embroiled in his own politics, maneuverings which, in an odd way, mirrored those of his father—hoping his friend's son had not gotten himself involved in something—irredeemable.

Dabble in the dark arts himself? Gods, no. Duran was like his father, a kindred soul of sorts, a throwback into the earlier days of Ancar rule, when a man *proved* himself, rather than talked himself into power. One could admire a soul like that. One had.

And here Hajun sat, about to look down from his high seat at the son of his friend, and make decisions he might not like, or even—personally—believe in.

Thunder rumbled overhead. Hladyr keep him from making hasty judgment, from letting himself

be maneuvered into something, or argued out of
justice—or into it—

He glanced at his wife, found her eyes on him,
and grimaced. This was not going to be an entertaining afternoon.

Somewhere, in the depths of his heart, he prayed
it would not be a tragic one, either.

Duran let the guards lead the way into the ducal
palace, shaking the water from his cloak as he
walked. He was dressed in his work clothes, thread-
bare but serviceable—hardly the attire he would
have chosen to attend his duke.

But if the need for his presence at court was so
demanding that guards had been sent to escort
him, Hajun would have to take what he got.

The guards stopped outside a heavy wooden
door, one of them rapping on it with a heavy fist.
Duran's knees had started to tremble. He had no
idea what was going to happen to him on the other
side of that door, but had a notion what it was
about.

His father's shade stood to one side, ghostly
against the stucco wall. *You are Ancar*, his father's
voice whispering in Duran's mind. *Remember that.
Whatever happens to you, remember your pride.*

The doors opened. Duran followed the guards
into the hall, keeping his pace even with theirs.
Let no one say Duran Ancahar had been a coward—
or flinched from a meeting with his duke.

And there, over to the far side of the room:
Ladirno and Wellhyrn. Duran nearly broke stride
when he saw them, their presence here throwing
his thoughts into disarray.

Nor was Brovor present, and Duran thanked every god he knew he did not have to cope with *that* complication while he spoke to Brovor's father.

"Your Grace," one of the guards said, saluting with his fist on the center of his chest. "Before you stands Duran Ancahar, come with no delay from Old Town to do you honor."

Duke Hajun's eyes met Duran's, his fingers moved slightly and the two guards stepped back in unison, then turned with a smart clash of metal and each took up a position slightly to the left of the high seat.

"Come forward, Duran," Hajun said, motioning to the foot of the dais.

Duran swallowed, stepped forward and stopped, looking up into the Duke's expressionless face.

"I apologize for bringing you here on such short notice," Hajun said, and Duran heard only sincerity behind the words. "But you've been accused of certain things that must not go unanswered."

Perhaps he was expected to reply. Duran kept silent.

The Duke cleared his throat. "What do you know of the dark arts?"

"With regard to what, Your Grace?"

"Have you ever had anything to do with use of the dark arts?"

"No, Your Grace."

"Never?"

"Never, Your Grace."

The Duke drew a deep breath. "On your honor as an Ancar, you can assure me of this?"

"Aye, Your Grace. I do. I have no such dealings. Nor know of any."

The Duke leaned back in his high seat, rested his chin on his fist in silence. Duran shifted his weight, glanced quickly from one side of the room to the other, in the direction the Duke himself was looking.

"Your Grace," Duran said softly.

"Aye?"

"Do I have the chance to know who has accused me?"

The Duke straightened in his chair. "Aye. You're Ancar. It's your right." He turned and gestured. "Ladirno. Wellhyrn. Attend me."

Duran's heart lurched. Why? Why had those two accused him of such idiocy? They knew him better than that. What in Dandro's hells did they think to prove?

The two alchemists stepped close to the high seat and bowed, neither of them meeting Duran's eyes.

"These are your accusers, Duran," the Duke said. "Would you question them?"

Duran smiled suddenly, recognizing one of the pivotal points of Ancar law. At a trial before his lord, the Ancar accused was not assumed guilty until it had been proved beyond a doubt—and as accused, he could question whoever had brought him before his lord's justice. He wondered if Wellhyrn and Ladirno—Torhyn themselves—were familiar enough with Ancar legalistic principles to know the old law, the rights of Ancar with Ancar lord. . . .

He turned toward his two colleagues of the Profession, folded his arms and smiled at the sudden confusion on their faces.

"What gives you the right to accuse me?" he asked—not the accent of Old Town, not Duran the apothecary—not at all.

Ladirno glanced sidelong at Wellhyrn, a flush reddening his face.

"By report, Sor Duran," Wellhyrn said in his most urbane tones. "We've had reports about you that lead us to believe you're involved in the use of the dark arts—with utmost concern for your soul . . ."

"A report. In other words, you have no *personal* proof of this. It's hearsay."

"Our source is impeccable."

"Who?"

"Your priest. Vadami."

"Vadami." Duran felt a tide of anger welling up inside: Vadami, aye, but urged on by Zeldezia, he had no doubt. He said, coldly, deliberately: "And by what right does Vadami, a Torhyn, accuse me?"

"By virtue of your continued association with the Sabirn. He's warned you, has he not, that dealing with the Sabirn is dangerous, that it puts your soul in peril? Yet you have ignored him, haven't you, and continued to deal with the Sabirn?"

Duran turned toward Duke Hajun. "My lord, what Wellhyrn says is true—up to a point. The priest Vadami *did* warn me to see less of the Sabirn."

"And did you follow his advice?" the Duke asked.

"No, Your Grace."

"Why not?"

"Because he couldn't prove to my satisfaction that the Sabirn were evil. All he could do was repeat the same, well-worn suspicions people hold concerning the Sabirn; and we do not, *not*, my lord duke, desert loyal servitors on simple hearsay."

"You've had dealings with the Sabirn for years now, haven't you?"

"Aye, Your Grace. And not once have I personally seen behavior that in the least indicated an interest in, or use of, the dark arts."

"Hladyr as your witness?"

"Hladyr as my witness, Your Grace. I will not lie, in any cause."

The Duke nodded slightly, then gestured one of the court priests forward. "Take note of this. Duran Ancahar, once Duran *vro* Ancahar, has sworn in Hladyr's name. As an Ancar, he has taken the oath against his soul."

The priest seemed only mildly interested, though Duran suspected otherwise. "It is so noted, Your Grace."

"Very well." The Duke turned back to Duran. "Your accusers also maintain that you habitually entertain the old man who frequents 'The Swimming Cat.' That you frequently take notes on this person's utterances. Tell me why."

Duran shot a glance at the two alchemists. "Someone must have nearly drowned himself to see that, Your Grace. I had no idea my humble life was interesting enough to draw an audience in a storm."

A low murmur of laughter ran through the crowd gathered to watch the proceedings. Both Wellhyrn and Ladirno frowned and drew themselves up straighter.

"As for taking notes, absolutely I do, Your Grace. For years, I've collected Sabirn legends and tales—a purely scholarly interest. They ruled a great empire. My hope is that, in some of their legends and stories, they've left behind truths that could help us in modern times."

"In what manner?" the Duke asked, a spark of genuine interest lighting his face.

"As Your Grace already knows, I deal in medicines. I dispense what help I can to poor folk in Old Town. It's been my hope to discover forgotten medicines in the Sabirn legends—medicines to ease suffering, medicines to equal what must have been in the old Empire."

For a moment, no one spoke or moved. The Duke leaned forward in his chair.

"But could we trust such medicines? The Sabirn are known to be demon worshipers, Duran. Necromancers! How can you deal with devils and do good?"

"To my observation, Your Grace, and on my honor, I have never seen, nor heard of, any Sabirn working with the dark arts. The Sabirn I know are far too busy surviving, to be using the amount of time necessary to perform such draining tasks; and I would reject anything that came from such sources."

"And how do you know dark sorcery would take such a great amount of time," asked Wellhyrn, a sly look on his face, "unless you've been involved in it?"

"Would you like to inform His Grace how long it takes for an alchemist to perform some of our simpler tasks? Or is it effortless? A snap of the fingers, perhaps?"

Wellhyrn dropped his eyes. "His Grace is already aware that we work very hard to produce what we give him."

"Then if you're working with nature and find things arduous and time-consuming, doesn't it make sense that any actions taken contrary to nature would be much harder?"

No one spoke. The Duke motioned one of his wizards forward.

"Jorrino. Is what Duran said true?"

The wizard bowed slightly. "He makes an uneducated guess, Your Grace, but—naively close to the truth."

"But—" Wellhyrn said.

"Wellhyrn," the Duke said, his voice gone very cold. "You've not been asked to speak."

Wellhyrn subsided, his face gone white with shame.

"All of which is getting us nowhere," the Duke said, leaning back in his high seat. "Wellhyrn, Ladirno. You told me you *fear* Duran may be involved in the dark arts. The key words here are 'may be.' You've no proof beyond hearsay. Is this true or false?"

"To our own concern, Your Grace—" Ladirno said. Wellhyrn seemed to have lost the faculty of speech.

"The priest Vadami has spoken to Duran about consorting with the Sabirn, and Duran has—for his own reasons, reiterated here—refused to comply. This is the central substance of your accusations. True or false?"

"True, Your Grace.—But—"

"None of you has *proven* that Duran is guilty of anything more than *speaking* with the Sabirn, and that in the course of master to servant. True or false?"

"On the surface, true, Your Grace, but his writing—"

The Duke turned to his wizard and his priest. "I find no guilt in this man, either of performing the dark arts, or of lying. Do you concur?"

"We find no cause, Your Grace," the priest said. "We have ways of seeing such things. He's telling the truth as he sees it."

The wizard nodded. "I don't sense he has ever dabbled in the dark arts, Your Grace, and we wizards have ways of seeing that, too."

Duran let loose his pent-up breath, his eyes fixed on the Duke's face.

"Then hear my judgment," the Duke said. "I find Duran innocent of all charges of dealing in the dark arts. I find Ladirno and Wellhyrn guilty of bringing unfounded charges against him. As for the priest, Vadami, I suspect him of being over-zealous."

The two alchemists stiffened in their finery, their faces gone pale and still.

"Duran Ancahar."

Duran stepped closer to the dais.

"I urge you to keep your dealings with the Sabirn to a minimum. They are not well-liked in Targheiden, and are—rightly or wrongly—suspect of nefarious dealings. I pass no judgement with present associations, but beware new relationships. Do you hear me?"

"I do hear you, Your Grace."

"Wellhyrn. Ladirno. —I assume you thought you had reason. But consider: bringing accusations against another citizen without adequate cause can be slander. By holy Scripture, slander is perilous to one's soul. Both of you are banned from attending court for the next ten days, during which time you may meditate on this. Do you hear me?"

"We hear you, Your Grace," Ladirno said faintly.

"Good," Hajun said. "You have my leave, gentlemen."

Duran's knees were shaking again, only this time from relief. His two colleagues bowed to the Duke, turned and stalked off down the hall, neither of them affording Duran so much as a glance.

Duran stood his ground and caught Hajun's eyes.

"Duran?" the Duke said, lifting one eyebrow. "You have something else to say?"

"Yes, Your Grace. It's good to see that Ancar justice has not died with the past. My thanks, Your Grace."

With which he bowed deeply, and turned away.

"That gods-be-damned, no-good, lying bastard!"

Ladirno sank back in one of the chairs in his apartment and let Wellhyrn rage, pacing up and down the room, his face livid with anger.

"Do you realize what he's done to us?" Wellhyrn howled, turning to face Ladirno. "He's *disgraced* us in the Duke's eyes, that's what he's done! We've been banned from attending court for ten days, Ladir! *Ten* days!"

"He certainly has," Ladirno said acidly. "Thank the gods it's nothing worse."

"I'll see Duran Ancahar damned before he gets away with this! I'm *twenty* times the alchemist he is! If he thinks Ancar blood can ingratiate him into the Duke's favor by disgracing us, he's got horse-shit for brains!"

Ladirno gazed out the window at an overcast sky, some disconnected portion of his brain marveling that all Targheiden had not begun to flood yet.

"Dammit, Ladir! Pay attention to me!" Wellhyrn stopped in front of Ladirno. "If I hadn't listened to you about taking our suspicions to the Duke—"

"Now you wait just a damned moment," Ladirno snapped, rising. "Don't you try laying the blame on me. It was your idea!"

Wellhyrn glared.

"Thank Hladyr's mercy our banishment wasn't permanent," Ladirno said, doggedly keeping his tone mild. "The Duke's not known for his sweet temper—no more than his father was."

"How did we know we'd get ourselves involved in some kind of damned Ancar trial?" Wellhyrn raged, pacing again, periodically slamming a fist into his open hand. "And Duran . . . can you believe it? He talked his way out of *everything!* —sweet as one of the Duke's own courtiers!"

"You forget," Ladirno said, still in the same mild tone, "that Duran's father used to be the Duke's companion and, as such, he was Ancar of the Ancar. What do you *think* that name means? Ancahar. That's *aristocracy*, man—blue-blood, to the utmost."

Wellhyrn's face grew red, and Ladirno allowed himself a small smile. He had always suspected that Wellhyrn hated Duran for once having thrown aside what he would give his soul to be—an Ancar lord of the highest degree. Title aside—Torhyn were Torhyn—and Duran had been *born* a noble.

Wellhyrn seized a book from Ladirno's table

and threw it against the wall. Ladirno winced, but kept silent, afraid of Wellhyrn's violence.

Wellhyrn spun around and faced Ladirno, his eyes narrowed to slits. "I'm not going to take this lying down," he snarled. "I'll get that son of a dog for this. I swear it!"

"And what are you going to do?" Ladirno asked, watching Wellhyrn pace.

"There's got to be a way we can get back at him without anyone knowing. And, by all the gods, I'll come up with one." Wellhyrn halted abruptly. "I've got it! By all that's holy! We'll set our wizards at him!"

Ladirno sighed heavily. "Would you get control of yourself, Hyrn? Stop raging and *think!* We can't afford to set our wizards at him. We have enough enemies of our own; diverting our wizards from *them* could be disastrous!"

"No more disastrous than letting Duran get away with what he's done!"

"He's done no more than defend himself," Ladirno said, "as you or I would have in like circumstances. He accused us of nothing more than inaccuracy—"

"Which could have gotten us banished for good! What's the matter with you? How can you speak in his defense."

"I'm trying to get through to you. Now . . . *sit down!*"

Ladirno had seldom used that particular tone of voice with Wellhyrn: in shock, the younger man drew a deep breath, then sat down in the matching chair.

"I don't mind hiring someone to set on Duran,"

Ladirno said, most reasonably, he thought. "But our resources are limited. And if ours are—his certainly are."

"Maybe you're right." Wellhyrn brightened. "He couldn't afford it. Gods, he couldn't hire a junior apprentice—and if we bought even an hour from a second-rate wizard—"

"Now you're thinking."

The old, malicious smile was back on Wellhyrn's face. "Then let's do it," he said, leaning forward in his chair. "Tomorrow morning." He laughed coldly. "We'll ill-wish that bastard. If Duran *is* treating the heir for the pox, maybe we'll get lucky and he'll fumble the treatment."

"Dammit, Hyrn! I don't care what you do to Duran, but don't even think of misfortune on the Duke's son! I won't stand for that."

"Take a joke, Ladir!"

Ladirno held Wellhyrn's gaze until Wellhyrn looked away. "Do you want to contact the wizards, or shall I?"

"You do it." Wellhyrn's eyes glittered coldly in the lamp-light. "I'll think of other ways we can get to this problem of ours. And believe me, I'll think of something!"

CHAPTER 10

"Duran."

Duran turned from his shelves to Kekoja, who was already spreading out the coppers he had earned on the counter-top.

"Good day?" Duran asked.

"Oh, aye." The Sabirn boy grinned widely. "You hear about that warehouse fire, next block over? Boom!"

"I heard. So water-logged it wouldn't burn, thank the gods. Rain's to *some* advantage . . . Well!" Duran counted up the coppers and shook his head in wonder. Thirty-one coins lay on his counter.

"Best yet," Kekoja said pridefully.

"Here, lad." He gave the boy his percentage, and deposited the rest in his belt pouch. "You did a damned fine job."

"Guess so. —Had many people in here today?"

"No." He knocked into a pot, grabbed after it before it went off the edge. "Damn! I've been so clumsy today!" He gestured at the waste-bin. "Two pots, *two!* I've broken."

Kekoja lifted an eyebrow. "Not like you," he said, not smiling in response to Duran's tale.

Duran looked at him with a sudden, cold thought.

Kekoja dropped his pay into his belt pouch. "You be careful," the boy said, wiping the dark hair back from his eyes. "Don't you do anything risky for a while. Nothing with the furnace—"

"The way my luck's running? Nothing dangerous today, I promise you."

"You 'bout ready to close up?"

"Aye. Pretty soon."

"Then I'll see you in the morning. —Duran? You *do* be careful—"

Duran waved him out: Kekoja left; and with a sigh, Duran sat down on his doorstep, content to simply sit, doing nothing.

Could it be someone had hired a wizard to ill-wish him?

One could guess who.

And if so, there was little he could do about it: he could afford no protection.

Damn them. He could not understand why he should threaten them—but they must see him as such: that was the only reason he could think of for them accusing him before the Duke.

And the prospect of some wizard's ill-wishing made him shudder. All sorts of things could go wrong in his business: a mistaken dosage and possibly kill a patient. He could drop acids on himself. A firing could explode. The house could burn down: in a neighborhood so closely, ramshackle-built—the whole of Old Town could go—

Or a nosy neighbor—might look out a window at the wrong time of night—

It needed so little—

All because he had saved a boy from a bad beating and possible death.

He sighed and closed his eyes. It was pleasant to sit here like this after such a muggy, tense day—unmoving. Breaking nothing. Making no disasters. Pedestrians passed him. He paid no attention.

"Duran."

Zeldezia.

Gods, some wizard *was* after him.

He opened his eyes: she stood there with her sleeves rolled up to her elbows in the heat, fists on hips.

"I heard you was called in to see the Duke."

He nodded.

She sniffed virtuously. "If you listened to folk—"

"So." Duran leaned his head against the door jamb, and looked up at her. "Then I suppose you know everything about it. I wouldn't bore you with the details."

Not what she hoped for. She set her jaw. "The Duke let you go."

"Of course." Duran gave her nothing satisfying, willing her to lose interest and walk away. Obviously *he* had no wizardry: she did not move.

"Ain't you going to reply to that?" Zeldezia asked.

"Why should I?" Duran kept his voice calm. "You know all about it."

"Duran. Listen to me if you won't listen to Vadami: he says if you repent an' give up seein' them Sabirn, Hladyr will still forgive you—"

"Oh? And does Vadami now have a special conduit to the Shining One? I didn't realize he had become so exalted in the past few days."

"You're mockin' at me," she said, her voice going cold. "An' at a priest o' god. That's what they done to you. One of these days, Duran, you're going to be so sorry, an' there ain't no one goin' to help you."

He looked her straight in the eye. "Are you threatening me, Zeldezia?"

"I ain't doin' no such thing. I'm just warnin' you, that's all. Hopin' you'll change your stubborn mind an' see the *right* way to live."

"It's the right way because *you* think it's so," Duran said, struggling to keep the anger from his voice. "Anyone who dares believe differently than you is a heretic."

"That ain't so! Vadami thinks the same way, too. Ever' right-thinkin' person thinks so!"

Duran felt a wave of weariness wash over him. "Then go talk with the good priest, Zeldezia, and have the courtesy to leave me alone."

"Ain't you concerned for your soul?"

"As much as anyone else. Now are you going to leave, or do I have to get up and slam the door in your face?"

Her eyes narrowed. "Don't insult me, Duran, who's tryin' t' help you—"

"Get! Leave me alone!"

She drew herself up, puffed as if she would say something else, then spun on her heel and went, hips swaying, down the street and into her shop.

Duran shrugged. There was no hope for it. He did not see how he could continue to live his life

the way he pleased *and* keep Zeldezia and the
priest off his back. He had received some protection in the Duke's decision, but he dared not fool
himself, trusting his luck would hold: luck in his
case was in serious question.

Dog came back, his tongue lolling out of the
side of his mouth, and walked into the shop. Duran
heard him settle down in his accustomed spot by
the counter. He reminded himself to pick up a
bone or two from Tutadar for Dog's dinner, stirred
on the doorstep, stood and fished for his key.

Ah well. A good meal and a fresh mug of ale
should lighten his mood. He drew the door closed,
locked it, and crossed the street.

"The Swimming Cat" was only moderately full: it
was early yet. Duran nodded to Tut and walked
back to his table. The other customers watched
him pass, a few nodding a greeting in his direction, but for the most part they were silent—as if
he had walked in on some discussion his neighbors
did not want him to hear.

Him, he thought. A man from Old Town did not
make a forced visit to the Duke of Targheiden and
return without comment.

Once Duran had seated himself, his neighbors
began to talk again, but their conversation was
muted, without its usual animation. Tut walked
over, wiping his hands on his apron. "Fish tonight, Duran?"

"Aye. Breaded, if I can have it. And a mug of
ale."

Tut nodded, went to the kitchen door and
shouted Duran's order to the cook. He brought a
mug of ale back to Duran himself.

"Have a good day?" Tut asked, pulling out a chair and sitting down, as he would, in slack moments.

"Good enough," Duran said. Perhaps he was too apprehensive that he read more into this approach.

On the other hand, judging by the expression on Tutadar's face—

"Duke lost himself another ship today," Tut said quietly. "Word come."

"Dandro's hells."

The innkeeper shrugged. "Duke, he's lost a damned lot of goods. Folk got a lot of hard luck— lot of hard luck. People get desperate."

Duran took a swallow of ale, then leaned forward on the table. "Is this news aimed at me, Tut?"

Tutadar dropped his eyes. "S'pose it is. *I* ain't believing, it, Duran, but—there's a lot of folks beginning to ask—where all this luck is comin' from. An' you can say it ain't Sabirn, but they ain't in the mood to listen. The Duke loses trade, Old Town loses business—hard times coming. Taxes'll increase to make up for the Duke's losses. We seen it before."

"They can't honestly believe any damn Sabirn has anything to do with the storms," Duran protested. Tutadar stared back. "Can they?"

"Startin' to seem that way. It ain't nature. It sure ain't any run of plain luck. Somethin's doin' it."

"Foreign enemies—"

"Sabirn are foreigners. Right among us. Here ever' day."

"Fools." Duran gripped his mug tightly. "Ignorant fools!"

"Then you're callin' me a fool, too, Duran,"
Tutadar said, lifting his eyes so he met Duran's
gaze. "I know you ain't a demon worshiper, an' I
know you wouldn't want to do anythin' that would
bring bad luck down on you, but, dammit, man,
you got a blind eye to them folk—an' I ain't sayin'
it's you, I ain't sayin' it's that boy, but it ain't real
discreet, you puttin' that kid up in ever'body's
faces—you havin' him real conspicuous—you givin'
him access to all sorts of shops an' places—he
works for you, but who knows who else he knows,
who knows who he talks to? Them folk all get
together. They all talk—"

"How in all the hells can you think that way,
Tut? You know me. You know I'm no fool. The
boy's honest; he doesn't bother people, and he's
helping me make the best living I've ever seen."

"Money won't buy your life, Duran."

"Gods, what are you talking about?"

Tut murmured, tapping his head, "I *know*, up
here, you ain't made no pacts with demons. But
here—" He tapped his chest. "—here, I'm scared.
You can't force folk, Duran. You can't force 'em
over night to change the way they been thinkin'
for hundreds of years. Some say—you can't fire
that kid. Some say he got a spell on you."

Duran stared, his heart chilling. "You're saying
I have to fire this kid, is that it? I have to run my
business the way Zeldezia's damn hate-mongering
wants?"

"It ain't all Zeldezia. I'm sayin' you got yourself
in big trouble, Duran, because I can't change the
way folk think, and you can't change 'em either.
Me and Ithar have kept tellin' everyone you ain't

changed none . . . that you're the same man they've
always knowed. But you *ain't* the same, deep down.
You been actin' real odd. Like this kid was real
important." He took a deep breath. "It ain't natural, folks to mix. I dunno what this kid prays to. I
don't want to know. I got me second thoughts
about Old Man—"

"Listen to me, Tut." Duran struggled to put
words to his thoughts. "I can't let the boy go now.
I have a debt of honor, since I've taken him on. I
made a vow to him; we sealed our agreement and
swore by the gods. I can't back off an agreement
because I'm *scared*, Tut. For better or worse, I'm
Ancar. You know what an oath is worth to me."

"You swore an oath like that to a Sabirn kid?"

"I swore. Zeldezia says my soul's at risk. My
soul's at risk if I break my word, Tut! I swore to
that kid and I'm not backing off because of any
threats! I can't! Maybe this neighborhood better
damn well understand *why* I'm not going to fire
that kid!"

"You never lied to me before," Tutadar admitted, "an', far as I know, you never lied to no one.
Look, why don't you tell the boy to go off for a few
days? Go somewhere no one can see 'im? That
ain't firin' 'im—send 'im off to the hills, have him
dig you some roots or somethin'—"

Duran ran a hand through his hair. "I'll think
about it . . . I really will. I understand your worry.
You think that would calm it down?"

"Chance it might. An' right now, if I was you,
I'd take it. If the storms keep up—"

"I know where they're coming from!"

"Zeldezia. Aye."

"The Duke heard the whole question—someone accused *me* of association with warlocks! He threw the accusations out of court—*and* threw out the accusations against the Sabirn!"

Tut shook his head. "Some'd say the Duke was makin' a big mistake about that last. Duran, Zeldezia ain't agin you. She's scared you're close to bein' damned."

"As if she was the authority!"

"Some of your neighbors been listenin' to her, Duran. Listenin' to her real serious."

"All right." Duran leaned back as Lalada brought his fish to him and set it down on the table. His appetite had vanished. "I'll send the boy off, Tut. Maybe I can do without him for a handful of days." He met the innkeeper's eyes. "Now you tell me, what's going to happen if the weather suddenly turns good? Will that convince everyone they're right about the boy being a demon worshiper?"

"It ain't going to make 'em happy, that's for sure. Now, if he come back an' the weather stays good, that's another thing."

"Or if the weather stays bad and he's nowhere to be seen." Duran spread his hands. "Damn! It's crazed, Tut, it's no damn sense!"

"Don't seem it is, does it?"

"Tut—do you believe this crap?"

"Me? I trust you, Duran, an' I speak for you, do ever'thin' I can to keep the neighbors calm. But I'm only one person, an' Ithar's only one person. We can't do more'n what we can do."

"That's all I can ask for."

Tutadar shoved his chair back from the table.

"You enjoy your meal, Duran, an' think 'bout what I said. At least it'd give the neighbors time to calm down."

Duran sighed, and began cutting up his fish. "I'll talk to the boy, Tut. I promise you."

Duran left the inn—heard the low rumble of conversation start up the moment he exited the door. He had stayed no longer than necessary. No. No. Not in that atmosphere.

Wind swept debris down the cobbles, rattled shutters. He turned his head from the blast, and blinked from a wisp of hair blown in his eyes, blinked again, seeing a gray-wrapped lump sitting against the wall of his shop, beside the steps.

Old Man—like sin come home to roost.

Had the neighbors driven him from the "Cat"? Duran wondered.

He fished out his key, opened the door as Old Man rose and stood beside him. "Come on in," Duran said—anxious to get him out of sight, quickly; and guilty and angry for that small, prudent cowardice. "I'll light the lamp."

He did that, turned, saw Dog had gone to stand by the doorway, his tail wagging uncertainly— held between duty and his usual foraging.

"Go, Dog," Duran said, waving a hand, "before it truly gets bad."

Dog obviously was of the same mind, for he trotted quickly off into the wind.

Duran shut the door. The air in the shop was close and still, smelling of shelves and shelves of herbs.

"Why weren't you at the 'Cat' tonight?" Duran asked.

Old Man said, "I may not be there much longer, Duran. I barely make enough to survive any more."

Duran frowned. "No one pays you for your stories now?"

"No one but you. No one else asks to hear them."

"Ah." Duran was at a loss for words. "I—should have guessed."

Old Man smiled slightly, a mere movement of the lips. "Perhaps it's just as well. You've too much else to account for with your neighbors—to be the only one giving money to a Sabirn."

Duran leaned back against his counter. "The neighbors aren't pleased with me on many counts, so I hear."

"You've heard right. They aren't. That's why I'm here."

Duran's shoulders stiffened.

"Your neighbors," Old Man said. "Your neighbors are talking about violence."

"You're serious, aren't you?"

"I've heard them discussing it."

"Was Zeldezia the ringleader?"

"She and the priest Vadami."

Duran clenched his hands. "Before or after I was called to the ducal palace?"

"Before *and* after."

"Hladyr bless!" Duran slammed his hand on the counter.

"It was serious, Sor Duran. This weather—they seem to think—"

"I know. I heard all about it. Tut advised me to send Kekoja off somewhere for a few days. He seems to think that might calm everyone down."

"Tutadar is a good man," the Sabirn said, "and more open-minded than the rest. But even he has his blind spots. I think things have gone beyond sending Keko off and bringing him back a few days later. If you value my advice, Sor Duran, you should start thinking about leaving town, *before* your neighbors do you some harm."

Duran was trembling now, his stomach was a hard knot, and his hands shook. Leave Targheiden? Leave everything he had known for thirty-five years? An Ancar run in cowardice from the town his ancestors had built? A wave of anger swept through him. By Hladyr's light! He *was* Ancar . . . he was of a noble house! He could not evade a fight like this. It was dishonorable . . . as dishonorable as negating the bargain he and Kekoja had struck.

O gods! Go off into the countryside—go back into exile. I had enough of that with my parents. Everything I know is here!

Everything I've built . . . all my work . . .

"Didn't you realize that this might happen?" Old Man asked.

"Maybe in my heart of hearts I thought it *could*," Duran said, "but I didn't . . ." He looked up at the ceiling, at the lamp-light playing with the shadows across it. "It happened to my father. I never thought it would happen to me."

"You make them nervous, Sor Duran. You traffic with demon worshipers."

"Bah!" Duran began to pace up and down in front of his counter. He heard a faint whine, a scratch at the door. He stalked over and jerked it open, let Dog and a gust of wind inside. "Sorry, Dog. Curse me for a fool . . . I forgot to bring you your bones. Perhaps some cheese until morning, eh?"

He went and got that. Dog wagged his tail, took it—more grateful and more faithful than others he had helped.

"All right," he said to Old Man. "You think the neighbors are going to run me out of town. So where the hells do I go? What will I do to survive?"

"You're a doctor. Whatever you choose to call yourself, you're better than most poor folk ever see. You'll never be hungry. A traveling doctor is always welcome, no matter where he goes."

"To what end? Old on the road and starving? I'm not an active man, I've no knowledge how to survive—I want my food from the tavern, my supplies from a market, I want a bed at night—" *I want my books. I want familiar things . . . I want to die somewhere I understand . . .*

"You want. It was no helpless man who rescued Keko from the thugs in the alleyway that night. And it's no helpless man who has the mind you have."

"What's *that* supposed to mean?"

"Keko tells me. Keko tells me how you make your medicines. How you have your little jars— your little jars with the old bread, the cheese— how you cured the smith with a salve of herbs and moldy bread—"

Duran shrugged, finding no hope in that, against the thought of exile.

"Our physicians understood molds. In the Empire they did. *We* use such remedies. But no Sabirn told you."

"It cures cuts," Duran said glumly. "It can't cure human stupidity, Old Man, it can't cure hate!"

"You have a mind. You want proofs, you want substantiation of things. You don't think like your neighbors. You look past what seems. You *think*."

"It does me no good."

"Do you want learning? Come with us, and we'll give you what knowledge we have."

Duran stared. "Come with you where? And who is 'us'?"

Old Man leaned on his walking stick. "Not all the Sabirn you see in Targheiden have lived here all their lives. We come and we go. No one notices. You remember when I came to the 'Cat' —not all that many years ago? I suppose you, along with everyone else, thought I came from some other section of town."

"Aye."

"I didn't. I came from elsewhere . . . from beyond Targheiden."

"Why?"

"To serve as a gatherer of information. To find certain trade stuffs we need and can't easily obtain. Targheiden is, after all, a shipping capital."

"What—trade stuffs?"

"Sulfur. Niter."

"For what?"

"I'll tell you—once we're outside Targheiden."

"We."

"As I said—time I was traveling again. You've asked questions. I'll answer them. I'll tell you stories you don't imagine."

It was the storyteller's voice, that mesmerized, that stole a man's sense about what was real and not real. It was a spell in itself—a spell—that broke down the lines between possible and impossible.

"Once," Old Man said, softly, "we had a ship that sailed with no wind."

"With no wind?"

"And no sails. Think about that, Duran."

"But—"

"We digress," Old Man said: the voice became sharp, incisive—commanding. "We were talking about your neighbors—and my advice. Will you take it? Are you willing to come with us?"

"But . . . who is this 'us'?"

"Targheiden doesn't love Sabirn." Old Man shifted, taking some of his weight from his crippled leg, and leaned back against the wall. "We've become unwelcome here—those of us that have become . . . too visible."

The Sabirn woman—hanged as a necromancer.

Duran's head spun. Thirty-five years of his life here—with his parents and on his own—in the same shop, the same small apartment upstairs. He had spent his youth here, had roots here, friends here. And. . . .

He could die here.

Possibly.

After what he had heard tonight, *more* than possibly.

"But I can't take all my things with me," he protested. "I have my alchemist's tools, my books, my notes, my medicines . . . Without those, I'm worthless!"

"We have a wagon," Old Man said. "We can get others. How much room do you need?"

Duran chewed on his lower lip. "But how in Dandro's hells can I move this much stuff without the neighbors knowing?"

"We'll help you."

"Who," Duran asked again, "is 'we'?"

Old Man waved a hand. "Myself. Kekoja. Several more. We have our own possessions to take."

Duran shook his head slowly. There *had* to be some other way to approach this. He could not run—merely because his neighbors were upset.

Or could he?

Was his pride worth his life? Was it worth all he ever meant to do, all the notes, the knowledge his father had collected, that he had added to over a lifetime, the pages and pages—

"It's simple, Duran." The Sabirn's black eyes glittered in the lamplight. "We know the dark ways . . . the streets the Guard never travels. We load your belongings—we go. That's all."

Duran shuddered.

"And," Old Man said, "we aren't without wizards of our own."

"Gods . . ."

"Them, too."

"You're asking total trust from me," Duran said at last. "*Total* trust."

"You have my true name," Old Man said with quiet dignity, "You *know* what I am. That is a sacred bond."

"Are you—"

"You know," Old Man said, in that Voice, "—what I am."

"I suppose I do," Duran said, and shivered. "When do you—suggest we start?"

"I don't think trouble's imminent. Not by what I've heard. And if Kekoja doesn't show up for work tomorrow. . . ."

"Wait. If Kekoja doesn't come to work tomorrow, won't the neighbors think something's strange?"

"You said Tutadar suggested you send him off. I would imagine he'll tell the other folk you're going to do something like that."

"All right," he said. He lifted his chin, decision made. "I'll start gathering everything I need tonight."

"Good. You have enough baskets for your medicines, don't you?"

"I'll manage."

"And your alchemist's tools?"

"The baskets I keep things in. But my alembics, my furnace—"

"We can make you new ones."

"And where is that? Where will we be?"

Old Man's face was very serious, still in the lamp-light. "A place where the mind can run free," he said.

Ladirno sat at his lately-habitual table in "The Golden Shoe," contemplating the walk back to his apartments, but dreading the unpredictability of his companion and looking, still, for some decision, some sense that things might have settled. Wellhyrn sat in a chair opposite him, looking frustrated and angry. As of yet, Wellhyrn had not come up with a suitable punishment for Duran—a revenge that nobody could trace back to its source. The lack of inspiration had thrown Wellhyrn into a beastly—and dangerous—mood.

Oddly enough, some small part of Ladirno took a bleak satisfaction in his companion's discomfiture—but he did not trust him.

Distant thunder rumbled and Ladirno winced. Gods-blighted storms! He, himself, chose to believe that no one controlled the weather, but he could not remember a stretch of weather like this.

Perhaps the Sabirn *were* behind the weather.

Perhaps.

A darkly cloaked man walked toward their table, and though Ladirno could see no face below the hood, he thought he recognized him. Wellhyrn lifted his head and stared, then smiled coldly, his face relaxing in dark pleasure.

"Ah, Mandani. Please join us."

Ladirno drew in his breath: Mandani, he recalled, was the name Wellhyrn had mentioned, the wizard he had set on Duran—and of wizards he had dealt with, this one—this man was *not* a comfortable drinking companion.

"I have interesting news," the wizard said, still not throwing back the hood of his cloak. "I believe Duran to be protected."

"What?" Wellhyrn's face stilled to a portrait in ice.

"I had an apprentice spell him in 'The Swimming Cat' tonight. Though I was still working on him, he didn't drop a thing."

Ladirno flashed a dismayed glance at Wellhyrn. "But he has no wizard—he couldn't possibly afford a wizard!"

"I don't know."

"We have to suppose," Mandani said softly, "that someone *is* protecting him. I don't know the nature of this wizard, I don't know where he is, or what he is, but he exists."

"Are you asking for more money?" Wellhyrn's

green eyes were cold in the lamp-light. "Perhaps it's *you*. Maybe you're not as good as you say you are."

"Hyrn," Ladirno said, shooting his younger colleague a silencing look, his heart beating in dread of this man. "Forgive him. Things haven't gone well lately. We're—in some personal difficulty."

Mandani's expression did not change.

"Do you think you might need help?" Ladirno asked carefully.

"Assistance might be useful. Assuming his adept has none."

"I don't see how he's affording *one!*" Wellhyrn snapped.

Ladirno signed him: caution. "All right. If you think two of you can get the job done, then choose your partner. The fee for his services will be the same as your own."

"Thank you." Mandani's deep voice never varied. "We'll start immediately."

He rose and walked away.

Ladirno stared at Wellhyrn. "It seems," he said, "Duran's not innocent."

CHAPTER 11

Hail fell—heavy, large hail that coated the streets of Targheiden with ice-white pebbles, shattered two panes of glass in the Great Hall, killed live-stock, killed an old man on the West Side.

Hajun sat and glared at the silent Hall. None of his courtiers were talking; stiff-legged, they stood with their backs to the wall, their expressionless faces telling him more than words. The priests stood in a corner, whispering among themselves—and not a wizard was to be seen.

Cowards.

A runner came into the hall—spoke briefly to the priests. Faljend, the chief priest of Hladyr, quickly left that cluster and approached the dais. "If I might talk to you, privately, Your Grace. . . ."

Hajun beckoned him closer, closer still.

"There's a certain panic, Your Grace," Faljend said in the faintest of voices. "People gathering in various places, in the markets—they're afraid—"

"So?" Hajun snapped. "Their shingles are lying in the streets—their windows battered—what's remarkable they should be afraid?"

"Gently, Your Grace. We must stand as an example—"

"How in Hladyr's name are we going to do that?" Hajun leaned forward. "The merchants are at each other's throats . . . they're ready to lash out at anything that moves. And, depending on shipping as I do, I know how they feel, dammit!"

"We priests are doing everything we can, Your Grace. We've had special prayers offered at the Temple. Common folk are praying for a change in the weather. None of this seems to have done any good."

Hajun grunted a reply.

"It's wizardry, Your Grace, it's the Sabirn!"

"I'm so damned tired of hearing everyone howl about the Sabirn I could puke! What do you suggest? That we round up every Sabirn we can get our hands on and hang them?"

"Your Grace, if something's not done soon, we could be facing riots in the streets. *Everyone's* suffering, everyone, from you, Your Grace, down to the smallest shopkeeper in Old Town. No one's immune."

Hajun rubbed his forehead, willing his headache to vanish. "So?"

"I know, Your Grace, I'm telling you nothing new. I do, however, suggest that you make a public plea for calm. Send your heralds among the people to tell them your concern. . . ."

"How am I supposed to do that in all this wind and rain? Who'll listen? Everyone's inside."

"They'll listen, Your Grace. When people become as emotional as they are now, they'll listen from their windows, to anything that tells them what they *want* to hear."

"Words! Words are nothing! The question is *doing*, priest!"

"Search out the necromancers—there's more than one, Your Grace, there must be a nest of them. And hang them, one and all!"

"If my wizards can't *stop* them, priest, how in Dandro's *hells* are we going to lay hands on them?"

"We have to try, Your Grace! We have to smoke them out, *divert* them with danger from different fronts—"

"Give me names, dammit, give me names!"

Faljend bowed deeply. "We have our spies, Your Grace, as I'm sure you know. We do know names, Sabirn who hold themselves out to be wizards and fortune-tellers. We know who they are."

"*Fortune-tellers* aren't the ones involved!" Hajun said. "You're dealing with a furtive people, you're not going to find anything!"

"Divide their attention," the High Priest said. "But first, Your Grace, first you have to have the people behind you."

Hajun scowled, smelling disaster, thinking of his ships. His hold on this city. "Huhn. All right. I'll write up a speech. My heralds will be out among the people by this afternoon." Rain spattered against the windows, thunder boomed, and Hajun gripped the armrests on his chair. "Damn them!"

*　　*　　*

Vadami stood in prayer in the cavernous Temple, his eyes shut as he sent his pleas to Hladyr the Shining. He could hear other folk around him constantly praying, their muted voices added to his own.

He gazed up at the altar, hoping that the sight of it would warm his heart as it had always done. Surrounded by hundreds of burning lamps, overlaid with pounded gold, it sparkled as with captured sunlight, and towering over it was the intricate mosaic of the Shining One himself, standing above the entire world, all creation at his feet. It was a masterwork—a young man in the prime of life, golden hair blown back from a divinely beautiful face, looking down on his worshipers, compassion in his eyes. On either hand, the gods and goddesses: beneath his feet, the dark regions of Dandro's hells.

A crash of thunder. Vadami flinched. Rain spattered against the costly windows.

The Sabirn were responsible for this, Vadami would stake his immortal soul on that. Dealers in darkness, they had brought this evil on the city. *Everyone* knew it now—

Except Duran.

Vadami said a brief prayer for Duran's soul, though he felt certain that soul was lost forever. Why had such a kindly man succumbed to the Sabirn and their dark ways? Why would Duran not listen to what might have saved his soul?

Duran did nothing but laugh in Vadami's face.

Duran blasphemed the Shining One.

And prayers went unanswered.

Duran was Ancar—was no Sabirn heathen, but one of their own.

That was the link the evil had. *That* was the linchpin of their plot—the seduction of one of the noble blood, the drawing-astray of an Ancar lord, the breaking of the bond between Hladyr and this city—

The Duke himself—had sent Duran away with only the mildest admonition to not seek out any new Sabirn to befriend.

Vadami lifted his head again, and stared at the image of Hladyr, terrified.

Lord of Shining Light, he prayed. *Give me a sign. Tell me what I should do about Duran.*

Nothing happened. No sign appeared. Vadami's heart felt cold and empty.

Then, of a sudden, a thought. Hladyr *has* answered. *I* know the truth. *I* know the source of the evil—at least where it lodges . . .

In my own flock.

Remove Duran: then Targheiden and its people might be saved.

He had spent hours upon hours, seasons upon seasons, trying to save Duran's soul. Some souls, it seemed, were destined not to be saved. By anyone.

Hladyr, guide me! I don't know how to kill! I don't want to hurt any of your creatures, and so far Duran himself is surely no demon worshiper— only perilously close. What can I do? What should I do?

The image stared back, aloof, unreachable by any man's prayers.

Duran stood in the center of his bedroom and stared at the baskets he had leaned up against the outer wall. In those baskets he had carefully packed his most precious possessions: his father's notes, his alchemist's tools, his collections of various metals, his vials, beakers, a few of his small alembics. In what space remained, he had tucked in other sentimental odds and ends he could not see leaving behind.

He shook his head at the sight, and looked around at the rest of the room . . . at those things he knew he could not take with him.

There was the bed his parents had brought with them from the Ancahar estate, along with its night stand. Next to it stood the old bookcase his wife had brought with her when they had married—the only thing of hers he had. They were among the last physical ties he had to those long-dead people he loved the most . . . the last things he could touch, knowing they had touched them, too.

He snarled a curse and turned away. He still could not believe he had agreed to leave town, no matter how desperate the reason: he could not conceive of himself living anywhere else but Targheiden—going—

Where? Old Man had never yet said.

But the danger Old Man had warned him of, what Tutadar had said, were obvious facts. Why the hells had he not been able to see this before? He had known when he had helped Kekoja that he was dealing with fire. He had known.

I suppose, he thought, *it's like everything else in life: we see terrible things; but* nothing *can happen to us.*

It had happened.

He had no choice. If he was going to live out

what years he had left of life in peace, if he was going to live at all—he would have to leave the city he loved.

And to do this, he would have to place complete trust in the Sabirn, in Old Man, in Kekoja. All last night, into the small hours, he had wrapped his prized possessions in water-proofed paper: his herbs, medicines, books, and tools. Then, after stowing everything in baskets, he had lowered three of those baskets out the upstairs alley window down into the alleyway and the waiting hands of gods only knew who. He had seen Kekoja, and someone he thought was a woman.

Where the Sabirn had gone with his baskets, he had no clue.

And now, he waited for darkness to fall again, so he could deliver the rest of his possessions into those same shadowy hands.

He began to pace, up and down, past the desk on which he had written so many things. Past the bookcase, nearly empty. Past the table on which his small furnace sat. He reached and ran a hand over the top of that furnace, remembering all the years he had worked in front of it, trying time and again to unlock the secrets of nature and of the gods. . . .

The enormity of it all was beginning to sink in. He would never stand in this room again. He would never see the same sights again. Never, as long as he lived, would he be able to walk across the street and spend an evening with his neighbors in the "Cat," spinning out the day's happenings, and listening to homely gossip. He would be severed from everything he had known since he was a boy.

Twice now, in his overturned life. Twice a pilgrim in the world.

It hurt, the thought of it . . . burned in his heart like a brand.

He stopped pacing, and considered the step he was taking. His standing here in his apartment, visually recording the sights and sound of it for the future, was like being present at someone's death bed. But it was his own death, so to speak . . . a personal death, an ending of all the things he knew.

But dying at the hands of a mob was no way for an Ancar noble to leave the world. He still had things he wanted to do, wanted to learn, wanted to see. And if the gods had decreed that he would have to do all that somewhere besides Targheiden—

There was no choice.

A crowd had gathered in the street outside Ladirno's apartment, some of them having to stand out in the rain, away from the protection of the second story overhang. Ladirno drew the hood of his cloak up over his head and pushed his way into the back of the crowd. He was taller than most, so he had some kind of view.

It was a ducal herald, on horseback. The fellow looked as miserable as the folk who had assembled to hear him. His royal green cloak was drenched and dark, his wide-brimmed hat drooped, a steady stream of rain pouring off one side. The sight was enough to amuse—except the extraordinary fact of a herald out at all, in streets littered with broken shingle, except the grim, rain-chilled pallor of the faces that nothing would cheer.

"Attention citizens!" The herald's well-trained voice boomed out in the street as thunder rumbled overhead. "I come to you with word from His Grace, Hajun vro Telhern, Duke of Targheiden. These are the Duke's words:

" 'All citizens of Targheiden: measures to bring an end to this freakish weather are being undertaken. His Grace the Duke, assures you he is confident that, by the grace of Hladyr the Shining, there will soon be an end to these storms. He urges you add your prayers to those the priests are offering. Rest assured that every wizard employed by His Grace the Duke is actively involved in turning this evil from the city.' So says His Grace, Duke Hajun vro Telhern."

A mutter ran through the crowd. The herald drew his horse's head about and rode on. Ladirno snorted under his breath. Prayers? One hoped for more than that.

And the Duke's own wizards. All the Duke's wizards trying to do what Mandani and his associate were trying—

But the Duke would not believe—not believe the source of the evil.

As if—Ladirno shuddered—the Duke himself had fallen under some spell.

The rain increased and Ladirno broke into a slow run. The sign outside the "Shoe" was just ahead; swaying in the gusty wind, it offered a haven from the storm, and a chance for much needed companionship.

The rain had driven Vadami into "The Golden Shoe" some time ago, but his cloak was still cold

and dripping. He sat at a small table toward the
rear of the common room, sipping on a glass of hot
mulled wine: such a drink had seemed right on
this dreary day.

He had spent as little time as possible in Old
Town today, visiting only the critically ill—sharing
the Shining One's words with any who would listen. He had dropped in at "The Swimming Cat"
for a brief while, and there had found out from
Bontido, the potter, that Tutadar had managed to
convince Duran to send the Sabirn boy away for a
handful of days.

Such news should have made him happy, but
Vadami had a certain feeling that as soon as things
began to settle down, Duran would have the boy
back in his place as a runner, and the neighborhood would be set off again. In all the years he
had spoken with Duran, Vadami had not seen any
urge on the other man's part to change his ways.

Especially now. Especially considering the influences being brought to bear on him.

He flinched at the measures that might be necessary. He shrank from the bloodshed that might
be necessary, to stop this, remove his heretical
thoughts from Old Town.

If there is a growth on a healthy body, don't
leave it there, maintained an old Temple saying,
cut it out.

And so he would have to make sure that Duran
was removed from Old Town.

He did not want to be responsible for such
decisions. He never wanted to harm anyone.

Why then, had the gods saddled him with this
problem? He attempted to talk to his Superior—

his harried Superior curtly bade him solve his own difficulties with his own district—

I have no time, his Superior had said, awash in papers, awash in petitions from priests in every district—for charity, for dispensations—

One thought Duran might have been called to the priesthood himself: if not for Duran, and Duran's charity, countless people who lived in Old Town might have died. The man had always seemed unconcerned for his own aggrandizement in the world, choosing to help those who lived in poverty. Such a person should have been highly respected by everyone.

Should have been. Such was the Sabirn evil they could turn aside even such an exemplary life.

And make him blaspheme . . .

Memories swept over Vadami—his own schooling, the years of hard work and study spent in preparing him to become a priest.

And to have Duran stand up to him—someone who had not endured the study, the fasting, the grueling examinations—and for Duran to turn the words of the Book of the Shining to his own advantage—

No! to *Sabirn* advantage—

That sophistry could not be tolerated. Priests were the only ones qualified to interpret those words. If everyone could choose a meaning for what had been written down in that Book, the cohesive structure of the Temple would be in danger.

For two reasons, therefore, Duran must be punished: his dealings with the Sabirn, and his most dangerous notion that he could interpret the Holy Words.

"Priest Vadami."

He looked up from his wine glass. The alchemist, Ladirno, stood before him, thoroughly soaked.

"May I join you, priest?"

"Aye. Please."

"Damned storm," Ladirno said, tossing his cloak back from his shoulders to let it rest on the chair. He turned to give his order to a waiter, then looked back. "What brings you here, Vadami?"

"The weather. And I needed somewhere to sit a while and think."

The waiter brought Ladirno his glass of wine, took the money the alchemist handed over, and disappeared back toward the kitchen. Vadami watched Ladirno—remembering he was Duran's friend.

Was Hladyr leading him?

Was it—guided, this encounter?

"Sor Ladirno. Do you mind if I share a problem with you?"

Ladirno quirked an eyebrow.

"It's about Duran," Vadami said and, as the alchemist's face went dead sober: "He's—gone far past anything we believed. I fear—he is irretrievable."

"In what regard?"

Even now Duran had friends, people who thought him a good man. It worried Vadami, and at the same time made his heart ache to see such loyalty about to be hurt.

"It's true. I fear—he has contact with Sabirn wizards. I fear they've snared him—corrupted him beyond what any reason can deal with. He dares to argue with me. He mocks the Scriptures. He despises reason."

Ladirno shook his head sadly. "I feared so, Father. I did fear it."

"I'm sorry." There was so much respect in this man, so much learning, so much concern, so much . . . stature. "Add to that his consorting with the Sabirn. Something has to be done. I'm very sorry. But—"

"Believe me, I do understand. But I fear—" Ladirno lowered his voice further, leaned across the table, whispered: "Father, the Duke himself met these charges. The Duke heard all the evidence—gave him only the slightest of reprimands. Dare I say it to you, Father—dare I say a terrible thing?"

Vadami's heart beat faster and faster.

"I fear—" Ladirno whispered. "I fear the extent of this influence . . ."

Vadami caught his breath. Someone who understood! Truly understood.

"Dark dealings," Vadami said, "understates it. I'm very much afraid—and I don't want to say this to you who are his friend—that Duran's gone, completely sucked into that darkness."

An odd look passed across Ladirno's face, quickly gone. "Hladyr bless, Father. I fear—I fear the same. If you're correct—if I am—then . . . anyone dealing with him could be led astray."

Vadami whispered, "The time has come, Ladirno, when we must move. We must keep Duran's heretical ideas from the rest of the people. We must *remove* his influence from Old Town."

"Remove . . ." Ladirno echoed, fearfully. "You don't mean . . ."

"Sor Ladirno." Vadami shook his head vehemently. "I don't want to hurt Duran. I truly don't. But he has to be *stopped*, removed from influence— before his corruption spreads. Before his blasphemous interpretations of the Shining One's words fall on fertile ground."

"What are you suggesting?"

Vadami took a sip of his wine, set the glass down, and consciously steadied both his mind and his voice. "If we were to run Duran out of Targheiden, we could solve this problem. As a weapon then, as a channel for darkness—he would be useless to them."

"Run him out of . . . ?" Ladirno rubbed his chin. "What about his friends? What about all those poor folk he's helped? Don't you think they'll prevent such a thing from happening?"

"I've taken that into consideration. Maybe if the weather was its usual fine self his friends would back him up. But no longer. More and more people are becoming convinced the Sabirn are behind the storms."

"Are you?"

"Is there another answer? They hate us. They deal in the darkest of dark arts. If they have wizards drawing directly from the demons of darkness, who's to say *what* they can do—with an Ancar to spread their poison?"

"I hear you. But, Duran . . . I can't believe *he's* wrapped up in such acts."

"He is. He's totally involved. How can he not be, seeing the Sabirn as he does? A rotten apple will spoil an entire basketful. Everyone knows that. What we have to do is remove that apple *before* it rots the others."

"Why are you telling me this?"

"For the same reason I spoke to you before about Duran. You're his friend. I need your help in getting him out of town without hurting him. I was hoping you'd have some ideas on how that could be accomplished."

Ladirno sat for a long while in silence, studying his glass held in his hands. Vadami's heart went out to the alchemist, so obviously torn between friendship and a sense of what was right.

"The people are disturbed, you're correct about that," Ladirno said at last. "Did you hear the ducal heralds?"

"Aye. In Temple Square. The crowds—just stood in the rain . . ."

"Father, the citizens of Targheiden are ready to take up stones. Running Duran out of town could get dangerous. If anything starts—one can't say how far it would go, with what bloodshed."

Vadami nodded. "If we think this through carefully, there's a chance the folk of Old Town will just want to persuade him away. To frighten him. He's done too much good there for them to want to do him bodily harm."

"I don't know. We'll have to be *very* careful. Have you ever seen a mob in action?"

"No . . ."

"Well, let me tell you . . . you want to pick your leaders. You want to pick them extremely carefully. They should be respected enough to maintain control. They should be respectable people— his neighbors, his friends—who, however they may be frightened right now—will not want to hurt a long-time neighbor. Or stir up wider disturbance."

Vadami rubbed his forehead. "Wise words. I think I have the very person in mind who could talk to Duran's neighbors. She's a seamstress and she runs her shop right next to Duran's. She's been trying to talk him out of this fascination with the Sabirn for years—a good woman, Sor Ladirno . . . she believes in the right things."

"You think she can stir Duran's neighbors up to a point where they'll act? And keep it going? Responsibly?"

"Aye. They're already riled up. Considerably. It won't take much to convince them they'd be better off without Duran around."

Ladirno slowly shook his head, a look of sadness in his eyes. "I was hoping I'd never see such a day," he said, his voice weary. "Duran's always been . . . a little strange. Every one his colleagues has noticed this. Some of us have even spoken to him about it."

"Hladyr will bless your intent."

"We so hoped he would listen to us, to the Duke, to the Duke's advisors. What we didn't count on was the man's flare for words, and the Duke's leniency." Ladirno smiled crookedly. "But then it's that bond between Ancar. Perhaps that's why Duran wasn't punished as he should have been."

"Perhaps. I pray so."

"If it has to be, it has to be. Duran can't go on working against—honest folk. That's for sure."

"Then you think what I'm planning is right? That it can work?"

"Aye. You have all the arguments on your side, Father. After all, *you're* the priest . . . you're the one to counsel these people—to counsel all of us.

And I think it can work, if you're very careful. My advice still stands: use this seamstress. Only agitate Duran's neighbors as well—be sure to involve as many of his true friends as you can gain—that way there'll be no question of sincere purpose in this—"

A warm feeling filled Vadami's heart. He was finally taking some action. He was given a chance to save an entire section of town from practitioners of the dark arts, a chance to redeem Old Town from heresies and to preserve the Scriptures against attack—surely Hladyr had to bless that—in many ways.

That was why the god had left him in this dismal post—for Hladyr's greater glory, for his ultimate good.

"Hladyr bless, Sor Ladirno," Vadami said, signing him. "And prosper you and yours. Hladyr has used you to advise me—though you're Duran's friend—and friendship is nothing to be scoffed at—you know what is right and just; and Hladyr will reward you."

"In my own humble way, I try," Ladirno replied.

Now that he had an active plan at hand, one that the alchemist agreed was viable, Vadami could hardly sit still. He gathered up his cloak, slipped it over his shoulders, and stood.

"A thousand thanks, Sor Ladirno," he said, bowing slightly. "You'll be in my prayers. I'll always remember your advice, your patience, and your intelligent suggestions."

Ladirno looked up, his face very serious. "Father, I'm sure you're doing what's right. You're being far more gentle in your solution than any

other law might be. Only be careful. Guard
yourself."

Full shelves—and hundreds of empty clay pots—
kept the shop looking normal. Duran stood, hands
on hips, and surveyed what was left downstairs,
what he could not take with him. He had delivered nearly all of his drugs, herbs and medicines
to the alley window, only leaving behind enough
to do the absolutely necessary routine business
from his shop.

But few customers had stopped by. With the
continuing rain and wind, his lack of business was
not surprising. And since Tutadar had told the
neighbors the Sabirn boy was going to be gone for
a few days, it should seem natural that deliveries
and solicitations should stop, and that the shop
would settle to a quieter routine.

One hoped—that that was the preception on the
street, at least.

But, thank the gods, the last of his belongings
would be smuggled out tonight, storm or no storm.
When he had gone to the "Cat" for his midday
meal, the looks he had received from his neighbors were not—neighborly.

That was certainly part of the strange sense of
urgency that filled his mind. And part of it, he was
sure, was a desire to be done with this: now that
he had decided to leave Targheiden, he wanted
nothing more than to do it quickly—like any parting: the longer it drew on, the more painful it
began to be; and the more a man tried to settle his
mind—the more the old place began to seem irrel-
evant and strangely disturbing to him.

Dog, too, seemed keenly aware something strange was in the wind. As Duran's books, papers, medicines, and alchemist's tools had disappeared into the baskets, Dog had walked from place to place, sniffing the emptiness left behind. More than once he had turned his head, looked at Duran in canine puzzlement, and whined softly.

He was taking Dog with him—damned sure. Dog was going to be of great comfort on the road and—wherever else . . . the only living contact Duran would have of what his neighborhood had once been like. But he could not tell Dog that; and perhaps Dog—having experienced loneliness before—could not trust in things.

Duran sighed, scanned the shelves again for forgotten details, things overlooked, things that he might still regret. There was nothing. The shelves with their false, empty containers, stood as a reminder to him of how empty his life had become.

The past was dead, the present was dying.

Only the future seemed of import.

CHAPTER 12

"Can you believe it?" Wellhyrn fairly shouted, pacing Ladirno's rug. "That damned man has *got* to have more than one wizard backing him! There's no other way to explain it!"

Ladirno leaned back in his chair, watching Wellhyrn sputter. His young colleague had burst in not long after he had gotten home, his handsome face red with rage and his hands clenched as if he were prepared to strike out at anyone who got in his way.

"Calm, calm," Ladirno said. "Be patient."

"Patient!" Wellhyrn cried, facing him. "We're near the end of our resources. Two, *two* wizards, who don't come cheap! And from what Mandani's spy tells him—nothing's working!"

"He has his eye on Duran, then."

"Evidently he's been to that inn for his midday meal. The spy says that it was the same as yesterday. Duran seemed quiet, but not moody—showing no signs of bespelling, nothing in the world *wrong!* What in Dandro's hells are we going to do? We can't afford to put *another* wizard on him!"

"We may not have to do anything at all," Ladirno said, taking a sip of his second glass of wine. "I think the little priest might have solved our problems."

"Vadami?" Wellhyrn was incredulous. "That priest?"

"Aye. I just happened into the 'Shoe.' Ran into Vadami. He's utterly convinced Duran's damned, that he's lost his soul to darkness by dealing with the Sabirn."

"So? We tried that argument in court, and it didn't get us anywhere."

"This isn't the Duke we're dealing with, Hyrn. This is a young, ambitious priest, who's *very* pious, and *very* interested in doing something that will draw that piety to the attention of his superiors."

"What has that to do with our situation?"

"He still thinks I'm Duran's friend," Ladirno said, "and I'm not going to dissuade him of that fantasy. He told me today that he's reached the end of his patience, that Duran's beginning to corrupt the minds of Old Town." Ladirno leaned closer and lowered his voice. "He plans to run Duran out of town."

Few things ever caught Wellhyrn at a loss for words, but this did. Ladirno found satisfaction at his colleague's stunned expression.

"He's what?"

"Planning on running Duran out of town," Ladirno repeated.

"Are you certain?"

"Aye, I'm certain. Vadami's going to talk to that shrew who has her shop next to Duran's. He seems to think she's the most pious woman he knows."

"The seamstress?" Wellhyrn curled his lip. "She's nothing but a gossip and a troublemaker. She's had that reputation for years."

"That may be. But this time, all her gossiping and trouble-making will benefit us. She's the one after Duran; she'll get the entire neighborhood stirred up against him." He took another sip of wine. "Trust me, Wellhyrn. Not everything requires wide actions. We'll be rid of Duran without having to lift a finger ourselves."

"And without any suspicion coming to roost in our nest."

"Exactly. —I'm only sorry if the Duke's heir *is* receiving treatments for the pox from Duran, there's no chance that Duran can finish. He won't have a chance to save Brovor's life—personally. But there are other doctors. And we can discover who."

Wellhyrn smiled coldly. "That's beautiful. We couldn't have thought up anything that would have worked as well. But do you think Duran's neighbors will act? After all, he's been a well-liked man. And that woman—"

Ladirno shook his head. "He's taken the Sabirn side against them—what do you expect they'll do? What any pious folk would do—and they are that, Hyrn, they are that. They don't know statecraft from hogswill—but they do know their own pocketbooks. Trust that."

"Then our wizards *are* working."

"Perhaps. Perhaps you have someone else to thank—but let's wait a day or two. At least until we know for sure that Duran's gone. He may have some protection—protection of a sort we'd rather not deal with. It won't hurt to keep ill-wishing him."

"It's money we can ill afford," Wellhyrn pointed out.

"Let me tell you—friend. You involved us in this. *I've* found our solution. I want you to remember that."

Wellhyrn gave him a hard-jawed stare. "You—"

"The storms, friend. You want to know why our wizards aren't having any luck. Perhaps it's because Duran *is* involved up to his neck. Perhaps it's because he *does* have protections—from wizards the Duke's own wizards can't beat. Personally I don't want to *touch* this mess—but we're in it; and being in it, we'd damned well better put somebody else between us and the trouble—somebody with special protections: let the Temple fight this thing."

"A petty priest."

"A very zealous priest. Duran's human. What's human has soft spots. There are things he cares for, things he cares about—that's where we can get him. That's where this priest can get him. *We* don't have to touch the situation. Whatever black arts are behind him—they'll lose him. They'll lose the only reason they could possibly have to pay attention to *us*, do you follow me, Wellhyrn? Have you thought—if Duran is protected like this—what he could do if he turned those wizards' attention on *us*?"

Wellhyrn's eyes glinted in the lamplight. "So we use the priest, the priest uses the woman, the woman—runs that whoreson Duran right out of town. And *his* notion of who's responsible has to be his own neighbors."

"Exactly. You see—I do think of things. Slowly, but I do think."

"Gods! I'd give a lot to be there."

"Which is precisely where we're *not* going to be. We want not the slightest hint that we had anything to do with this!"

"Aye, aye. But our wizards can do a little something to speed things up."

A cold shiver ran down Ladirno's spine. "What are you thinking about?"

"Nothing that can be traced back to us. I'll make sure of that. What I have in mind will simply make the neighbors a bit more—nervous about Duran."

"You're not going to do anything illegal, are you?"

"I won't answer that. This way, you won't know."

"Dammit, Hyrn! Think things through! Just give it time, let things work the way they will—let the priest handle it!"

"Because I want this nailed down," Wellhyrn said, a cruel smile twisting his lips. "And I want to make sure this works. Damn Duran and his airs. An Ancar noble. I'm five times the man he'll *ever* be."

Ladirno met and held his colleague's eyes. "Don't let revenge get you in trouble. Don't. Stay away from this!"

"Pfft. You're getting jumpy as an old woman. I won't have anything to do with it."

"You've got a cruel mind," Ladirno said, eyeing the smile on Wellhyrn's face. "Damned cruel."

Wellhyrn leaned back in his chair, and lifted his wine glass in a graceful hand. "Oh, aye, I do. And isn't it wonderful?"

The rain had momentarily stopped; the sound of it running from the eaves down into rainbarrels was loud in the comparative silence of Old Town.

Vadami walked slowly through the cloud-covered twilight, his eyes roving around the street. He was cloaked against more than the rain: it would do him no good to be noticed right now. He walked till he saw Zeldezia's sign swaying in the wind, and made for her door with all the stealth he could manage.

Duran's door was shut, which either meant he was sequestered inside, or that he had gone across the street to the inn. Good, Vadami thought. He wanted no contact with the man tonight—just a word with the good woman.

The evening weather was warm. Zeldezia's door stood cracked open, and lamplight spilled a gold sliver onto the wet cobbles.

"Zeldezia!" he called out softly, and rapped softly at the door. "It's Father Vadami. Are you there?"

He heard footsteps, and the door opened. Zeldezia opened it wider, swept her skirts out of his way, dropped an anxious little curtsey—pleased to see him, worshipful of his office: she always was. "Father! Come in, Father, please, an' get yourself out of the weather!"

Vadami entered the small shop. As always, he could have eaten off the floor. Everything shone, from the wooden floor to the tables laden with sewing, to the good brass lamps hanging from the ceiling.

"An' what can I do for you?" Zeldezia said, offering him one of two chairs that sat by a table. "Can I get you some cakes? Some wine?"

"No, no," he said, sitting down. With a rustle of her skirts, she took the chair opposite. "I've come to you out of concern, daughter—perhaps for a little help in a situation. I need someone—brave and committed to Hladyr's commandments. I think you're that woman."

Her dark eyes glittered. "Ask, an' if I can, I'll help. How could anyone turn you down, Father?"

"It's about Duran."

Her face hardened and her mouth curved down into a deep frown. "Duran! If I hadn't owned this shop long's I have, I'd move! I don't want no dealin's with 'im, Father, I truly don't, I avoid 'im as I can—"

Vadami leaned close briefly and patted Zeldezia's hand. "I know, I know, daughter. And surely you're not the only one. I fear—I fear there's worse than we thought."

"Oh?" She sat up straighter in her chair, her hands nervously playing with the tongue of her fine leather belt. Her eyes were frightened. "What could be worse?"

"Actual practice of the dark arts."

"Next door?" Zeldezia wailed.

He kept his voice calm, tried to assure her by his steady gaze that he was doing what he thought was best. "That's what we have to stop, Zeldezia. For your sake—for the sake of everyone involved."

"You know he sent that Sab kid somewheres?" she asked. "But, mind you, that kid'll be back, an' we don't know what devilment he's off to—or who he's dealin' with! Father, we got to do somethin'."

"I know. That's why we have to break up this Sabirn nest, Zeldezia. I don't want to hurt Duran, and I don't think you do. But for the safety of all concerned, for the souls of the folk here about— Duran's already lost, Zeldezia, and he's spreading his corruption. He's perverted holy Scripture. He's blasphemed. All these things he's done—but what his Sabirn allies have done—"

Zeldezia signed herself nervously.

"They're aiming at the Duke himself, Zeldezia. It's power they want. They're *using* Duran's Ancar blood to find and curse things they couldn't touch. He's the canker that will spread, spread through all this town—"

"What can we do?"

"Get him out of this neighborhood! Out of Targheiden!"

She sniffed quietly, gnawed her lip, twisted at the fringes of her shawl. "I been thinkin' the same thing for a long time now, Father. I been worried, oh, I been worried! But Duran's got hisself some good friends. He got Tutadar and Ithar, two of the most respectable folk in this neighborhood. Gettin' them to go along with your plan ain't going to be easy."

"Maybe there are some we can't trust. Maybe there are some we shouldn't tell. But surely there are those that will do Hladyr's work . . ."

Zeldezia nodded vigorously. "If you bless us, Father, if you tell them yourself that the Sabirn

are behind all this wickedness, if you say it—aye!"
She squared her shoulders. "Some of 'em may not
like me, but I got a good reputation! I make more
money than a lot of 'em. I'm a respectable woman.
An' with you, Father—"

Vadami nodded. "Exactly. Exactly. Go to your
neighbors. For their soul's sakes."

"I will! I will, Father! Bless us!"

"Hladyr bless you," Vadami said. "You're a good
woman, and a pious soul. You have to be discreet."

"Aye, aye, I know who to talk to, an' I know
what words to use. I done it before an' they listened. They only got to look around 'em and lissen
to the thunder. I'll do it, Father, we'll see there
ain't no more sneakin' Sabs among us. . . ."

Duran walked into the "Cat," ignoring the coldness from his neighbors; Tutadar was one of the
few even to acknowledge his presence. Duran
sighed softly and continued on to his table.

He knew Tutadar had spread the word that he
was going to send Kekoja off for a few days; he had
hoped that would calm things.

It seemed they had miscalculated. Badly.

Several gloomy fellows sat in a far corner of the
common room, merchants, by the cut of their
tunics, harbor traffic—which could not be happy.
They looked to be Sacarreans, most likely, from
the looks of them. Probably in town to trade their
spices for grain and metals mined to the north. If
that was so, they had been marooned here in
Targheiden for days now, unwilling to chance pas-
sage across a storm-ridden sea.

Damn the weather. Damn all this wretched summer, its storms, its ill humors, its frustrations and its angers: in any better season no one would have faulted him hiring Kekoja to serve as his runner. The customers Kekoja had taken physics to had not complained. Several of Duran's neighbors—Ithar and Edfin the baker—had been happy to see Duran making a good profit.

That was the way life had always been in Old Town. When one of your neighbors was doing well, you wished him all the best of luck, hoping some of it would rub off on you. Good business in one trade had a habit of begetting good business in another.

But the weather had soured that. For good.

And changed everything.

He looked up as Lalada came to his table with a mug of ale. She did not meet his eyes; she merely set the mug down on the table, took his order for breaded fish, and walked away, dumb as a post. Duran watched her go, a sadness creeping into his heart. He had cured the bad humor that had afflicted her head, and she no longer sniffed and sneezed. That should have been enough to convince her she was safe in his presence. Obviously not.

Then the thought reached him that this might be the last evening he ever spent in "The Swimming Cat." Suddenly, everything took on a new importance. He stared at the old wooden table top, gouged here and there by knives. He heard the squeak of his chair as he changed position. Everything—the flickering lamplight, the sawdust spread on the floor, the two grey cats who slept in a far corner, the sound of muted conversation— seemed magnified. The relative calm of the common room, the friendly atmosphere that was usually present . . . all those things would dwell only in his memory.

He rubbed his eyes. He *was* growing old. He cheerfully admitted it. And, as the proverb assured him, it was far easier to teach a young dog new tricks than an old one set in his ways. A piece of his life—a major piece of his life was going away from him—or he was going away from it—and he was less interested in looking to the future than in looking at what he was losing . . .

Was that not the attribute of age? He was forty-five: that should have been still young. But it was late to be starting over. It was late to lose everything. There were not enough vital years left—to build a life on.

So what did one do? Exist. Exist was all, without a past, with only a dozen or so baskets holding his whole damn life—

And no interest in where he was after that.

Maybe it was better to stay, fight it out, die here, if that was what it came to—

Except the books—

"Duran."

He looked up. Tutadar had brought his breaded fish; the innkeeper set the plate out before Duran, then pulled out a chair to sit down facing him.

"Thanks, Tut." Duran began cutting up the fish, and lowered his voice. "I hoped the neighbors would at least be easier with the boy out of town. What's going on?"

"I don't know," Tutadar said, crossing his arms on the table. "Hail this morning. Warehouse roof collapsed, folk goin' about the Slough in boats, f' gods' sake. That's gettin' close to home, you know what I mean?" He nodded toward the front door. "Nobody been givin' Old Man a copper. Not a one. Maybe I misjudged everyone. I'm sorry. I did hope they'd look on you kinder. But folks is scared. Folks is scared an' mad an' they got nowhere to send it."

"Tut, I've lived here, I've dealt here, I've barely kept my head above water for years. I get the kid and I do—well—for the first time in my life. Is that evil? Is there any evil influence in that?"

Tut shrugged uncomfortably.

"Today I only had six customers—and them up from the harbor. Not my neighbors. I don't understand that, Tut."

Tut shrugged and never met his eyes. "Don't know. Don't know, it's what I said, folks is just nervous. I'm sorry about the kid. I am. You know it ain't me holds agin him. I don't want t' see you hurt, Duran!"

Duran stared at his friend. He hated pretending this night was like any other night. He wanted more than anything to confide in Tutadar, tell him where he was going, make some tie he could keep. . . .

But he dared not. For the first time in years, a hint of distrust had entered Duran's heart, even toward Tut. Even as he despised the feeling, he recognized prudence when he saw it.

"Well, so we keep our heads down. What happens next?"

"Hard tellin'." Tutadar looked ceilingward. "Long's the weather stays bad, I don't think you got a chance in Dandro's hells of keepin' 'em happy with you."

"Tut, I want you to listen to me carefully. If anything happens to me, I—"

"Don't you go talkin' like that, Duran!" the inn-keeper interrupted. "Nothin' going to happen to you if *I* have anythin' to say 'bout it. Or Ithar, for that matter."

"Thank you, Tut. And I know you mean it. But hear me through, if for nothing else than amusement. If anything should happen to me, I want you to take care of Dog. He knows you and trusts you, and he makes a good guard. And sell what I own, down to the shop itself, and give the money to some young doctor who might want to make a few trips to Old Town."

"Duran." There was a warning in Tutadar's voice. "Don't you bring no bad luck on yourself by talkin' this way."

"All right." Duran let a smile touch his lips. "Just you and Ithar keep in mind that you've been good neighbors all these years. That I've been proud to know you."

Tutadar blinked rapidly. "That's somethin', ain't it, when an Ancar noble says he been proud to know Old Town rats like us."

"This Ancar noble's one of those rats, too, courtesy of the old duke."

Thunder rumbled loudly. Duran and Tutadar both flinched.

"I confess," Tutadar muttered, "I don't trust

these storms no more. They been gettin' real nasty. —An' I know you ain't goin' to agree, an' I know you're going to hate me for sayin' it, but I still think Sabirn're involved somehow."

"I can't seem to convince you, can I?"

Tut shook his head. "Now, I *will* admit they ain't all bad. I never did mind Old Man. An' that kid who been workin' for you, he never been nothin' but polite to me. But that don't take into consideration the rest of 'em. I can't. I can't like 'em, I can't deal with 'em. . . ."

"I wish I could make you understand," Duran said. "I hope someday you'll find a reason to believe that because a man's different doesn't make him a bad fellow—just different."

"They're *too* different. They're spooky."

Duran smiled and took another sip of his ale. "Enough of this gloomy talk. I don't want to go home with a bad taste in my mouth. I like you too much, Tut."

Thunder rumbled again. "Sounds like you're going to go home with rain on your head. 'Less you want to stay 'round here."

"I'm afraid not." Duran sighed, gulped down the rest of his ale. "I think I'll be going to bed early tonight."

"Probably not a bad idea." The innkeeper shoved his chair back from the table and stood. "You take care of yourself, hear? An' don't you go givin' me any money for your fish. The meal's on me."

The sound of a rock thrown against the shutter of his apartment woke Duran from a sound sleep. He sat up in bed, rubbed his eyes, and stood.

Fully dressed, he walked through the darkness to the back window, and threw open the shutters.

It was raining again—which actually reassured him, for no one in his right mind would be out on the streets in this downpour.

"Hssst! Duran!"

Kekoja's voice. Duran could make out the Sabirn lad standing directly below the window, along with another man. Duran waved, and felt his way back across the room, while rain blew in on the gusts.

The last few small items, were packed—everything in four remaining baskets. He lifted one, grunting slightly under its weight: the last of his books and writings, this one. Walking back to the opened window, he carefully balanced the basket on the sill, tying the rope about it for a sling.

"Hssst!" He saw Kekoja lift his head, hand held over his eyes to shield off the rain. "Heavy!"

Kekoja waved and Duran eased the basket out of the window, bracing himself against the wall below it with his knees and feet. Gently as he could, he lowered the basket into Kekoja's hands, then watched Kekoja untie the long rope. The other man took up the basket on his shoulder and trotted off into the darkness and falling rain.

Duran hauled up the rope, returned to his baskets and readied the next to be lowered—a lighter one: it contained all his clothes, his blankets and what linen he possessed. He lowered the basket out of the window, Kekoja untied it, shouldered it and with a wave, disappeared around the corner into the deserted street.

It would be some time before the two Sabirn returned, so Duran dragged one of the chairs over to the window, sat down in the water-laden draft, and stared off into the darkness. Lightning flashed overhead, subdued, and the thunder that followed, a gentle rumble. Thank Hladyr. Conditions could not have been better for the task at hand. Maybe something was going right. Maybe the gods did not disapprove what he was doing.

They showed no lights: the bedroom was dark. Even so, he saw the long, narrow room in his mind's eye as if the sun were shining. It was his last night here. The last time he would sleep in his own bed. The last time he would listen to the homely creaks and groans of the building—*his* home, his shop—

A wave of sadness filled his heart. If only things had turned out differently. If only his neighbors could see that the Sabirn were little different than themselves.

If only. If only Hladyr could come down from heaven and walk among men again: it would take a miracle of the same magnitude to turn the hearts of his neighbors.

He heard the scuff of steps on wet cobble. He stood, looked out to see Kekoja and his companion returned from whatever hole they had nearby. He prepared the next basket, his alchemist's tools, mainly vials and beakers.

"Fragile!" he whispered down. "Glass!"

Kekoja received the basket: his partner took it.

The last, then. Duran hauled the rope up, tied it to the last basket—and this was the hardest to see go—this contained his father's weapons, the sword, the daggers, all had been passed down from father to son for generations of Ancahar noblemen. Heirlooms of the heart—his mother's carefully wrapped jewelry: he had never sold them—no matter how desperate things became.

Maybe things would have been different if he had. With those jewels, he could have bought a far better shop and not lived so near to the edge of poverty.

Maybe.

The sword, the jewels, his father's notes—all that was irreplaceable.

"Hssst!" He saw Kekoja lift his head. "You sleep on this one, hear? Take care of it."

Kekoja lifted his hands, received the basket—and the rope, this time.

Duran stood in the window after they had gone—realizing suddenly he was standing in a house bereft of everything he owned . . . everything that was valuable to him. All of it carried away to gods know what destination in the hands of the Sabirn. And he had to trust them. He had no choice. He was empty-handed now. They had everything.

Name-brothers, Old Man had said. Old Man had talked about trust. About friendship. But so had Tut. So had his neighbors—once.

He sighed and drew the shutters. There. It was done. He could not turn back now; he had committed himself to the most unsettling future he had ever chosen in his life.

"Oh, gods!" He rested his eyes against his hand in the dark, shook his head. Brovor. Brovor would have to seek another doctor to treat his pox. He *had* to do that. He had only a few treatments left, but it was vitally important he receive them. Brovor had to understand that—and he dared not, *dared* not send any message to him.

There was Mother Garan. Who would help her?

Thunder rumbled distantly. The rain poured down outside the window, the sound of it hitting the roofs and pavement, unnatural, malevolently persistent.

At least Kekoja had gotten the baskets away. Duran thanked the gods for this one small favor.

And prayed for Brovor's good sense, and an old woman's comfort.

At this late hour, in this downpour, the few souls on the streets walked briskly to their destinations. A fool would be standing here in the rain: but Ladirno did—in the shadows of the alley across the street from Wellhyrn's rooms. He could not sleep. His instincts, his curiosity, had finally driven him out at this ungodly time of night to take up this watch—

All because of the threat Wellhyrn had made.

Ladirno had no idea what Wellhyrn proposed to do to Duran, but if it *was* against the law, he wanted to know. He had suspected Wellhyrn in the past of shady dealings he had never been able to prove—but in this, for various reasons—

This time if Wellhyrn was being a fool, he fully meant to disassociate himself—leave Wellhyrn to twist in the wind, if that was the case.

He froze, leaned closer against the wall: a man approached Wellhyrn's building, obviously taking his time and appearing slightly drunk. Ladirno glanced up at the doorway, and saw Wellhyrn step outside. Head bowed, a purposeful gait to his walk, Wellhyrn left the doorway and stepped directly into the other man's path.

The two of them collided, and the drunk staggered, nearly knocked from his feet. Ladirno held his breath, hoping to hear something . . . anything.

But no words were exchanged, aside from a muffled curse or two. Wellhyrn reached out to steady the drunk and quickly dropped something into the man's hand. Ladirno drew a sharp breath. The lamps which burned at the doorway to Wellhyrn's apartments lent a fair amount of light to the street, and in this light he had seen the glint of gold.

The drunk snarled something at Wellhyrn, appeared to get his directions totally mixed up, then lurched off again, this time headed down the hill toward Old Town.

Wellhyrn glanced up and down the street, while Ladirno held his breath, plastered against the side of the building, and praying his colleague would not look his way.

Some bored god must have heard his prayer, for Wellhyrn turned around and went back inside.

For a long moment, Ladirno stood shivering against the wall. What was it that Wellhyrn had paid this man for? He had seen the flash of at least one gold donahri, sufficient price for a murder in some quarters.

A sour taste filled Ladirno's mouth. Ladirno spat into the street, gathered his cloak tighter, and hurried off into the dark down the alley.

A bell rang somewhere. A distant bell, muffled

and indistinct. The sound of it filtered into Duran's sleep and woke him from a dream of rain.

He sat up in bed, his heart pounding. He listened, unsure whether the bell had rung only in his mind, or in the real world.

No. There it was again—the "Cat's" bell—that only rang for theft and fire—

Duran sprang from bed, and ran toward the front window. Flinging open the shutters, he stared down into the street.

The rain had stopped. Torchlight from the "Cat" lit up the street, people running—

But not only that light—

"Fire!" someone called—Ithar, he thought. "Get buckets!"

Duran cursed aloud, lit his lamp with shaking hands, flung his clothes on, grabbed the lamp and rushed down his stairs—Dog was barking now, frantically. Duran set down the lamp, grabbed his cloak, unlocked the door with trembling fingers.

He stepped into a scene of chaotic motion. People ran here and there, searching for buckets. He could see the flames now, and his heart lurched. The fire burned up against the walls of Zeldezia's shop.

Duran glanced around and found Tutadar. The innkeeper was standing in the center of the street, directing his fellow neighbors to various rain barrels, instructing them where buckets were kept.

"When did it start?" Duran yelled over the commotion.

"Don't know! But it's burnin' good!"

Duran stared at the fire. The blaze was impossible—in a puddle-filled alleyway, debris soaked and sodden—

"Dammit!" He ran to Tutadar's side. "Don't throw water on it, Tut! Call back the buckets!"

The innkeeper stared at Duran as if he were mad.

"It's an oil fire, Tut! For gods' sakes, don't throw water on it! Can't you see? It's too damned wet for anything but oil to burn like that!"

Tutadar narrowed his eyes and looked back at the fire.

"Wait!" he bellowed, his voice carrying over the yelling of the neighbors. "No water! You hear me? *No water!*"

"Get mud, get dirt. Flour! Something that will smother the flames!" Duran glanced around. "Find Bontido. He's got to have something like that around his shop!"

Several of the neighbors were beating at the fire with heavy blankets now. Someone ran off with Bontido toward the potter's shop. Zeldezia stood in the street, her hands clasped, wailing in a shrill voice. A man ran back from the inn, struggling under the weight of a heavy bag of flour.

"Hurry!" Tutadar hollered. "All of **it!** On the fire!"

The man approached Zeldezia's shop, held the bag firmly, one hand keeping it open, and began tossing flour onto the fire. The flames fell back some, but did not die.

"Move aside!"

Duran stepped back as Bontido and two other men pushed a manure wagon full of soaked stable-dirt toward the shop. One of the men grabbed a shovel and started tossing the dirt onto the flames. Duran watched, his heart pounding raggedly. How the hells had an oil fire got started?

Who would have done such a thing to Zeldezia?

A ragged cheer went up from the neighbors as the fire guttered and slowly began to die. Duran drew a deep breath, not surprised to find his knees shaking.

A hand landed on his shoulder. He turned to face Tut. "That 'n was set," Tut said grimly. "Ain't no accident."

Duran nodded, still shaking.

"Damn you, Duran!" Zeldezia's shrill voice penetrated the voices of the crowd. "This is all *your* fault! Sabirn-lover! They witched my shop, they tried to burn me in my house!"

"Gods," Tut murmured, holding tight to Duran's shoulder.

The seamstress elbowed her way through a crowd grown suddenly silent.

"You brought this here fire on me!" she raged. "You an' them damned Sabirn!"

"Calm down, Zeldezia," Ithar said, reaching out to take her arm.

She yanked away from the smith, her eyes narrowed to slits. "You think I don't know! That I can't guess! You—"

"Zeldezia, shut up!" Tut roared, leaving Duran to step between. "You shut your damned mouth! You been nothin' but trouble the past few days, an' now you're accusin' the man who had enough sense to know what that damned fire was, and how to fight it!"

Zeldezia backed up a step. "What d'you mean—he knowed what it was?"

"It ain't sorcery! It's an oil fire. If we'd poured water on it, we'd've made it worse. You got Duran t' thank we saw it in time!"

"He *knowed* what it was! How'd he know? Oil don't get on the side of a body's building by fallin' from the sky!"

"For the gods' sake, Zeldezia, if he'd started that damned fire, he wouldn't've tried to stop it—"

Zeldezia spat at Tut's feet. "The Sabs started that fire—probably that damn boy's skulked back t' get me, near burned the block down! An' you, Duran, you're guilty along with 'em! Ever since I started tryin' to change your ways, you been settin' 'em on me— They wanted to burn me out, that's what, they know what I know—that they been witchin' the weather, that it's them plottin' agin us—"

Duran kept silent. Anything he said at this point would only make matters worse.

Tears were running down Zeldezia's cheeks now. "You low-down scum . . . you Sabirn-lover! I *hate* you for this! An' you'll pay, Duran! You'll pay!"

She spun around, ran into her shop, and slammed the door.

For a long moment the street was silent, so silent Duran could hear the water dripping from the eaves.

"She's crazy," someone muttered. "Damned woman's crazy."

"Maybe not," somebody else said.

Tut gripped Duran's shoulder. "Duran, I think you'd best go back inside. Hear?"

Duran nodded, turned and walked slowly to his shop. Dog stood in the lighted doorway, his tail wagging slowly now that the noise had died down.

Duran shut the door behind him, leaned up against the counter, staring off into the shadows.

Someone had deliberately started that fire.

Kekoja?

Gods, no, no. Not Kekoja, not Old Man—not fire, that could have burned Zeldezia alive.

Who would do such a thing? Who in the world would do a thing like that?

A jar was out of place on the counter. It weighted a paper.

It said, in a boy's uneven letters, *The river gate. Tomorrow sundown. Fire not ours.*

CHAPTER 13

It came down to waiting now—only waiting—wondering over and over again where Old Man was, why they waited at all—

Duran sat on his stool and listened to the work going on next door. Since morning, people had been over at Zeldezia's shop, removing the burned and scorched manure and flour, and washing down the wall with—the gods knew—no shortage of water.

He stayed to his shop, kept the door cracked—indecisive between the pretense of being open for business and the fear of his neighbors.

Mother Garan was the only visitor, desperate, on the edge of one of her headaches.

He gave her the whole pot of willow-tea, he held her gnarled hands and impressed on her as gravely as he could the danger of too much use.

He scared her, perhaps. She looked as if he had.

He wanted not to charge her, wanted to give her some money to go to an uptown doctor—but he knew her pride; and he feared she might spread that story.

Zeldezia had spent little time in her shop. Duran had seen her wandering up and down the street, whispering to various people, and throwing hateful looks in the direction of his door. Gods alone knew what she was telling everyone, what charges she was making.

He could not believe that Zeldezia had any enemies who would take the time *and* the risk to set a fire.

Could it have been someone after him, confusing his shop with Zeldezia's? He shuddered at the thought. Whoever had been the target—

If it had a bit more time to burn, it might have caught the second story on fire, and then gods help everyone up and down the block.

Now, seated on his stool, waiting as the day drifted on to afternoon—waiting, and not knowing—he simply hoped.

Tonight—he and Dog would take a walk. Lock the door to delay anyone finding him gone—

And just walk away.

"Have you seen the priest today?" Wellhyrn asked, swirling the wine around in his glass, his legs stretched comfortably before him. It was Ladirno's apartment. It was mid-afternoon.

"No. And neither have you, I suppose."

Wellhyrn shook his head. There was a curious expression on the younger man's face this afternoon, a look of smug, predatory satisfaction. Ladirno had heard the news from Old Town already, and it took no great wit to add things up.

"I know what you did last night," Ladirno said.

A look of surprise widened Wellhyrn's eyes. "What—do you mean?"

"There was a fire at the seamstress' shop. A very suspicious fire."

"Bad luck, I suppose."

"Luck had nothing to do with it. You're very smart, Hyrn—but *not* smart enough, not smart enough to cover your tracks—not smart enough to know me. I'm not as stupid as you think I am."

"I never thought you stupid," Wellhyrn protested.

"You made mistakes. You said yesterday you were going to make Duran suffer. As happens— you've pushed a situation already about to move. But let me tell you, friend, there's someone knows how that fire started. Your reputation is in those hands. That's a *fool*, Wellhyrn. And I'm not a fool. I won't stand for it."

For a long moment, Wellhyrn stared at Ladirno. He blinked twice and then smiled. "You did that with remarkably few clues, Ladir. I'm amazed."

"You aren't upset. You aren't even upset."

Wellhyrn lifted a velvet shoulder. Gold chain glinted in the light.

"Fool," Ladirno said. "You're brilliant, Hyrn, in your work, but leave politics alone. In that you are most definitely a fool."

"Ladir, Ladir." Wellhyrn's voice warmed to a companionable tone. There was just the slightest hint of patronization in it. "I turn your statement around . . . do you think *me* that stupid? The fellow I hired is a lackwit—"

"Wonderful."

"I made sure he left town," Wellhyrn said, lifting an eyebrow. "I had someone follow him this morning. It'll be taken care of— "

"And where does it *stop*, Wellhyrn?"

"It stops. It will stop." The assurance was gone from Wellhyrn's face. His lips made a thin line.

"You listen to me. We may fool people out of money now and again, the Duke being no exception, but by the gods! we haven't *robbed* them of it. And we don't murder."

"Getting soft, aren't you?" Wellhyrn sneered.

Ladirno got up, walked up to Wellhyrn, reached out and grasped Wellhyrn by the front of his tunic. "You listen to me," he hissed. "*I* made you at court. *I* took you on as my apprentice. And I can just as easily dump you right back where you came from. Of the two of us, you tell me who the Duke respects most!"

Wellhyrn reached up and removed Ladirno's hand from his tunic. His face was white.

"You keep that in mind, boy," Ladirno said, standing over him. "And don't try to get back at me in any way. By now, I know your tricks. And, if you try to take revenge, *I'll* go to the Duke with what I know. You might be surprised just how much that is."

A hint of genuine fear crossed Wellhyrn's face.

"You listen to me, and listen well. The Duke won't stand for your kind of goings-on. You may think you can deny it, but I caution you again. Do you want to face up to the Duke's wizards? *They* can get the truth out of you."

Wellhyrn shook his head slightly.

"We can go far, you and I," Ladirno said, letting warmth re-enter his voice, "but you need to learn to control your ambition. You're a damned fine alchemist. You could be one of the best. Don't ruin your chances by overstepping yourself. Or by underestimating others. Do you understand me?"

For a moment, Wellhyrn held Ladirno's gaze. Then he seemed to shake himself from his fear: his smile came back. "Ah, well. There won't be need— once Duran's gone. Will there?"

Vadami looked at the crowd which had gathered before him. A sidelong glance at Zeldezia sent a cold chill down his spine: the woman seemed utterly changed since they had met last. Her face was stoney, her eyes narrowed, and when she spoke, there was a terrible violence in her voice.

He supposed it was to be expected, having lived through the attempted burning of her shop last night.

That was what things had gotten to—the Sabirn *knew* there was movement against them—and they struck.

And they all had cause for fear.

He had tried to calm Zeldezia, he had attempted to keep her on the path of Hladyr's will—keep her from the sin of hate in what she did—

"Do you understand what we're to do?" he asked of the gathered men and women. No one answered, but he saw several nods. "And you understand that we do the will of Hladyr. What we do we do for his sake—for the sake of souls' salvation— drive away the sin of hate, drive out the demons—"

"Who else *but* the Sabirn would do something

like that to me?" Zeldezia cried above his voice. "Who else but Duran, who shelters 'em?"

"Tut ain't going to like this," one man warned. "He's a friend o' Duran's."

"Aye," added another. "Him an' Duran sit together all the time at the 'Cat.' He won't go for this."

"What Tutadar thinks isn't important now," Vadami said quickly, before other members of the crowd could agree with the speaker. "What's important is saving this neighborhood! Fire and flood! And Hladyr only knows what next?"

"The Duke," a woman shouted, "he let Duran off when 'e 'ad 'im—"

"Duran witched im!" someone shouted.

"Demon worshipers!"

"Maybe if we *asked* 'im to leave," another man said, "he'd—"

"No. We don't want him coming back. And he would, once the furor dies down." Vadami drew himself up. "Forget all the good things Duran did for you in the past. He's not the same man any more. He *hired* a Sabirn to work for him. He even had that same Sabirn *live* with him! What does that tell you?"

Suddenly, Zeldezia stepped forward. "Father Vadami ain't tellin' you all! I seen—I *seen* them Sabirn look at Duran like he's some kind of a lord of theirs. I *seen* that old man hangin' 'round his shop. I *seen* Duran talkin' to any Sabirn he can lay a hand on. He's a wizard! Ain't nobody can tell me otherwise."

"Zeldezia—"

"I heard that damned Sab boy playin' his flute!

Music gave me the creeps! It was demon music, on my soul it was! I seen him look at me, that kid, with nothin' in his eyes but darkness."

The crowd murmured louder now. Vadami felt sweat break out.

"Kill that Sab-lover!" Zeldezia cried. "Ain't no pity—he never showed *me* no pity. I asked him to save his soul by givin' up seein' the Sabirn, an' look what 'e did to me!"

The crowd stirred now; their voices had grown deeper, had grown ugly.

"Ever since that Sabirn kid showed up, we ain't had nothin' but evil weather!" Her voice went shrill as she turned to the crowd. "You lost business? Your customers been stayin' away! It ain't *your* fault you been goin' hungry. Duran's done this to you, an' you know it! I say, let's go after him an' give 'im back some of what he's given us!"

"I hear you!" a few men called back. "Let's get that bastard!" others growled. "Burn 'im out!"

"Wait!" Vadami took a step toward the crowd and lifted both hands over his head. "Stop! Think what you're going to do! Don't start anything the Duke's Guard will have to deal with!"

"Duke won't care if we get ourselves a demon worshiper!" Zeldezia shouted. " 'Less he's witched, too!"

"Get 'em all!" someone cried.

The crowd surged forward, their faces distorted with anger, following Zeldezia who had started off toward Duran's neighborhood.

"No! Stop!" Vadami was pushed aside. Sweat ran freely down his face now. Gods! It was getting away from him—totally out of his hands. He gulped down a huge breath, and sprinted off after the crowd. Maybe . . . Oh, Hladyr make it so . . . he could keep them from undirected violence—

Gods above and below! What *had* he done?

Duran stepped outside, turned and locked the door behind him. Dog sat waiting close by, panting in the sultry heat. The storm still had not broken, but thunder muttered ominously in the distance.

The street was strangely deserted for this time of day. The men had stopped work at Zeldezia's shop, and he saw life at only a few of the neighboring buildings.

He shrugged. It would make it easier if he could leave without seeing any of his neighbors. He pocketed the key, aware of the uselessness of the act, took up his staff he had leaned against the wall, and started off down the street.

He had written Tut a short note, explaining that he was leaving and why . . . that he did not hold anything against Tut or Ithar: they had been the truest friends, in good times as well as bad.

He reached the corner, paused, and turned around. His eyes misted slightly, and he blinked. *That was your shop*, he thought, *your home. And now it's nobody's. You're done here, Duran, through. Leave it in the hands of the gods.*

He sighed and started off down the street that ran perpendicular to his, headed east. He had a good half hour of walking before he reached the east side of town where Kekoja and Old Man would be waiting for him.

He quickened his pace, Dog running along ahead, anxious now, only for it to be over. . . .

*   *   *

The Great Hall was nearly empty at this hour—
Duke Hajun himself had come from his dinner-
table. He stared at the young guardsman who
stood panting before him, having spilled out his
news—

A mob—gods. . . .

Loose in Old Town?

"No idea what stirred them up?" he asked, and
the Captain of the Guard, who had brought the
boy—

"Sabirn, Your Grace."

"Damn. —Where are they headed?"

"South, Your Grace. Toward the harbor." The
Captain licked his lips. "It's a small mob, Your
Grace, and we—"

"I don't give a damn if it *is* a small mob! Get
your butt moving! I want a squadron dispatched!
Get it stopped!"

"Aye, Your Grace."

"Reasonable force! You hear me?"

"Aye, lord."

The Captain saluted, the young officer saluted,
and ran from the hall.

Hajun found himself shaking. A small mob? There
was no such thing.

Duran kept to the center of the street, avoiding
the standing pools of water, and quickened his
pace to a fast walk. He did not want to be caught
by darkness outside his own neighborhood. Strange
streets always made him nervous, a good indica-
tion of how limited his world had grown.

He had not traveled this far east in a long time,

but the streets and the buildings looked much like those in his own neighborhood. Dog seemed to think the walk to be a holiday of sorts. He frisked and danced down the street, his tail wagging, every once in a while barking for the sheer joy of it.

Duran calculated he had been walking close to a third of an hour now. The clouds had grown thicker and thunder rumbled incessantly. He noted people had begun to light lamps in their homes and shops, though they kept their doors and windows open in the heat.

He looked ahead and saw a slight figure waiting by the edge of a house, a shadow in the early twilight. His heart raced. A thief? He thought of his moneybelt, and tightened the grip on his staff.

Dog, however, had recognized the figure, and ran ahead, tail wagging. The person reached down and patted Dog's head, then straightened.

Kekoja!

Duran quickened his pace again. Why was Kekoja here, instead of waiting at the edge of town?

"Can you run far?" Kekoja asked with no preamble.

Duran blinked. "Why?"

"Because there's a mob after you, Sor Duran, an' it's an angry mob, an' I don't want to stay around an' see what happens."

A bolt of fear struck through Duran's heart. A mob? Who had raised it? After what had happened last night, he knew the answer even as he asked himself the question.

"Let's go!" he said, and set out after Kekoja at a slow run.

Why, why, why? he asked himself in time to his

running footsteps. *Why couldn't they just let me go?*

His breath came harder now, and he felt the sweat run down his sides. Dammit! He was getting too old for an all-out run like this. His heart beat raggedly. Maybe he would die of heart failure and save the mob its trouble.

He concentrated on Kekoja running before him, on the long thin legs pumping tirelessly up and down. There was more strength in that wiry body than many people could guess. *Just stay with him,* he urged himself. *Don't fall too far behind!*

The moneybelt felt like it weighed as much as a heavy stone, and bumped up and down on his waist. He was burning hot, and wished he could stop long enough to remove his cloak. Several passers-by turned in amazement to watch the race, and a strange one it must have appeared to them: a large yellow dog far out in the lead, a dark-haired boy loping along, and a middle-aged man bringing up the rear. If Duran had not been running for his life, he would have found it amusing.

He heard a muted roar off to his left and chanced a hasty glance in that direction. His heart lurched. Coming down the street he and Kekoja were passing was the mob.

"Here they come!" he called out, his breath growing shorter. "I think . . . they've . . . seen us! Run! I'll make it . . . fast as I can!"

"Not far," Kekoja shouted back over his shoulder. "Three more blocks."

Three more blocks. Gods! He would die before then. He reached down inside himself to gather needed strength. *You're Ancar,* he told himself.

An Ancar doesn't tire in a race. An Ancar will die on his feet rather than give up! Keep going! Make your ancestors proud!

He stumbled once, caught himself, and ran on. Dog had sensed his master's panic, and stretched out a dead run, ready to turn and fight if need be. Kekoja began to pull away, and Duran knew he would be left behind.

"Keep going!" Kekoja called over his shoulder. "I'll get the others ready!"

The others? Duran dimly wondered how many "others" there might be. As many as made up the mob? He doubted that.

As he very much doubted his ability to run those three blocks more.

Vadami had caught up to the head of the mob before they had gone very far, but that was all he had been able to accomplish. He had tried reasoning with them, but the men and women who stalked along after Zeldezia were beyond reasoning now.

He and Zeldezia had called the men and woman together in a neighborhood far to the east of Duran's, so no casual observer could guess what was going on. They had started off to the west, traveling a route that would bring them into Duran's neighborhood several streets to the north. Along the way, they had added a few more people to the mob, and Vadami estimated their numbers were now forty-five strong.

He did not understand how he had gotten into this position. He kept thinking of going off to the side and returning to the Temple. No one was listening to him. Everything was—

"There he is!"

The mob roared. Vadami could barely make out a distant figure several blocks south, down the street headed east.

"After him!" shouted the burly fellow who had been so vocal earlier. "Don't let him get away!"

"Wait!" Vadami yelled in a very unpriest-like voice. "Listen to me!"

Thunder rumbled overhead and lightning lit the sky. People began to run, waving sticks, pausing to gather up loose cobbles.

Then Vadami heard another noise over the thunder, the noise of hooves. Several other people had heard the sound, too, and they broke stride as they ran to glance around.

Suddenly, the street that crossed directly in front of them was filled with horses, and on those horses sat the green-cloaked Guard of the Duke himself.

"Halt!" their commander bellowed over the thunder. "Stop where you are, in the name of His Grace, the Duke!"

The mob halted and began to mill around; some men and women looked frightened, while others seemed increasingly defiant.

"Down with the Sabirn!"

Zeldezia's screech split the heavy silence. She darted off to one side, somehow escaped the arms of a guard who leaned halfway off his horse to catch her, and pelted down the street.

Her action spurred the mob into unthinking motion. Several men charged at the guardsmen, brandishing rocks they had picked up in their hands.

"Swords out!" the Guard commander roared.

Even over the yelling and the rumble of thunder, Vadami heard the rasp of steel on steel as the guardsmen drew their weapons.

The mob howled.

"Death to the Sabirn!" someone yelled.

The commander brought his hand down. "Engage!"

Vadami closed his eyes at the sound of the first scream. Confusion reigned: horses neighed, people cursed and screeched. A body pitched into Vadami, a horse went down—Vadami started to run, heart pounding in his chest, in the direction Zeldezia had taken, fear giving him a speed he had not known he possessed. His legs ached, and he wondered how Zeldezia could keep up the pace: others did—men passed him, with sticks in hand—

Hladyr . . . Shining One! Help me to stop this!

Only the thunder answered him, thunder and the sound of Zeldezia's exhortations.

A large wagon stood in the center of the road. There were no buildings around Duran now, only the ancient arch of the river-gate, the harbor, and the fort built there to protect it. He ran—hearing the shouts closer and closer behind him—the pelting of stones—Dog loping, panting, beside him—

"Duran!"

Kekoja was with the wagon! The sight of the boy frantically beckoning him on gave Duran new energy: he ran, his ears ringing, and small black specks beginning to dot his vision. Behind him, he heard the shrill voice of a woman crying out for death to all unbelievers—

Zeldezia. He would have recognized that crow's voice anywhere.

He stumbled, staggered, caught himself painfully, and kept running—

"Duran! Hurry!"

Kekoja's voice. A stone hit to his left—he threw himself into final effort toward that wagon—ran and ran until he lost his vision, lost his footing entirely.

Strong hands lifted him up. He hung in their grip, limp.

"Get him into the wagon," another voice said. Old Man. Old Man had made it to safety, too.

"They're on us!" Kekoja cried.

"Aye, I see them."

Duran was half-dragged, half-carried over the side of the wagon—tried to help himself as men lifted him up and then unceremoniously dumped him down on his baskets—his baskets—!

Dog landed in the middle of him—

Stones hailed about them, the shouts grew— Duran looked down the street, and his chest tightened: men running at the wagon, armed with knives and large stones. In the forefront ran Zeldezia, her dark hair come loose from its ribbons, streaming out behind her like a storm cloud.

And Vadami.

Duran closed his eyes. He had never particularly liked the priest, but he had not thought Vadami one to stoop to mob violence.

"Ready?" Old Man called.

"Aye," someone answered.

Three Sabirn men stood at the side of the wagon, long metal tubes held in their hands.

Old Man stood facing the mob, not moving, not saying a thing. Duran wanted to yell, to curse, to do anything but lie in a shivering heap in the wagon, waiting for the mob to take him.

"Now!" Old Man said.

Duran had been in situations of danger before, and knew that time could do one of two things: it could speed up so he had taken action before he knew it, or it could slow down so that each moment felt like an hour.

The thunder cracked close at hand: all of Dandro's hells seemed to explode from the tubes—smoke, and fire, and screams from the crowd. Smoke cleared on the wind—there were people on the ground—the crowd running in terror—

The men scrambled aboard, Kekoja and Old Man, too. The wagon jerked into motion, wheels rumbling on the cobbles, and Duran held onto Dog, held onto him for dear life.

He had finally seen true wizardry, he thought: he had seen it with his own eyes.

EPILOGUE

Not more than two leagues off from Targheiden, beneath a sky that poured cold rain, Old Man brought the wagon to a stop. Duran and Dog sat covered by a tarp in the rear among his baskets; Duran's head still spun, but his breath came evenly again.

"Will anyone follow us?" Kekoja asked Old Man.

"In this weather?" Old Man shook his head. "I doubt it. Not the mob and not the Guard. I don't think they'll dare. I only regret we had to let them see the weapons—"

"They'll call it sorcery," one said.

The other Sabirn standing alongside the wagon laughed. Duran stared at them in wonder. How casually they acted after having delivered fire from their hands—hard men, dangerous men. He shivered, held to Dog's collar, sitting in his nest of baskets.

The rain slacked to a drizzle, and the thunder

and lightning diminished. Even so, Duran agreed with Old Man: no one would come after them. No one in his right mind, at least.

"And now, Sor Duran," Old Man said, turning sideways on the wagon's seat, "we'll try to make amends to you." He glanced at the other Sabirn. "Hear me," he said, "this one is called Duran. He has my name and Kekoja's. You now have his. The only thing lacking is for you to tell him your names."

"Fenro," one of the men said.

"I'm Domano," another.

"Aladu!" called the third man from the other side of the wagon.

The woman who shared the wagon-seat with Old Man smiled in the rain, her black hair plastered to the sides of her face. "I'm Turchia," she said. Her voice was low-pitched for a woman's.

Duran remembered what he had told Dajhi, Old Man, what seemed a lifetime ago. "Your names are safe with me," he murmured, touching his heart.

He sensed the Sabirn relaxing, saw the sudden warmth in them—though he was certain Old Man had told them this Ancar was different from most.

"There's a small grove of trees down the road a ways," Aladu said. "Let's make camp there."

There were no more questions until Old Man stopped the wagon for the night. The men dragged out another tarp from the wagon and secured it to three long staffs of wood, making a tent of sorts out from the wagon. A third tarp they spread on the ground so everyone could sit in comfort.

With a minimum of fuss, Fenro had started a

small fire. Duran and Dog settled: Kekoja scurried about on small errands—but among the first he brought Duran a cup of heated wine.

"My father," Kekoja called him—"my second father—"

At which Duran found his eyes stinging, and his throat tight, and the wine most welcome to hide the fact.

"Now for questions," Old Man said. White teeth flashed in the firelight as Old Man smiled. "One of mine first. Then, I promise you, I'll answer anything you want."

Duran nodded. "Ask."

"Did you have any enemies who would have been able to hire wizards against you?"

Duran started to shake his head in denial, then nodded slowly, seeing Wellhyrn's face, and Ladirno's, in his mind.

Kekoja reached out and tapped Old Man's knee. "I *told* you."

Old Man smiled.

"But I was only clumsy for a day," Duran said, recalling everything he had dropped and tripped over. Suddenly, why things had returned to normal dawned on him. His skin tightened. "You knew," he said softly, his eyes holding Old Man's gaze, "and you counteracted the ill-wishes aimed at me. Who was the wizard, and how did you afford him?"

Old Man smiled.

"But, Ladirno and Wellhyrn could afford some of Torgheiden's best. . . ."

"Then I'm complimented," Old Man said. "Next question. Ask."

"What you did . . . back there . . . the mob."
He looked from one dark face to the next. "What
in Dandro's hells was it?"

"*That* wasn't wizardry," Old Man replied, "but
just as well they think it was. You're an alchemist.
You've seen things explode."

"Aye—"

"Explosion in an open-ended cylinder—" Old
Man opened his fingers. "Boom! A pellet flies—"

"Set that damned mob running, that's for sure,"
Domano said.

"I'm sorry I had to do it, though." Old Man's
voice was soft. "Now life for the Sabirn of Targheiden will be even more difficult. Perhaps impossible. There'll be blood. There already has been.
It may shake a throne—"

"Was it you—the weather?"

Old Man had no expression. He only sipped his
wine.

"Did you?" Duran demanded to know.

"Say that times change. Kingdoms end. This
one—has run its course. All the accumulated
magic—all the spells against it—call it nature. Call
it a run of luck. No. I didn't. Their own wizards—
wished the luck on their enemies. They feared—
and they hated; and they wished with all they had.
And their enemies—are *in* the city: do you see?
Their enemies—"

"—were themselves," Duran said, with a chill.

"There are those worth saving," Old Man said,
"those that aren't so blind. When we come across
a mind like yours—we make every effort to draw it
to us: we make no difference of race."

"We," Duran said, and looked at the dark faces
in the firelight. "Who is this—we?"

"Northeast of here. We've a place there. If this kingdom falls—we'll not be part of it. We'll wait. We've waited before. A thousand years."

Duran's head spun. The Old Empire—

"Dajhi," Duran said. "Are there—alchemists where we're going? Are there those—who can transmute metals—turn base metal into gold?"

Old Man laughed. "Once an alchemist, always an alchemist. No, Duran, I'm afraid not. That's something no one has ever been able to do."

"I wonder why?" Duran mused, staring into the flames.

"Maybe that's something *you'll* discover," Old Man said.

Silence fell, and in that silence Duran heard his pulse beating in his ears. He was not so old. He had his medicines and his alchemist's tools. He had his Sabirn friends—

A cold nose touched his hand. He put an arm around Dog's neck, and stared off to the west where Torgheiden lay, hidden by the darkness and rain.

Strange: he mourned the loss of home with a real grief, but at the same time that life seemed pale and distant. Few men were ever given the chance to start their lives over.

Duran smiled, and turning his eyes east, began to dream of what he could find.

Paksenarrion, a simple sheepfarmer's daughter, yearns for a life of adventure and glory, such as the heroes in songs and story. At age seventeen she runs away from home to join a mercenary company, and begins her epic life . . .

ELIZABETH MOON

THE DEED OF PAKSENARRION

"This is the first work of high heroic fantasy I've seen, that has taken the work of Tolkien, assimilated it totally and deeply and absolutely, and produced something altogether new and yet incontestably based on the master. . . . This is the real thing. Worldbuilding in the grand tradition, background thought out to the last detail, by someone who knows absolutely whereof she speaks. . . . Her military knowledge is impressive, her picture of life in a mercenary company most convincing."—**Judith Tarr**

About the author: Elizabeth Moon joined the U.S. Marine Corps in 1968 and completed both Officers Candidate School and Basic School, reaching the rank of 1st Lieutenant during active duty. Her background in military training and discipline imbue The Deed of Paksenarrion with a gritty realism that is all too rare in most current fantasy.

"I thoroughly enjoyed *Deed of Paksenarrion*. A most engrossing, highly readable work."
—**Anne McCaffrey**

"For once the promises are borne out. *Sheepfarmer's Daughter* is an advance in realism. . . . I can only say that I eagerly await whatever Elizabeth Moon chooses to write next."
—Taras Wolansky, *Lan's Lantern*

*   *   *   *   *

Volume One: Sheepfarmer's Daughter—Paks is trained as a mercenary, blooded, and introduced to the life of a soldier . . . and to the followers of Gird, the soldier's god.

Volume Two: Divided Allegiance—Paks leaves the Duke's company to follow the path of Gird alone—and on her lonely quests encounters the other sentient races of her world.

Volume Three: Oath of Gold—Paks the warrior must learn to live with Paks the human. She undertakes a holy quest for a lost eleven prince that brings the gods' wrath down on her and tests her very limits.

*   *   *   *   *

These books are available at your local bookstore, or you can fill out the coupon and return it to Baen Books, at the address below.

All three books of The Deed of Paksenarrion _____
SHEEPFARMER'S
  DAUGHTER   65416-0 • 506 pages • $3.95 _____
DIVIDED
  ALLEGIANCE   69786-2 • 528 pages • $3.95 _____
OATH OF GOLD 69798-6 • 528 pages • $3.95 _____

Please send the cover price to: Baen Books, Dept. B, 260 Fifth Avenue, New York, NY 10001.
Name_____
Address_____
City_____ State_____ Zip_____

THE KING OF YS
POUL AND KAREN ANDERSON

THE KING OF YS—
THE GREATEST
EPIC FANTASY
OF THIS DECADE!

by Poul and Karen Anderson

As many authors that have brought new life and meaning to Camelot and her King, so have Poul and Karen Anderson brought to life a city of legend on the coast of Brittany . . . Ys.

THE ROMAN SOLDIER BECAME A KING, AND HUSBAND TO THE NINE

In *Roma Mater*, the Roman centurion Gratillonius became King of Ys, city of legend—and husband to its nine magical Queens.

A PRIEST-KING AT WAR WITH HIS GODS

In *Gallicenae*, Gratillonius consolidates his power in the name and service of Rome the Mother, and his war worsens with the senile Gods of Ys, that once blessed city.

HE MUST MARRY HIS DAUGHTER— OR WATCH AS HIS KINGDOM IS DESTROYED

In *Dahut* the final demands of the gods were made clear: that Gratillonius wed his own daughter . . . and as a result of his defying that divine ultimatum, the consequent destruction of Ys itself.

THE STUNNING CLIMAX

In *The Dog and the Wolf*, the once and future king strives first to save the remnant of the Ysans from utter destruction—then use them to save civilization itself, as the light that once was Rome flickers out, and barbarian night descends upon the world. In the progress, Gratillonius, once a Roman centurion and King of Ys, will become King Grallon of Brittany, and give rise to a legend that will ring down the corridors of time!

Available only through Baen Books, but you can order this four-volume KING OF YS series with this order form. Check your choices below and send the combined cover price/s to: Baen Books, Dept. BA, 260 Fifth Avenue, New York, New York 10001.

ROMA MATER • 65602-3 • 480 pp. • $3.95   _____
GALLICENAE • 65342-3 • 384 pp. • $3.95   _____
DAHUT • 65371-7 • 416 pp. • $3.95   _____
THE DOG AND THE WOLF • 65391-1 •
544 pp. • $4.50   _____

WHAT OUR READERS SAY ABOUT

LOIS McMASTER BUJOLD

"I read [THE WARRIOR'S APPRENTICE] very carefully with an eye on making criticisms based on my experiences as a former military officer, but each time I found something, you repaired it. . . . I could find nothing to fault in the story. It was well done and well written."
　　　　　—Kevin D. Randle, Cedar Rapids, Iowa

"I am reading Lois Bujold's THE WARRIOR'S APPRENTICE for the third time. . . . The girl [sic!] plots intricately. I love her writing, and will buy anything she writes."
　　　　　—R.C. Crenshaw, Eugene, Oregon

"You may be off on a new Space Patrol with the Dendarii Mercenaries. It will strain my purse, but I should cut my eating anyhow!"
　　　　　—John P. Conlon, Newark, Ohio

"I have been recommending [SHARDS OF HONOR] to my friends, telling them that the book is about personal honor, love, duty, and the conflict between honor, love and duty. I am looking forward to your next novel."
　　　　　—Radcliffe Cutshaw, Boca Raton, Florida

AND HERE'S WHAT THE CRITICS SAY:

SHARDS OF HONOR

"Bujold has written what may be the best first science fiction novel of the year."
—*Chicago Sun-Times*

"A strong debut, and Bujold is a writer to look for in the future." —*Locus*

"An unusually good book."
—*Voice of Youth Advocates*

"Splendid . . . This superb first novel integrates a believable romance into a science fiction tale of adventure and war." —*Booklist*

THE WARRIOR'S APPRENTICE

"Highly recommended for any SF collection."
—*Booklist*

"Bujold continues to delight." —*Locus*

"Bujold's first book, *Shards of Honor*, was called 'possibly the best first SF novel of the year,' by the *Chicago Sun-Times*. *The Warrior's Apprentice* is better." —*Fantasy Review*

ETHAN OF ATHOS

"This is Ms. Bujold's third novel, and the consensus of opinion among those who enjoy watching the development of a new writer is that she just keeps getting better." —*Vandalia Drummer News*

"An entertaining, and out-of-the-ordinary, romp." —*Locus*

"I've read SHARDS OF HONOR about twenty times; THE WARRIOR'S APPRENTICE not so repeatedly but I'm working on it. If [Ms. Bujold] can maintain the quality she'll rank with Anne McCaffrey and C.J. Cherryh." —Aeronita C. Belle, Baltimore, Md.

"I just finished your book SHARDS OF HONOR. It was so good I almost don't want to take it back to the library.... Keep up the good work." —Jan Curtis, Delaware, Ohio

---

MAGIC AND *COMPUTERS* DON'T MIX!

RICK COOK

Or ... do they? That's what Walter "Wiz" Zumwalt is wondering. Just a short time ago, he was a master hacker in a Silicon Valley office, a very ordinary fellow in a very mundane world. But magic spells, it seems, are a lot like computer programs: they're both formulas, recipes for getting things done. Unfortunately, just like those computer programs, they can be full of bugs. Now, thanks to a *particularly* buggy spell, Wiz has been transported to a world of magic—and incredible peril. The wizard who summoned him is dead, Wiz has fallen for a red-headed witch who despises him, and no one—not the elves, not the dwarves, not even the dragons—can figure out why he's here, or what to do with him. Worse: the sorcerers of the deadly Black League, rulers of an entire continent, want Wiz dead—and he doesn't even know why! Wiz had better figure out the rules of this strange new world—and fast—or he's not going to live to see Silicon Valley again.

Here's a refreshing tale from an exciting new writer. It's also a rarity: a well drawn fantasy told with all the rigorous logic of hard science fiction.

February 1989 • 69803-6 • 320 pages • $3.50

Available at bookstores everywhere, or you can send the cover price to Baen Books, Dept. WZ, 260 Fifth Ave., New York, NY 10001.